"GOOD, YOU'RE UP AND ABOUT.
YOU MAY LEAVE NOW."

Lilian let out a small scream at the unexpected arrival of a man, no doubt Lord Granton from his clipped and precise speech. She'd screamed not only because he'd startled her, but because she was standing wearing nothing but her shift and bloomers. Did the man not believe in knocking? Keeping her back to him and turning her head slightly, she said, "Sir, can you not see that I am unclothed?"

"I'm covering my eyes with my hands," he said blandly.

Lilian peeked behind her and gasped. "You are not," she said. He was not smiling, as one would expect from a man who was such a prankster. He simply stared at her, his expression unreadable, almost as if he were completely unaware of how improper his behavior was . . .

More Historical Romance from Jane Goodger

Lady Lost

JANE GOODGER

LYRICAL PRESS
KENSINGTON PUBLISHING CORP.
http://www.kensingtonbooks.com

LYRICAL PRESS is published by

Kensington Publishing Corp.
119 West 40th Street
New York, NY 10018

First Electronic Edition: October 2016
eISBN-13: 978-1-60183-789-9
eISBN-10: 1-60183-789-5

First Print Edition: October 2016
ISBN-13: 978-1-60183-790-5
ISBN-10: 1-60183-790-9

Published in the United States of America

Chapter 1

Lilian would never forget the first time she encountered Marcus Dunford. He was naked and glistening with sweat and the most glorious thing she had ever seen.

Not entirely naked. Had that been the case, she might have fainted dead away and been discovered, no doubt from the thump that would have sounded when she hit the marble floor.

She was eighteen and hiding from His Grace, the Duke of Weston, who for some odd reason had set his sights on her the very first day of the Barrington summer party, the first such event Lilian and her mother and sister had ever attended. Lilian had come out just that spring, and her debut had been underwhelming to say the least. They hadn't any money, nor real connections, so the number of events they had attended had been woefully limited. Still, her mother had saved and scraped for years in order for her to have her season, so Lilian had tried her best to attract, if not a titled man, then at least a rich one. As the daughter of an earl, her mother had expected that Lilian would receive far more interest than she had. But the truth of it was, the Martins had been out of society for so long, no one knew who they were. Those who did were not particularly impressed by her pedigree, given it came with no money and little influence. The new earl, a second cousin who had inherited the title following the death of Lilian's father ten years prior, was a religious fanatic who most would rather not be associated with. Worse still, Lilian, with her riot of multicolored hair that went from nearly blonde to red to brown, and gowns that were less than the height of fashion, wasn't at all considered *au courant*. It also hadn't escaped Lilian that, with her willowy figure, she looked quite a bit younger than her years. More than one person had wondered why she was coming out at all, thinking she was nearer to fifteen than eighteen years old.

Lilian was aware of all this even before the season started, but her awareness had only grown as the weeks and months went on. This house party that marked the end of the season was to have been her last hurrah before the three headed back to Cornwall and their crumbling manor house and their quiet, dull lives. What a miracle, then, that the Duke of Weston had chosen that very same party to come out of his prolonged exile from society and immediately and quite aggressively set his cap on Lilian. Her mother, of course, was thrilled. Lilian, far less so. It wasn't that the duke was old (which he was) or that he was not at all handsome (he was quite plump), but rather the way he looked at her. It made her skin crawl.

But she would marry him if it came to that. She would have to, for her mother, Anne, was dying and Anne's greatest wish was to see her daughters settled before she passed. That hopeful look in her mother's eyes tore at Lilian's heart as nothing else could. Her mother was desperate for her to marry, for her younger sister, Theresa, to be safe and cared for. The thought of the two girls being under the direct care of the current earl was just too much for Anne to bear, and she'd wept more than once at the mere thought of it.

If only her mother could live a few years longer, the girls would be financially set. Their grandmother had settled quite a large sum of money aside for her only grandchildren, but it would only be available to them after they turned twenty-five, and that was seven long years away. Lilian would have happily lived in Cornwall in their little manor house if only her mother would live just a bit longer. But she would not. As much as Lilian tried to deny the truth, it was difficult to ignore that Anne was withering away before her very eyes and it wouldn't be long before she was bedridden.

Which was why Lilian would say yes if the Duke of Weston proposed and also why, when she saw him talking to another gentleman in the hall, she quickly ducked into the nearest room and hid. Not very adult of her, but there it was. And there she was when two strapping young men entered the room, unbeknownst to Lilian, bragging about which one could do more push-ups.

Lilian had hidden herself behind the curtains of a bow window and was quite obscured by bushes from anyone who might pass by outside and by the heavy velvet curtain from anyone inside. What she hadn't realized was how very warm she would be in her little hot-house of a hiding place. She quickly became drowsy, and fell asleep, only to be awakened by the low tones of two men, one of whom was counting.

"Fifty-four, fifty-five. No, fifty-four, you didn't go all the way down, Marc."

"The hell I didn't," said another man.

"Fine. Fifty-five. Give up?"

"Never," the other man growled.

Lilian sat up as quietly as she could, painfully aware that the sun, which had been beating down on her mercilessly, had now reached the other side of the house entirely while she'd slept.

"Fifty-five, fifty-six. Your arms are beginning to shake, old man."

Lilian sat forward just enough so that she could look through the thin space between the curtains—and there he was in all his mascu-line glory, naked from the waist up, muscles bunched from the exer-tion, back glistening from sweat, chiseled jaw set with determination. She hadn't known men had so many muscles. His arms alone were a wonder, thick ropes of pure power, pistoning up and down in a way that made her feel decidedly odd. She suddenly found it difficult to breathe. His hair was dark and curling, slightly damp along his nape and forehead. His long body was prone before her, so she couldn't get a good look at his face, could only study his profile, his straight, masculine nose, his well-defined jaw, his strong chin.

He was the most beautiful man Lilian had ever seen in her life.

"Fifty-nine. Give up now, Marc, you'll never do it."

"Marc" shot a look at the other man, then lowered himself once again. The other young man was hunkered down beside Marc, his shirt open, his chest glistening slightly, and Lilian supposed he had already had his turn. He was a fine-looking man, but her eyes kept straying to the man on the parquet floor, lowering himself down, and then up, his muscles straining with the movement. For a fleeting moment, she wished he were completely unclothed, but she quickly pushed that horribly improper thought away.

"Sixty. Sixty-one. Damn it, Marc, do you have to best me in every-thing? Sixty-two. All right, you've won, you can stop now." Marc did one more for good measure, then pushed himself to his feet as if he could have done dozens more push-ups without a problem. The man called Marc laughed, and took up his shirt, wiping himself with it before putting it on.

"I fear Mr. Courtland is going to be quite unhappy with me when he sees my shirt," Marc said, looking down at the rather limp garment. He pulled on his braces with an easy gesture, and Lilian watched, fascinated. She had almost no experience with men, and here she was, watching one dress himself. Lilian couldn't recall seeing him during the season; she felt she would have noticed him if she had. The sun was behind him so she still was unable to get a good look at his face, and she had a moment of pure panic that she might see him again and not recognize him.

It suddenly became very important that she did.

"Lilian." She turned to find her sister waving at her from the wide door that led to the gardens outside. Though she was fifteen, Theresa looked like a tiny fairy princess in her white gown and golden ringlets and could have easily passed for a far younger girl. She had the boundless energy of a puppy, and whenever she entered a room, she drew the attention of anyone who was about. Back home, the servants indulged her shamelessly, and her mother could never say no to her. Theresa was slim (a wonder, given how many sweets she accumulated from the adults she met), and purely adorable—most of the time. The fact that Theresa could not participate in most of the season's events had been torture for her poor sister, who was used to getting everything she wished, be it strawberry tarts for dessert or a new ribbon for her hair.

Even though Lilian walked toward her sister, Theresa gave her a look of pure impatience. "Lilian, hurry."

There was to be a croquet match, and the two had planned to watch it together with their mother. Sighing, Lilian went to her fifteen-year-old sibling, whose enthusiasm over attending this two-week house party knew no ends. Poor Theresa had watched Lilian prepare for the few social gatherings she'd been invited to with unabashed jealousy, and Lilian had thought more than once that her younger sister, had she been old enough, would have been much more suited to a season than she herself was. Theresa adored everything that went into having a successful season, including the fashion and the flirting. Her sister didn't realize she was flirting, of course, but she had a natural way of charming everyone around her that would bode well for her when it was time for her to come out. In contrast, Lilian saw her season as a task that she must complete in order to make certain they would not be forced into abject poverty—at least until the sisters could obtain their inheritance at age twenty-five.

"Where *were* you? The match has already started," Theresa said, grabbing up her sister's hand and tugging.

"The match will last for at least an hour, Theresa. I'm certain we didn't miss much."

"Mother was nearly frantic because I couldn't find you and is now abed. Not from being frantic," Theresa added when she saw Lilian's look of concern.

Lilian grinned. "I was in the library. Hiding from His Grace." Lilian made a face and Theresa giggled. Lilian and Theresa had giggled in bed more than once in the past few days talking about the duke, whom Theresa had yet to meet. The croquet match was the first event that children were allowed to attend with the adults. "And while I was hiding, I fell asleep. Can you guess how I was awakened?"

Theresa shook her head, her eyes wide. "Not the duke!"

"No. By the most beautiful man I've ever seen in my life. At least I imagine he must be beautiful." She leaned to her sister's ear and whispered. "He hadn't a shirt on."

Theresa let out a satisfying gasp of shock. "Did he see you? Who was it?"

"That's just the thing. I haven't any idea other than his name is Marc. I didn't get a good look at his face, but he must be attending the croquet match, don't you think? He was . . . perfect."

"Are you in love?" Theresa's eyes danced. Nothing captivated her interest more than talk of young men and marriage.

Lilian laughed, but her heart gave a small, ridiculous wrench. "Of course not. There's no such thing as love at first sight."

"Let's see if you can spot him," Theresa said, with unsuppressed excitement. "And then he'll see you and fall instantly in love, too."

The two sisters walked with exaggerated sedateness toward the small crowd watching the croquet match, and every once in a while Theresa would say something to the effect of, "Is that the one? In back, with the blond hair."

Lilian couldn't stop her stomach from being a jumble of nerves. She scanned the crowd, trying not to look as if she were actually looking for someone. Her eyes lit on the duke and quickly skirted over him lest he make eye contact with her. And then she saw *him* and clutched her sister's hand.

"I see him." He stood with the other man who had been in the library, and it appeared the two were having a serious and heated conversation. Lilian furrowed her brow, for it was unlikely such scowls from the two could possibly be due to the croquet match, which had not even begun yet despite Theresa's concerns that they'd missed the beginning. He was just as magnificent fully clothed as he was half naked. He wore the summer uniform of the well-dressed male, light fawn trousers, a single-breasted frock coat of blue, and a cream-colored vest. His hair beneath his straw boater appeared tamed from his earlier exertion, and he was still too far away to clearly see his face. Though what Lilian could see was pleasing: square jaw, straight nose, even features. She longed to make her way to the other side of the croquet field so she might get a better look, but was terrified that he would somehow know what she was about.

"Which one?"

"The tall gentleman in the boater. Blue coat. He's next to a man wearing an awful plaid coat."

Theresa clutched at her arm. "I see him." She squinted. "He doesn't seem all that special to me."

Lilian almost reminded Theresa that she hadn't seen his glistening and muscular torso, but thought better of it; Theresa was far too young to know such details.

"Shall I find out what I can? Mary Watworth is standing right by him. She might know."

Lilian pressed her lips together. "Yes, do. But be discreet, please."

Theresa gave her a look that said, *Of course I will be,* and headed in the direction of her man of interest. From the corner of her eye, Lilian could sense the duke looking at her and she did her best to ignore him. Her mother, of course, would have been exceedingly angry with her for not encouraging the duke's affections. But Lilian simply could not bring herself to do it, though she knew eventually she would have to.

"Married? He's *married?*"

Marcus Dunford, Lord Granton, the man she'd decided to marry, was already married. Lilian sat on a bench between her mother and sister, who had just gleefully imparted this information. Their mother had joined the sisters shortly after the croquet match ended, and they were now sitting on a bench beneath an arbor.

Theresa also discovered Lord Granton's sister had once been engaged to Weston, the very same duke pursuing Lilian. This Rose was, in fact, the very reason the duke had been out of society for so long. Theresa didn't know the details, but apparently something quite awful had happened between the two, and now, even though Weston and Granton's family were neighbors, they did all they could to avoid one another. Lord Granton, Theresa announced with no small amount of glee, had already left the party. Lilian was not amazed at the sheer amount of information Theresa was able to ferret out; she had a knack for it.

"Or perhaps he found out you're in love with him and he was trying to escape," Theresa said, and then, because she found herself so amusing, she clutched at her stomach in a vain attempt to stop laughing. At that moment, Lilian fervently wished Theresa had not been allowed to join her mother and her at the house party. She realized too late that while Theresa could be great fun, she was also rather adept at exposing one's weaknesses and capitalizing on them. And it was obvious that she would delight in torturing Lilian about her minor crush on Lord Granton.

"Why don't you go back to the nursery and play with your friends," Lilian said.

Theresa scowled. "You know I'm far too old for the nursery."

"I don't know, you may be nearly sixteen but you *look* ten."

Theresa stuck out her tongue and pouted, indeed looking like a young child. Lilian made a face at her little sister and was about to say something more when their mother interrupted her.

"Lilian, don't be mean to your little sister. I remember quite well what it was like to have an older sister who got to go to all the balls whilst I had to stay home. It seemed like forever before I had my own come out. Please do try to be more understanding. And what's this about a Lord Granton?"

"She's in love with him," Theresa sang.

"Lilian is not in love with Lord Granton," her mother said firmly.

"Yes, she is. She was staring at him all day. Like this." And Theresa promptly made her face go slack and her eyes go dreamy before she burst out into laughter. Her mother pressed her lips together, but Lilian could tell she was trying not to laugh. Encouraged,

Theresa stood up and batted her eyes at the imaginary Lord Granton. "Oh, sirrah, I do love your curls and your broad shoulders."

"Stop it, Theresa. Mother, make her stop. I only wondered about the gentleman, and I had no idea he was married."

"Theresa, that will be enough," her mother said, then jerked her head so that Theresa would sit on the bench. "His Grace is coming," she whispered, then gave Lilian a frantic look, as if she could somehow tame her hair in two seconds. Indeed, the Duke of Weston was strolling toward them, a smile on his face as if finding them was a delightful surprise.

"Ah, three beautiful ladies," Weston said, bowing before them, and Theresa giggled, quickly stifling herself when Lilian gave her a small nudge.

"And who is this?" Weston asked, taking up Theresa's hand and bending over it. Theresa blushed, and Lilian smiled, thinking His Grace kind for making such a fuss over Theresa. Not too many gentlemen would have done more than acknowledge such a young girl.

"This is Lady Theresa Martin, my younger daughter."

"A pleasure, Lady Theresa. I do hope you will save a dance for me this evening."

Anne started. "Your Grace, Theresa has not yet come out. She is but fifteen, sir."

"Balderdash," he said without rancor. "This is a house party. Rules are far more relaxed than in town."

Theresa perked up, like a puppy being offered a prize bit of prime rib. "Oh, Mother, could I? I would be the happiest girl in the world. And no one would mind. I don't have to stay for the entire ball, and if His Grace says it's fine, surely no one else will care."

Anne furrowed her brow. "I don't know, Theresa. You are really far too young to attend such an affair."

"I insist," His Grace said. "Have no worries. I will talk to Lady Barrington and make certain she understands that Lady Theresa is attending the ball at my request." His Grace smiled then, and Lilian felt a small fissure of unease, though she couldn't say why.

That night at the ball, Lilian couldn't help but look for Lord Granton, but it seemed as if Theresa was correct. The gentleman was nowhere to be seen so must have departed. She told herself she was being silly to search for a man who was married, but she simply couldn't help herself. It wasn't as if she would have pursued him, but she did wish she had gotten a good look at his face. If she were to run into him somewhere, she would not recognize him, which was probably for the best. No doubt if they happened to meet, she would not have been able to rid herself of the image of his glistening back and well-formed . . . everything. Just the thought made her cheeks heat.

Theresa, wearing her best gown, stood beside Lilian trying her best to, well, not be Theresa. But the poor girl was so filled with excitement, she could hardly stand still. Nor be quiet. Every woman or man who passed elicited some sort of comment from her, and no matter how many times Lilian or her mother shushed her, she simply could not contain herself.

"You are not to dance," Anne admonished her younger daughter.

"What about His Grace? He specifically asked that I save him a dance," Theresa said, just one small note away from a high-pitched wail.

"You may dance with His Grace, as it appears he may one day be your brother-in-law, but no one else."

"Mother, I hardly think any man here will ask a twelve-year-old to dance," Lilian said, just to get her sister riled up.

"I'm nearly sixteen, and you're jealous that His Grace asked me to dance and not you."

"He was simply being kind to my baby sister," Lilian said, with emphasis on the word "baby."

Lilian swore she could see steam coming from Theresa's ears, so she relented. "You don't look twelve at all. I was only teasing. And that dress is very becoming on you, Terri, truly."

Mollified, Theresa looked down at her white dress, trimmed with a bit of lace and light blue satin ribbons. "Are you certain? This is such a little-girl dress."

"You look lovely," said her mother, whose voice sounded slightly strained. "Lilian, a word if you please."

Lilian could tell from the forced smile on her mother's face and the fine sheen of sweat on her forehead that she was not feeling well. She was always trying to hide her illness from Theresa, though Lilian was painfully aware that her mother would not be with them long. It was she, after all, who had spoken with her mother's physician.

"I don't believe I'll be able to stay for the entire ball," Anne said.

"I want you to look after Theresa and make certain she doesn't get into any trouble."

"Yes, Mama. Don't worry." She searched her mother's face to determine just how ill she was feeling. Most times, her mother could struggle through, but it was clear she was feeling particularly ill.

"Thank goodness His Grace is here to watch over the two of you."

Lilian gave her mother a small smile before the older woman turned to leave, the weight of what was unsaid not lost on her.

"Where is Mother going?" Theresa asked when Lilian returned alone.

"She's feeling a bit under the weather," Lilian said with forced brightness. "I think perhaps she had too much sun today. It was dreadfully warm."

Theresa nodded, accepting the explanation without a word, and turned back to the throngs of the wealthy and powerful before her. The orchestra had begun playing nearly an hour earlier, and Theresa basked in the experience of being part of such an evening. "It's so exciting, is it not?"

"I suppose." Lilian looked around the room and didn't see a single familiar face—or at least no one she could comfortably walk up to and converse with. At that moment, she longed for their home in Cornwall with its lichen-covered stone walls and riot of roses that seemed to climb over every surface. She felt as if she didn't belong here, with these finely dressed people, no matter that her father had been an earl and her mother a countess. Her memories of their grand home were few, and so she didn't miss the lavish lifestyle she might have experienced had her father lived. While the Martins had not wanted for life's necessities, and indeed lived better than most in their tiny village, they had not participated in society and watched nearly every penny spent. They had a handful of servants and new dresses when they outgrew the old, but they'd never experienced anything as lavish as the house party they now attended. She ought to feel as excited as Theresa, but the truth was, Lilian missed her friends and their sedate and simple life. "To be honest, Terri, I'm looking forward to returning home. I haven't had a good strawberry tart since we left."

"I'd rather have a single ball than a dozen strawberry tarts," Theresa said feelingly. "You're such an odd bird."

Lilian secretly agreed. She'd participated in the season only to please her mother. She had tried to be charming and demure on the rare occasions when a gentleman had shown interest. But it appeared she lacked the social skills to garner more than a single dance or perhaps a cup of punch. It wasn't until the Duke of Weston that any gentleman had come round more than once. Lilian couldn't help but wish almost any other gentleman had shown her interest. As her mother had pointed out, beggars could not be choosers, and Lilian very much fell into the category of beggar, at least when it came to men. And having a duke express interest was far beyond anything she could have imagined. Why, then, was she so reticent about a future with him?

Theresa clutched her arm suddenly, bringing her out of her small bout of self-pity. "His Grace is coming."

Indeed, the Duke of Weston was making his way toward the pair, his eyes sparkling and completely on Theresa. "I think he's come to claim your dance," Lilian said indulgently. "And then it's off to bed with you. Mother's orders, you know."

Theresa instantly pulled a pout, but quickly lost that expression when she looked at the duke.

"Lady Theresa," he said, grandly sketching a bow. "I request the honor of your hand for this dance."

Theresa curtsied nicely, and shot a look to Lilian as if to say, *Isn't this the most fun ever?* Lilian grinned at the pair and gave her little sister a wink. Really, the duke was being so sweet, asking her little sister to dance a waltz with him.

Lilian watched as they danced, feeling a small swell of pride at how happy Theresa looked, how well she danced, and how expertly she charmed the duke. It really would be too bad if Theresa could not have her own season when the time came. If her mother was wrong about the duke's interest, Lilian would not marry, and Theresa would have to wait to be introduced to society until Lilian came into her inheritance. By then, Theresa would be twenty-two and far too old to have her first come-out.

If the duke did not propose, Lilian had no idea where they would live when their mother died—something Lilian did not want to think about at all. Wishing her mother would not die with all her heart would not change the truth of how ill she was. Lilian had prayed and prayed until tears streamed down her cheeks, but her mother had grown only sicker. This trip had been especially taxing for her, and she'd spent more time in bed than out of it. Times such as that afternoon, when her mother had joined her daughters on the garden bench, had been rare indeed.

Sometimes, when her mother looked at Lilian, she'd seen in her mother's eyes the desperation she felt. The house they lived in was part of their cousin's entailment, and he could decide it was unseemly for two young girls to continue to live there alone. Indeed, he'd hinted at as much in a recent letter, which was why it was so imperative that Lilian marry, and marry quickly.

Lilian forced her thoughts away from her dire predicament and to the man who had shown such interest in her in the past week. They had gone for walks, they had danced, and played cards, and spent an almost unseemly amount of time together. And now he was being so charming by entertaining her little sister. Really, Lilian thought, she could do far, far worse than to marry a kind duke, no matter that he was so old and a bit plump. After they were done with the waltz, the duke dutifully returned Theresa to her.

"His Grace has asked that I accompany him to dinner," Theresa gushed. "Oh, please, Lilian. Mother would say yes, I know she would."

Lilian looked from Weston, who was giving her an almost apologetic look, to her sister, who looked happy enough to fly to the moon without wings, and simply could not bring herself to say no. "Very well, but this is our secret. Mother will be quite vexed with me—and you—if she finds out."

Weston looked slightly contrite. "I do apologize for putting you in such a difficult position, my lady. I hope I can remedy this transgression with a dance."

Shaking her head and smiling, Lilian extended her hand and placed it on Weston's arm just as the small orchestra began playing a country dance. "Of course, Your Grace."

Lilian was at dinner, thinking the duke would make a rather nice husband, when the first hint of concern struck her. She sat across from her sister and the duke, who had been positioned side by side, Theresa on the duke's right. Lilian had never seen Theresa look happier. She was fairly glowing under the attention the duke was giving her. Every once in a while, Weston would look up at Lilian and wink, as if acknowledging that he was secretly suffering from not being in Lilian's company.

It wasn't until the third course that Lilian noticed her sister's coloring was unusually high. And that Weston's right hand appeared to be . . . not where it should be. Lilian stared for a moment, then looked away, trying to tell herself that appearances could be deceiving. No one else at the table seemed to notice anything amiss. The ancient baron to her left was far too interested in his meal to even say more than a polite "good evening," and the gentleman to her right was engaged in conversation with the lady next to him.

Biting her lip, Lilian kept stealing surreptitious looks at Weston and his hidden hand, which by all rights should be holding his fork. Instead, His Grace ate with his left, and Theresa had stopped eating entirely, her entire body gone still. Gathering her courage, Lilian dropped her napkin to the floor and made a small show of being miffed at her own clumsiness. Then she dipped down to retrieve it and looked beneath the table.

Weston's large hand was, indeed, resting on her sister's thigh, shockingly high up. As she looked, he caressed her, moving his hand between Theresa's legs and Lilian got the horrible feeling he knew she was watching. Grabbing up her napkin, Lilian sat back up and stared at her plate, her face red, her heart beating madly. What should she do? Confront the Duke of Weston now, during dinner? Breathing became difficult and her hands shook in her lap as she clutched the napkin.

Finally, she looked up at Weston, who stared across the table at her.
And smiled.

Chapter 2

Three years later

"I seen her standing over His Grace, holding that gun. She turns to me and she says, 'His Grace is dead,' cool as you please." Bessy Wilson, upstairs maid to His Grace, the Duke of Weston, was rather relishing her role as Birmingham Town Police Department's best (and only) witness to murder. "Just like that. No emotion, no tears. It gives me the shivers, it does. But I'll tell you what. If Lady Lilian did do it, I say good for her."

Constable Toby Conroy looked over his notes, rubbing his large mustache. "Did you hear gunfire?"

Bessy shook her head. "No one heard a thing, not even Her Grace, who was in the room next door. When I seen poor Lady Lilian standing over the body, I run to Her Grace, you see. She was asleep and not too happy to get woken up, I'll tell you. Then I tell her what I seen an' off she goes, running into His Grace's room, screaming, 'You murdered him, you murdered him.'"

A woman wailed from the second floor, a sound of abject despair, and the two lifted their heads and looked up. To Conroy, who had investigated more than one murder in his day, the display of grief seemed a bit excessive, as if Her Grace were an actress on a stage. A bad actress. Her Grace was, of course, far too upset to submit to questioning, but Conroy did get a glimpse of the young woman as she sat upon a chair in her room, dabbing at eyes that appeared to be completely devoid of tears. He could have been wrong on that account, but he'd noted it.

"What was Her Grace wearing?"

Bessy looked shocked. "What kind of a question is that?"

"Please just answer it, Miss Wilson."

The maid screwed up her freckled face in thought. "Now that is a bit odd, isn't it?"

"I don't know," Conroy said, smiling and patient.

"She were wearing her robe."

"That's not unusual," he said lightly, but he made a note of it. Now, if she'd been fully clothed, that would have sounded an alarm in his head. "And what did Lady Lilian do when her sister confronted her?"

Bessy lifted her chin. "Poor thing denied it, of course, while holding the pistol standing next to his bloody corpse. It were awful, it were. Her Grace started screaming, calling her sister a murderer, saying she'd always hated His Grace for choosing her over Lady Lilian. It's no secret, you see, that His Grace was first attracted to Lady Lilian but turned his sights toward Her Grace when he saw her." Bessy made a face of disgust before schooling her features. Conroy had spoken to half a dozen servants and had quickly realized they adored Lady Lilian and were less than charitable to the new widow.

"And what did Lady Lilian say? Can you recall?"

"She said, 'You know I didn't do this, Terri, you know I didn't.' And then Her Grace got madder than a hornet and calls her a murderer and says she's sending for Scotland Yard and that she'll hang, and that's when Lady Lilian left. She drops the pistol and runs. That's the last I seen of her."

Conroy thanked Bessy, closed his notebook, and tucked it and his pencil into his coat pocket. It seemed like an open-and-shut case, and a murderess was on the loose. Why would Lady Lilian run away if she were innocent? No doubt, innocent or guilty, the threat of a hanging was more than enough to cause a young lady to run away. He tried to picture events as if Lady Lilian was innocent. She heard a sound and, curious, she went into the room and found a pistol, picked it up, and hurried over to His Grace to see if he was well. And that was when Bessy entered the room, later followed by Her Grace. In her robe.

Conroy had been a constable for a long time—nearly as long as the police force had existed—and something wasn't sitting quite right. He let out a deep sigh, wishing this case were as cut-and-dried as it appeared on the surface. The only thing he knew for certain was the Duke of Weston was dead and the duke's sister-in-law was missing.

Chapter 3

Marcus Dunford, Viscount Granton, was in a particularly foul mood, which was saying quite a lot as he'd felt wretched most days for nearly five years. He sat in the damp, dark interior of his well-sprung carriage, lumbering through the North York Moors on his way home from a brutally trying interview with his dead wife's parents.

They were outraged that, upon the death of their daughter, Eleanor, he'd immediately stopped the five hundred pounds he'd been paying them monthly as part of his marriage contract. Marcus had been avoiding the meeting for a year, but decided to have done with it as they had threatened to visit him at Merdunoir and he wanted no one in his home. As it was, it was already getting overcrowded, what with two full-time servants.

"How could you be so cruel? Isn't it bad enough that you crushed poor Eleanor's spirit and now are punishing us for her one small transgression?" Lady Hartwood had said, tears streaming down her face. The lady, no doubt, had been lamenting the fact that she would no longer spend luxurious vacations on the Continent due to a sudden lack of funds.

"I counted no less than five small transgressions," Marcus had said, keeping his temper in line. It would never do to show emotion before these people. "And as Eleanor is no longer my wife, I am under no obligation to make good on our wedding contract."

"Our daughter is dead, God rest her soul. And you, sir, are a cold bastard," Lord Hartwood had said, staring daggers at him.

Marcus had simply looked from one to the other. "Yes, I am. Good day, sir, madam."

He'd stood and made a proper bow before departing, leaving

them both sputtering their indignation. Had they really thought he would continue to pay the stipend? Hell, the first time he'd discovered Eleanor in another man's bed, she had broken the marriage contract and he would have been within his full rights to sever payments to her parents then and there. But he had been kind.

Now Eleanor was dead, having had the ill timing to smack her head fatally on her lover's bedside table, no doubt during a particularly acrobatic lovemaking session. When Eleanor had been drunk, she had been an accommodating lover with everyone but her husband. When she'd been sober, which was rare toward the end, she had been life itself, charming and beloved by all. Even him—at least in the beginning. It was only after the wedding—actually their wedding night—when Eleanor had informed him she had been forced by her parents into a marriage that she had been vehemently opposed to. What a fine actress she'd been while he'd been courting her, for, until that moment, he'd thought she'd been in love with him.

Her parents blamed him for her death. They all did, pitying her for having married such a cold, unfeeling bastard. Simply because one did not express every emotion one experienced did not mean one did not feel it. He could not be like his brother Adam, who allowed every emotion he felt to show clearly in his animated face, who gushed poetic about how much he loved his wife. One look at Adam gazing adoringly at Georgette, and a person knew immediately he was in love. Marcus had always schooled his features, good practice when dealing with businessmen, peers, and cheating wives. No one looking at Marcus at that moment, as his carriage rattled through the barren landscape toward his home near Whitby, would know he was wishing he were the sort of man who could commit murder.

"She suffered," Eleanor's mother had said. "All she ever wanted was love, and you couldn't even give her that."

It was true, of course. He hadn't loved her, at least not the way wives apparently wanted to be loved. But he'd always believed they were a good match, compatible, and that perhaps they would come to love one another in time. It did happen on occasion. When he was in a particularly foul mood, as he was now, he tortured himself with the thought that she'd never wanted to marry him, that the very idea had been abhorrent. She'd made him the object of ridicule and pity, and a man's pride could only take so much before, well, before he hid himself away in some godforsaken, rundown estate.

Suddenly, his driver heaved back on the reins, and the carriage rocked and lurched to the left before coming to a stop, listing slightly to one side.

"My lord," his driver called down. "I've struck a woman."

A woman? Out here? There was no town nor house for miles. Marcus climbed down from the carriage and jumped to the spongy ground, taking care not to crush an early bell heather that lent a bright bit of color in this otherwise gray day. His driver stood looking down at an object lying in the road; from where he stood, it resembled a pile of clothing. Hell, he hoped they hadn't killed whoever it was. That's all he needed.

Marcus walked over and looked down to see a woman wearing a dark blue, mud-stained dress, her auburn hair a riot of tangled curls surrounding a pale face. She looked dead. Marcus nudged her a bit with his boot.

"Is she dead?" his driver asked fearfully.

Marcus watched as her chest rose and fell. "No. She's breathing." He let out a curse. Now that he gave it some thought, it would have been easier if she'd been dead. He could have heaved her body into the carriage and delivered her to the mortuary in Whitby and been done with it. As it was, he was now saddled with an injured woman, and he'd have to bring her to Merdunoir, as it was far closer than the township. Marcus got down on one knee, grimacing when the water-soaked ground immediately went through his trousers and dampened his skin, and examined the lady lying prone and unmoving on the rutted road. She was wearing an expensive dress, but she carried no reticule and wore no jewelry. She was pretty enough, he thought dispassionately, with fine features and full lips that seemed unnaturally pink against her pale face. She was thin, her cheekbones showing more than they ought. Her dress was loose and ragged despite its quality, and a small tear revealed a bit of her corset and the creamy top of one breast. Marcus looked pointedly away from that bit of flesh. It appeared the lady had been wandering the moors for quite some time, for the bottom half of her dress was completely caked with mud; her shoes, impractical things for a walk on the moor, were literally coming apart at the seams. He could see no damage to her person, and if not for the fact that she was lying still in the middle of the road, he would have said she was sleeping.

"Are you certain you struck her, Palmer? I see no injuries."

"I'm not certain, my lord. When I came over the rise, she was there, beside the road, swaying like, and then she fell right in front of the team. I near fainted myself."

Marcus tapped her on the cheeks, and her burnished lashes fluttered slightly. He struck her harder, the sound overloud in the quiet. She opened her eyes and Marcus reared back slightly, the air sucked from his lungs almost forcefully.

Palmer let out a low whistle. "Gor," the driver muttered.

Indeed. The lady had the most remarkably colored eyes he'd ever seen, a brilliant aqua color that he'd only seen on the wings of the morpho butterfly on display at the Victoria and Albert Museum in London.

"Are you injured?" he asked, but the lady continued to stare at him as if she either was blind or didn't understand God's English. "Are you injured?" he repeated, louder this time.

"Help me." He saw her lip movements more than heard the words, and then the lady closed her eyes, for which Marcus was quite grateful. He didn't want to think she was lovely. Hell, he didn't want to have to save her. *Help me.*

Bloody hell, he'd have to.

"Help me with her, will you Palmer? Into the carriage."

Palmer wrinkled his nose in distaste at the thought of picking up the lady's less attractive end, likely not wanting her muddied shoes and skirt to get on him. Marcus placed his gloved hands beneath her arms and they lifted the lady, who hung like a corpse between them. Marcus didn't know what was wrong with her, but it didn't seem as if she was long for this world, and he prayed he wasn't signing his own death warrant by helping her. They placed her unceremoniously on the front-facing seat, ever the gentlemen, and arranged her the best they could so she wouldn't tumble to the floor. Lifting his seat, Marcus brought out a blanket and covered her. She smelled of mud and moor, not an entirely unpleasant combination.

"Drive on, Palmer, and do try not to hit another pedestrian."

Palmer looked momentarily horrified, until he realized his lordship was jesting. "Yes, sir."

For the next hour, Marcus watched as the lady was jostled back and forth on the seat. At one point, he had to save her from falling to the floor by heaving her back up. One hand, pale and limp, dangled off the seat. Though her nails were dirty, she had the hands of a lady, smooth and fine, with no signs of labor. What the hell was she doing out here? Who were her people? And what would he do if she died before he got any answers from her? If he had Palmer bring her to the nearest mortuary, she would be buried in a potter's field, unnamed, unmourned. For some reason, that bothered him. Quite a bit more than he wanted it to.

When they reached his estate—a lofty word for this run-down manse that hadn't many modern conveniences—she stirred, rubbing her eyes with one hand and letting out a small sound.

"Miss," Marcus said, to give her forewarning that she was not alone. "We have reached Merdunoir." Some clever ancestor had combined *mer du noir*—sea of black—as homage to the sea over which the home looked.

"No," she said, her eyes opening wide as if in a panic.

"I assure you, yes."

She looked momentarily confused as if trying to recall him and how she'd ended up inside a carriage. "Murder?"

Now, that was odd. "Mer-du-noir," he said, enunciating each syllable. "My estate."

The lady, who looked quite young now that her eyes were open and she was moving about, tried to sit up, then clutched her head as if the movement made her dizzy. "I feel rather ill," she said, looking as if she might lose her accounts. She swallowed convulsively.

"If you don't mind, may we do that outside my carriage?" Marcus asked calmly.

She looked at him as if he was exactly what he was: a cold bastard.

"Here," he said, sighing. "Give me your hand. I shall help you."

She did, with hesitation that was slightly annoying, allowing Marcus to touch a woman's hand for the first time in more than a year. He didn't like it, but gritted his teeth and allowed it, if only to keep his carriage clean. Thankfully, Palmer had dropped the stairs and was waiting for them to disembark. He handed the lady off to his driver/butler/groom/valet.

"Where am I?" she asked, looking around her.

"Merdunoir, miss," Palmer said.

"No, I mean what county? What part of England?"

"York, near Whitby," Marcus answered. "Are you injured? You fell in front of the carriage and we thought perhaps you'd gotten stomped on by one of my team."

"I did?" She looked down at her ruined gown, swaying, as if she were atop a cliff and experiencing vertigo. "I don't . . . I don't recall." And then she fainted dead away, back into the arms of Palmer, who caught her, then didn't seem to know what to do with her.

"Pick her up, Palmer," Marcus said, walking toward his front door, assuming Palmer could carry her. She was merely a slip of a girl and shouldn't overburden his burly employee. "Put her in . . ." Damn, there were no rooms made up except for his. ". . . my room." This last was said begrudgingly. He would have no place to sleep this night and he was bloody tired. But the sooner she was well enough to travel, the better. He didn't want anyone in his home, and especially not in his bed, no matter how pretty her eyes. He wanted, above all things, to be alone.

"I'll get Sadie, shall I, sir?"

Sadie was Marcus's cook/housekeeper/maid and Palmer's older widowed sister, a woman Marcus begrudgingly allowed to stay, mostly because she was a better cook than Palmer. "Fine idea, Palmer."

Good. Between Palmer and Sadie, they could take care of the girl until she was gone. He wondered if he should send Palmer for a physician, then almost immediately rejected the idea. The closest physician was fifty miles away and was eighty-three. The man was a menace who clung to old ideas and probably killed more people than he saved. Sadie was good with medicinal concoctions, so whatever was ailing the girl, she'd be in better hands with Sadie than the doctor, at any rate. Also the doctor was a drunk, and Marcus found he had little tolerance for anyone who over-imbibed on a regular basis.

Alive or dead, Marcus wanted only for the girl to be out of his house as quickly as possible.

As had happened every time Lilian awakened since that terrible night two weeks prior, a heavy dread filled her. This time, it was worse, for she found herself in the dark, in a bed, with absolutely no idea where she was or how she'd gotten there. *Think, Lilian.* The last two weeks were a haze of hunger, thirst, and endless terror. She didn't know where she was going, who could help her, and so she just walked as far and as fast as she could. Her money, just a tiny amount she'd been able to grab before running away, had gotten her as far as Harrogate and then she'd walked most of the way, thinking vaguely of going to Scotland, where her uncle now lived with his new wife.

Uncle Stanley wasn't even a true relation, but she had no one else, no aunts or uncles, no grandparents. Only her sister.

It was foolish to think she could walk to Scotland, but where else could she go? Everyone likely thought she was a murderer. Terrifying images crowded her mind, of Weston, bloody and still, of Theresa screaming at her. Did Theresa truly believe Lilian would murder Weston? It was beyond absurd. She couldn't think about it all now, not when she didn't even know where she was or whether she was in danger.

Lilian turned to her side, feeling weaker than she ever had in her life, trying to remember where she was and how she'd gotten here. She was in a bed; that was all the information she had. She reached out her arm to the right and didn't touch the other edge or a wall. A large bed with well-laundered blankets that smelled and felt clean. Letting out a gasp, Lilian felt beneath the covers and sighed with relief to find she had on her shift and bloomers, though someone must have removed all her other layers. Surely she would have remembered getting undressed. Closing her eyes, she concentrated on the last thing she recalled. A carriage, a man. No, men. Reaching out her left hand, she felt a side table and, thank the heavens, a glass, heavy with some liquid. She lifted the glass to her nose and sniffed, smelling nothing, then took a small sip. "Thank you," she said, lifting the glass and taking a deep drink. Had any water ever tasted as sweet as this?

"You're awake."

Lilian screamed at the sound of a woman's voice, for she'd thought herself quite alone, and started so much she lost most of the precious liquid in the glass.

"Definitely awake," the woman said with a chuckle. She had a broad Yorkshire accent and sounded amused. "I'm Sadie Barnes. I'm housekeeper an' cook here. Let me light a lamp so I can get a better look at ya and you can get a better look at me."

Lilian shielded her eyes from the sudden bright light, then found herself looking at the smiling face of a woman who was perhaps twenty years her senior. Her face was shiny and smooth, as if she'd scrubbed it not long ago. The woman had the sort of smile that immediately put a person at ease, and Lilian, despite her situation, found herself relaxing slightly.

"We don't have your name," she said, "and we're wondering if you might have people worried about you."

Lilian shook her head, thinking it would be foolish to tell this woman her name, especially if she was wanted. Feeling a sense of inevitability, she said, "Lilian Martin," holding her breath and waiting for Sadie to screech in recognition. In the silence, her stomach gave a loud grumble.

"Well, Miss Martin, how long has it been since you've had anything to eat?"

Lilian furrowed her brow. "I don't know." Days, it had been.

"Let's get you fed, then. Here, I'll leave the lamp with you and I'll go fetch you something quick."

After Sadie had gone, Lilian drank the rest of the water that hadn't spilled, hoping the woman would bring more. Was this Sadie's home? She raised the flame on the lamp so she could get a better look at her surroundings. The bed was large, with intricately carved posts that were thicker than her legs. Directly across from the bed was a large, cold fireplace, surrounded by white marble, with brass andirons that gleamed from a good polishing. The floor was covered with a thick carpet—Aubusson, she thought. This was a wealthy person's home. But whose?

Sadie bustled into the room humming a tune Lilian didn't recognize, carrying a tray piled with food, including a pot of tea and a pitcher of water. Oh, wonderful woman. Bread, cheese, a slab of cold ham. Lilian felt as if she were in heaven.

"Is this your home?" she asked as Sadie positioned the tray on the side table.

"Goodness, no. This is Lord Granton's home. Merdunoir."

Lilian felt the blood drain from her head and she very nearly fainted. Again. She had never met Lord Granton, but she certainly knew of him. Over the years, she'd learned much about the man she'd so admired that day during the Barrington house party. Following the house party, her mother had fallen gravely ill and had been so relieved to see one of her daughters marry a duke, she'd never considered why Rose Dunford, Lord Granton's sister, had chosen to run rather than marry the duke. Her mother had called Lady Rose foolish.

"But her loss is our gain, as they say."

They had gained an immoral monster. Lilian was glad he was dead; she simply wished she was not the one everyone thought had murdered him. Just one night before he'd been shot, Theresa, her changeable sister, had come into her room crying. Weston had called for Theresa and she had found him in bed with two young maids. He'd wanted her to join in and had become exceedingly angry when she had not. Her sister sported a bruised cheek for her disobedience. Lilian hated Weston, yes, but so had a dozen other people.

And now she was in one of the homes of Weston's neighbor, a man who most certainly would be keenly interested in His Grace's murder. She was doomed.

"Lord Granton's father is my sister's neighbor, though I've never met his lordship," Lilian said, deciding to be as honest as possible without divulging to this kind woman that she was wanted for murder. It wasn't supposition; she'd used a bit of her dwindling funds to buy *The Times*. Reading those words in the newspaper that called her a murderess had made it seem so real; it was as if her mind hadn't truly been able to believe what had happened that terrible night until she'd read an account of it in the newspaper.

"What a coincidence," Sadie said, apparently delighted.

"Yes. And his lordship, is he in residence?"

"He's the one what found you on the moor, dearie. Thought you was struck by his team or ill, but I'm thinking you were just starving, poor thing."

Lilian tried to remember what she knew of Lord Granton (other than his fine form), but her information was woefully inadequate. She thought she recalled that his wife had recently died, but that's all she knew. She took a large bite of ham and closed her eyes at the loveliness of it.

"Take your time, dearie. Your stomach may not be ready for a lot of food."

After slowly devouring nearly everything on the tray, Lilian was overcome with sleepiness. She was soon fast asleep and didn't even hear Sadie removing her tray. Her last thought before she drifted asleep was that she needed a good bath and must ask Sadie's assistance in the morning.

"How is your patient?" Marcus asked that morning when Sadie delivered his breakfast.

"Much better after a good meal last night, that's for sure. She was asking for a bath and food. I think the poor lass was just faint from hunger and thirst."

"That's good. I wouldn't want her spreading some disease," Marcus said blandly, ignoring Sadie's tongue-clicking. Sadie was never shy about expressing her opinion, often acting more like an aunt than a servant.

"As soon as the lady can walk without fainting, please let her know she may leave," Marcus said, looking over his correspondence. His brother, Adam, continued to forward his mail, including social invitations, even though he had little interest in rejoining society. He wished people would simply leave him alone and allow him to live his life. Even his sister, Rose, who lived in America and had married their former groom, had the audacity to criticize him. To be honest, she hadn't truly been as critical as she had been concerned, no doubt fired up by his youngest brother, Stephen. The very same brother who'd come unannounced four months prior and tried to see him.

That had been a rather dark time for Marcus, and though now he regretted—slightly—pretending he was not at home, he'd been in no shape to see anyone. He still truthfully didn't want to see any of his family. Not yet.

"I don't think she'll be ready to travel for days, sir. She's weak as a kitten, she is."

Marcus set aside a letter from his solicitor and stared at Sadie until the older woman worried her hands. "Kittens can walk."

Sadie clicked her tongue and was about to say something when they were both startled to hear a knock on the front door, a booming sound that echoed through the empty halls. Other than Stephen, no one had bothered Marcus at Merdunoir, and he wondered what brave soul was daring to do so now.

"I'll see who that is, my lord," Sadie said quickly, likely grateful to escape Marcus's company.

She returned moments later, an odd expression on her face. "There's a woman to see you, sir. Says it's important."

Marcus immediately noticed two things: Sadie had said woman, not lady, and if he wasn't mistaken, his housekeeper looked positively livid. "I'll see no one, Sadie, you know that."

"There is a child with her," Sadie said, unable to meet his gaze. "A small child."

For another man, having a strange woman appear unannounced at his doorstep with a child would have been terrifying. But Marcus, in all the years of his marriage, had never strayed, even when he knew

Eleanor had. "I can't imagine what a woman towing a child would want with me," Marcus said, his tone unbending. "Send her away."

"Yes, sir."

Marcus sat and waited, having a feeling that Sadie would be returning, looking even more harried. He was correct.

"She won't leave. Says if she does, she'll leave the poor little mite she brought with her on the doorstep."

Marcus threw down his napkin and stood. By God, would no one leave him in peace? He stalked to the door, ready to blast the woman standing there, but something about the little face of the girl peering up at him made him stop. The pair stood there, just outside the door, the soft morning light doing nothing to soften the woman's appearance. The girl child stood beside the woman, holding on to the woman's coat lightly, just a thumb and forefinger, as if she didn't want the woman to know she was holding on. The girl wasn't his, he knew that for a fact, but she was just a little thing, perhaps four or five, and she looked rather pathetic standing there next to the large matron. As he approached, the little girl tugged on the woman's coat and the woman batted the child's hand away roughly.

"Madam," Marcus said, and something in his eyes made the woman back up a step. Perhaps it was that he'd wanted to strike the woman for slapping the little girl's hand, but what kind of example would that have set? "May I ask why you are on my doorstep with that child?"

"My name is Susan Broom." When he gave her a blank look, she huffed out a breath. "She's yours."

Chapter 4

Mrs. Broom shoved the girl toward him. She was a large, brutish woman, with a fine mustache above her thin lips and thick, bushy brows over cruel brown eyes.

"I assure you, she is not mine."

"Well, she ain't mine. Unless you want to pay me for her upkeep. You're past due."

Marcus furrowed his brow. "I believe you are mistaken, madam. I have no child."

The woman laughed, revealing a mouthful of brownish, crooked teeth. "You're Lord Granton, ain't ya?"

"I am."

"And your wife is Lady Granton."

"My wife passed away more than a year ago."

Her eyes widened. "That explains why I haven't been getting paid. This is her brat. I been taking care of it for more'n four years now. Feeding and clothing it, and I ain't gonna keep doing that if I ain't getting paid. You owe me fifty pounds, plus travel. I've come all the way from Northumberland. I had to leave my own precious children behind and spend my own money to find where you were."

Marcus looked down at the little girl, who looked up at him, her face solemn. *My God, she very well could be Eleanor's child;* she had her hazel eyes, her light brown hair. They had spent months apart on several occasions, so he supposed it was possible. And this vile woman had called her "it."

"What is the child's birth date? Do you know?"

"May 2, 1875 was the day Lady Granton brought a baby to me and it was just born then."

"Surely you don't expect me to take the child without proof,"

Marcus said, keeping his tone level, if only for the sake of the child. Inside, he was reeling, for a quick calculation made him realize the little girl could have been conceived when he was in America with his sister, Rose. Soon after he'd returned, Eleanor had announced she was heading to Italy because she dreaded the coming winter. At that point in their farce of a marriage, he wouldn't have cared if she'd said she was going to the other side of the world. Now her trip made much more sense, as well as the fact this woman hailed from Northumberland. Eleanor's family had a home in Northumberland, rarely used, where she could have lived in secret until the child was born. No doubt she'd been terrified at the prospect of telling him she was carrying another man's child. Eleanor had been an intelligent woman. Even now, the rage that coursed through his veins nearly made him ill, made his hand shake when he took the documents Mrs. Broom smugly held up for him.

Marcus laughed lightly as he examined the certificate of birth, a sound that held little humor, and Mrs. Broom backed up another step, looking at him warily, as if he were a madman. Just when he thought he couldn't be more humiliated, Eleanor had reached out from the grave to do this. He held a letter clearly written by his wife, for she had purely awful penmanship, the sort no one would be able to duplicate easily. In it, she detailed the arrangement with Mrs. Broom, the promise to pay the woman fifty pounds a year for the care of a female child.

"Fifty pounds. Plus travel. It's fair, my lord."

He looked at the little girl, who wore a ragged, faded dress and clutched what looked like a misshapen stocking in her hand. She wasn't starved looking and her hair was clean, if a bit tangled. And he knew if he gave the woman money, she would leave.

Bidding her to stay at the door, Marcus disappeared, returning moments later with a pouch containing seventy-five sovereigns. Handing them to the woman, he said, "You will never darken my doorstep again and you will never tell a soul about this child. Do you understand?"

"Yes, my lord," the woman said, but her gaze skittered away from his and he had a feeling she'd already told more than one person about the origins of this little girl. There was nothing Marcus could do about that now, he thought fatalistically.

"Where are her things?"

The woman looked at him blankly. "Things?"

"Clothing. Shoes. Toys. Is she trained to use a chamber pot?"

"Yes. She's very nearly five," she said. "She has nothing else, sir." She placed the pouch into a large carpet bag and, giving the child a cursory glance, bade him good day.

Marcus, who wasn't a particularly sentimental man, found it difficult to believe any woman could leave a child she'd been raising for over four years without some form of good-bye. But the woman continued down the drive without a backward glance, and the little girl stood still, watching her walk away. Marcus stood there in rapt disbelief, resisting the urge to call her back, until he felt a little hand in his.

He looked down and forced his lips into some semblance of a smile.

"My name is Mabel," she said, her expression still solemn. "Are you my papa?"

"No."

His response garnered no immediate reaction. Then, "But Mrs. Broom said you were my papa." She called the woman who'd raised her Mrs. Broom? Good God.

"I am not. I am sorry, but I do not know who your papa is." How could even Eleanor have done such a thing? Surely someone knew of the child's existence. Her maid, Miss Cates, might know who the father was. It didn't matter, though. Any child Eleanor had borne during their marriage was legally his responsibility, legally his child, whether he liked it or not.

"Did your mama ever visit you?"

Mabel shook her head. "Mrs. Broom said I was too naughty and my mama didn't want me."

Marcus's blood began to boil, and he wished, not for the first time, that he was not a gentleman, for he very much would have liked to have throttled Mrs. Broom for speaking such nonsense. "Poppycock," he said, making Mabel smile.

Mabel looked back a bit fearfully at the cavernous foyer behind them. Marcus supposed Merdunoir would be a bit frightening to a little girl. The house was large and rambling, perched on a cliff overlooking a sea that on this day looked dark and forbidding. He was beginning to love the old place, and just this past spring, he'd started thinking about renovating it. But that would mean workers about, bothering him, and he just hadn't had the stomach for it.

Still holding her hand, he turned and walked into the dreary-looking house, and Mabel followed without hesitation. Something shifted in Marcus's chest. What a brave little thing she was. She hadn't shed a single tear. One would think a child would have grown attached to a woman, even one as foul as Mrs. Broom.

What was he going to do with a little girl? Where would she sleep? He supposed he could have a cot set up in his room for now. . . .

"Dammit!" The woman was already in his room. He'd completely forgotten about her.

Mabel flinched slightly at his outburst, and Marcus stifled another curse. He stopped and hunkered down to her level. "I do apologize for startling you." The girl looked terrified, so he forced another smile, hoping it looked genuine. She clutched the small bundle in her hands tightly against her chest. "What is that?" Marcus asked, indicating the thing in her hands.

"My dolly." She held it out for his inspection. It was a stocking with something stuffed into the end and twine tied around it to form a sort of neck. It had no hair, no eyes, nothing to indicate it was supposed to resemble a human form.

"It's a stocking."

"It's a dolly," she said adamantly, and hugged the thing against her again.

"If you will." He eyed the thing skeptically, trying not to smile at her fierce expression.

He was completely out of his element. He supposed he could hire a nanny. Children had nannies, did they not? He knew nothing of children, particularly little girls, except what he remembered of his sister Rose. He'd been so much older than she, he'd spent little time with her, especially when she was a small child. Food. Children liked to eat. Sadie would know what to do with her.

"Are you hungry?"

"No, sir."

He gave her a grim smile. "Let's take you to the kitchen at any rate. That's where Sadie is, no doubt. She's my housekeeper and cook, and she makes the most delicious little tea cakes. I think you'll like them."

"I don't like tea," Mabel said.

"You'll like tea cakes, however. I'm sure of it."

The kitchen was perhaps the only part of the house that his father had bothered to introduce to the nineteenth century, and so was a warm and inviting place. One wall was lined with windows, too high to see out of but letting in a comforting light, even on a cloudy day. The brick floors, unlike most of Merdunoir, were immaculately clean, scrubbed and swept daily. When they entered, Sadie was standing by the large, wooden table, beating a pile of dough that she was likely imagining was Marcus's head.

"You sit here, child," Marcus said, lifting her up to sit on a stool, grimacing at how thin she felt beneath his hands. Perhaps she had been starved, after all. "A word, if you will, Sadie."

Marcus drew Sadie to the furthest corner of the kitchen to explain the situation.

"The poor, wee mite," Sadie said, looking over at Mabel, who sat at the stool, swinging her legs and talking to the stocking.

"Is there anyone in the village who would make a suitable nanny? I certainly cannot ask you to fill that role with everything else you do."

Sadie shook her head. "The villagers, well, sir, you should know they think Merdunoir is haunted. They won't step foot in this house in the daytime, never mind spending a night. I'm afraid you're going to have to advertise in London."

Marcus was taken aback, for he'd never heard of such a thing. "You can explain to them that this home is not haunted. They'll believe you, won't they?"

Sadie simply stared at him, her face turning slightly ruddy.

"Do you mean to tell me that you believe the house is haunted?"

She nodded, once, quickly. "But I figure something dead can't hurt me and I need the position, I do. You won't find another soul in Whitby who will work here. Even the name frightens them. Sea of black. Gives you the shivers, it does."

"And your brother? Does he also think Merdunoir is haunted?"

"No, he does not, my lord. Stubborn fool that he is. He thinks we're all crazy, but I've heard the ghost, sir. Haven't you? The moaning, the footsteps?"

Marcus let out a sharp laugh, recovering quickly when he realized Sadie wasn't joking. "No, I have not. At any rate, I'm glad you can overlook the house's uninvited guests. Speaking of which, have you told the lady she may leave?"

"Not with all the excitement, sir."

Marcus let out a sigh. "I'll see to it. In the meantime, could you please give the child something to eat?"

"Certainly, sir."

Marcus felt an odd hitch in his chest looking at Mabel, and he wondered what the hell he was going to do with her.

Lilian had never felt quite so out of sorts in her life. Her head still reeled when she stood, and she'd nearly fainted dead away after she'd used the chamber pot. What a fine thing that would have been, to have someone come in and find her so discomposed. With the morning light, she could see she was in a large, masculine-looking bedroom containing thick wooden furniture from some previous century. The bed was huge, its intricately carved headboard soaring nearly to the ceiling, its footboard a shrine to opulence. She'd laughed aloud when she saw it, knowing that never in her life would she sleep in such a creation again. What sort of person purchased such a monstrosity?

With bare feet, she carefully padded over to the window and drew back the thick, velvet curtains, revealing an overcast day and a stunning view of the North Sea. Lilian had never seen anything quite so lovely as when a sharp needle of sunlight pierced through a rare opening in the clouds and lit a patch of the turbulent water below.

"Good, you're up and about. You may leave now."

Lilian let out a small scream at the unexpected arrival of a man, no doubt Lord Granton from his clipped and precise speech. She'd screamed not only because he'd startled her, but because she was standing wearing nothing but her shift and bloomers. Did the man not believe in knocking? Keeping her back to him and turning her head slightly, she said, "Sir, can you not see that I am unclothed?"

"I'm covering my eyes with my hands," he said blandly.

Lilian peeked behind her and gasped. "You are not," she said. He was not smiling, as one would expect from a man who was such a prankster. He simply stared at her, his expression unreadable, almost as if he were completely unaware of how improper his behavior was. "Will you please turn around so that I may get back into bed, Lord Granton?"

He gave her a small bow, then turned. Lilian sidled to the bed, just in case his lordship decided to spin around, but he remained still, almost at attention, as she moved as quickly as she could to the bed and pulled the covers to her chin, her head spinning slightly from the movement.

"You may turn around now."

"May I?" he said, mockingly. "Thank you. I am glad to see you up and about. As I said, you may now leave."

He'd not moved further into the room, but remained just inside the door, looking at her with a frown as she efficiently bundled her thick curls into a loose bun. He was a tall man and younger than she'd thought, with thick dark hair and piercing eyes that were an unusual golden brown. As nervous as she was, Lilian couldn't help but note he was uncommonly handsome, though he was in need of a shave. Three years ago, she hadn't gotten a good look at his face, which in hindsight was a good thing, indeed. Had she, she might have made even more a cake of herself over him, for his features perfectly matched the fine physique she knew was hidden beneath his clothes.

"This is my room," he said as explanation.

"Oh, I'm so sorry, my lord. I didn't know. I do appreciate your hospitality and, of course, saving me from the moors. I fear I don't remember what happened or even how I came to be here."

"I'm afraid you have me at a disadvantage, as you know my name, but I do not as yet know yours. Who are you?"

"Sadie did not tell you?"

"Obviously not, as I am asking you." His smile was painfully polite.

Lilian swallowed down a bit of fear. Lord Granton was known to be a hard man, and she was certainly seeing proof of that now. What would he do if he knew who she was? Perhaps Sadie had not heard of the duke's murder, but Granton certainly would have. Feeling tears pressing against her eyes, she looked down to the coverlet and worried the soft material between her fingers before looking up again, straight into his stony expression. "I am Lady Lilian Martin."

She watched him carefully. She'd certainly surprised him, but that was all. "Your sister is Weston's wife. And you are the older one, the one who escaped."

Oh, God. He knew. He knew and he would turn her in. Of course, he would. That's what any man confronted with an accused murderess would do. "Yes," she managed to say, though her throat was constricted with fear.

"I pitied your poor sister," Marcus said blandly. "My own sister barely escaped marrying Weston. Do you know that story?"

Lilian was besieged with confusion. Why was he talking about his sister escaping . . . ? He didn't know! He'd been talking about escaping marriage, not the authorities. She nodded quickly, trying very hard not to smile, for that would have been completely inappropriate given the topic of their conversation.

"What are you doing out here, my lady? I daresay it is not the usual place to find the daughter of a peer."

Lilian had a strong distaste for lying, and so gave the gentleman an honest answer. "I was living with my sister and we had a falling-out," she said, swallowing down an unexpected and horrifying urge to laugh. Certainly, it was better than telling him the full truth. *I am the prime suspect in the murder of one of the highest members of the peerage and will likely hang if I'm discovered.* No, that would never do. "I was on my way to visit a family friend in Scotland but ran out of funds."

"And clothing."

She could feel herself blush, for the way he was looking at her, it was as if he could see through the bedcovers. "I left rather hastily, my lord."

"Indeed."

Lilian tried not to fidget beneath his level gaze, but it was impossible not to. He had a way of looking at a person that somehow made one feel self-conscious.

"It appears you have recovered adequately," he said after a long moment. "You may leave immediately. I can have my carriage bring you as far as Whitby, where you can take a train wherever you'd like. I don't enjoy guests and am not set up to receive them. I have no other room for you." He moved his lips slightly upward, and Lilian thought that perhaps he was attempting to smile politely to lessen the blow of his words.

"I would like nothing more than to be on my way," Lilian said. "But I have no clothes and no shoes. Certainly you would not send me out onto the moors in my shift."

Something dark flickered in his eyes. "No, I would not. I will talk to Sadie about procuring an appropriate dress." He looked as though he were about to leave, but stopped. "You fainted twice, my lady. Is there any chance you could be with child?"

Lilian's jaw dropped slightly. "There is none. Unless it is a second Immaculate Conception, my lord."

He gave her a long look before letting out a soft burst of air, almost a laugh but not quite. "If I don't see you again, my lady, I wish you well on your travels."

He stepped out of the door, a short journey indeed, for he hadn't come into the room more than a few feet, leaving Lilian to stare at his departing back in shock. Had she ever in her life met a more disagreeable man? Actually, thinking of Weston, she most certainly had.

Marcus stepped out of his room more determined than ever to have the lady gone. When he'd opened his bedroom door to find her there, silhouetted against the window, her auburn curls a wild mass down her back, he'd briefly lost his ability to draw air into his lungs. It had been longer than he wished to consider since he'd been with a woman, and to have one as lovely as Lady Lilian running about half naked was a temptation he could do without. He'd stood there far longer than the lady knew, far longer than he should have, gazing at her like some adolescent boy catching his first sight of a woman. If he chose to think of her feature by feature, she was not a particularly remarkable woman. He didn't really care for red-toned hair, and her jaw was a bit too square, her nose too strong, her mouth too pink. But somehow all her features came together to produce something rather astoundingly beautiful.

Most remarkable of all, he had a feeling she was completely unaware of this fact. She was also a terrible liar. He had no idea what she'd been doing walking on the moors by herself, but it certainly wasn't because she'd had a "falling-out" with her sister. More likely than not, it had probably been something to do with Weston. With that old goat's penchant for young girls, it was likely the duke had had something to do with her mad rush to get away from Mount Carlyle.

Marcus went directly to the kitchen, where he found Sadie and Mabel chatting, an empty plate in front of the girl.

Mabel turned to see him and smiled, and Marcus was struck by the thought that he couldn't remember the last time he'd entered the room and someone had looked pleased to see him.

"You were right, sir. I do like tea cakes. They don't taste like tea at all," Mabel said, making Sadie laugh.

"I am correct about most things," Marcus said solemnly. He turned to Sadie, who was frowning at him, probably for ruining the happy mood in the kitchen. "Lady Lilian needs her clothing and shoes so she can leave. Would you please deliver them posthaste?"

Sadie immediately found a light dusting of flour on the table distracting, and began sweeping it up with her hand. "I burned the dress, and the shoes are beyond repair, my lord. I'll have to go to Whitby tomorrow and buy her something. It's far too late to set out now. Truly, I don't know what I'll be able to find at any rate. Certainly nothing befitting a fine lady. I could travel to Pickering, perhaps. Then again, Mrs. Thornbush, she's a fine seamstress and could probably fashion something suitable for the lady in less than a week."

"A blasted *week?*" Marcus said, earning him another frown. "Why on earth did you burn her dress? All it needed was a good cleaning."

Sadie sniffed. "Less than a week, my lord. And the lady's dress, it were ruined, my lord, beyond my abilities to repair. I'd loan her one of my own dresses, but I hardly think that would do."

No, it would not. Sadie was probably not much taller than five feet and rather plump, and Lady Lilian was tall and lithe. The image of her standing before the window was etched in his brain so vividly that, if pressed, he could probably tell the seamstress her dimensions. Putting her in one of Sadie's dresses and sending her on her way would be impossible.

"Give her my robe for now," Marcus said, intending to retreat to his study.

"And what of Mabel, sir? What shall I do with her?"

Her question stopped him cold, left him staring at the old wooden door that separated the kitchen from the rest of the house, its lower half dented and smooth from years of servants entering and leaving. He wanted to leave, to ignore Sadie's question, but he turned instead, spying his wife's daughter looking up at him with wide eyes. Hell and damnation, he didn't need all these complications. If the lady was going to stay in his room, the girl could stay with her. It was certainly a large enough bed. And he could stay in his study on that damned uncomfortable settee that was far too small for his frame. He'd hardly slept at all the previous evening.

"We need a day maid, sir. I can't do it all, you know. I can't be cook and housekeeper and maid and nanny all in one. And perhaps another strong back around here. My brother isn't getting any younger, you see. I could convince someone to come out during the day, as long as they could return to the village before the sun sets."

"You mean before the ghost appears."

"Ghosts, sir," Sadie said, eyes looking about as if she feared the apparitions were listening in.

What was the good of being a recluse in a house full of other people? Marcus thought darkly. It seemed he was no better at being a recluse than he was at being a husband. Or a brother. Or, he thought, looking at Mabel, a father.

"Very well, Sadie. A maid and a footman would be in order. Two maids, if you can find them. I'm of a mind to open up a few more rooms." He ignored Sadie's beaming smile.

"I knew she was a good omen."

"The child?" he asked, looking skeptically at the girl.

"No, sir, Lady Lilian."

Marcus scowled at his cook. "Would you mind very much introducing the child to our guest?"

"Oh, no, sir, I can't leave my bread." Sadie made a show of checking the large oven, where, indeed, several loaves of bread were baking.

"Very well. You may come with me," he said to the little girl. "I want you to meet Lady Lilian. You will be sharing a room with her until we can set something special up for you."

"In the attic?" Mabel asked, looking slightly fearful as she peered up to the ceiling.

Sadie, who had been wiping down the table, stopped as if she was holding her breath, as if he actually would put a tiny girl child up in the attic, where the ghosts apparently resided. Mabel, who had climbed down from her stool, stood holding her stocking against her stomach.

"No. You shall have a pretty room on the same level as I."

The little girl smiled, showing a dimple in her right cheek, and Marcus's heart wrenched just the smallest bit.

"I lived in the attic back home," Mabel said happily, as if living in an attic weren't awful. She skipped up to Marcus, holding out her hand for him to take. Good God, Mrs. Broom would pay for mistreating this child.

"I see."

"There were rats." This was said with a certain amount of gleeful disgust.

"I detest rats," Marcus said.

Mabel giggled. "Me too. Are there rats here?"

"Not that I've seen. I don't allow them and certainly not near little girls."

"Good. Mrs. Broom said they might eat me. I shouldn't like to be eaten by a rat."

Marcus made a mental note to write to his solicitor and inquire about how he could most harm Mrs. Broom without sending himself to prison. He now regretted giving the harridan even one penny. Still, Mabel seemed like a sweet little thing, unaffected by her terrible upbringing, and he wondered if there had been someone else in the household who had been kind to the child. There must have been. It would be unthinkable if there had not been.

The two began walking up the stairs, and when Mabel struggled a bit to keep up—it was a rather long set of stairs—Marcus hoisted her up so that she clung to his neck, her little legs wrapped around his torso as best she could, which was to say not very well.

"Who is Lady Lilian?"

"An unwanted guest," Marcus said, knowing the child likely wouldn't understand what he meant. "She was ill, but is feeling better now. Nothing contagious, I assure you. She'll be leaving soon enough."

"What's 'tagious?"

"She doesn't have an illness that you can catch."

Marcus knocked this time, slightly irked that he was forced to knock on his own bedroom door but not wanting to catch the lady in her shift again, and only went in when Lady Lilian called out for him to enter. She was sitting up in bed, the covers pulled up to her chin, and her hair was slightly tamed into a knot at the base of her neck. Next to her was a thick volume, which could only be Marcus's collection of short stories by Edgar Allan Poe, perhaps not the best thing to read whilst in an old, decrepit mansion reported to have ghosts.

"Lady Lilian, may I present Miss Mabel Dunford," Marcus said, setting Mabel onto the carpet. "You may curtsy." He gave these instructions even though he wasn't entirely certain the little girl would know what he meant, but was pleasantly surprised when Mable executed a passable curtsy, even still clutching his hand and holding on to her stocking.

"Hello, Mabel, it is a pleasure to meet you." Lilian looked up to Marcus, obviously waiting for some explanation as to whom the child belonged, but Marcus remained silent. "How old are you, Mabel?"

"Very nearly five," she said, looking up to Marcus as if for approval. He nodded, and she shuffled slightly closer to him, her little body nearly an attachment to his right leg. His first instinct was to step away, but he decided quickly he could tolerate her nearness and so remained in place.

"As you may be unaware, my lady, sleeping accommodations at Merdunoir are very few. I would appreciate it if the child could share a room with you at least until I am able to enlist additional servants to ready two more rooms. Apparently, you will be forced to remain here until we can procure you clothing." He felt his face heating slightly, though why he couldn't say.

"I am very grateful for your kind hospitality, sir. I do recognize this as an inconvenience for you."

"It is more than an inconvenience, my lady, and it is not kindness that has forced this decision. It is damnably bothersome, but as I have no choice in the matter other than sending you on your way unclothed, I will allow you to stay."

Mabel tugged on his arm to get his attention. "That's a naughty word," she whispered.

"Not for me. You may not say it, however."

Marcus thought he heard what sounded like a soft snort coming from the direction of the bed, and he glared at the lady, whose face was carefully blank.

"In the meantime," he continued, as if he hadn't been interrupted, "you may wear my robe if you are inclined to walk about. I shall return momentarily with it. You two ladies may become better acquainted until I return."

Lilian watched with a small amount of bemusement as the gentleman walked from the room. She had a feeling that, as acerbic as he seemed, he wasn't as awful as she'd originally thought. Any man who would carry a small child up the stairs, then allow said child to hold his hand, couldn't be all unkindness. It was quite obvious he didn't want her here, and to be honest, Lilian didn't want to be at

Merdunoir either. But as Sadie had burned her clothing, she hardly had any choice in the matter but to accept his hospitality, such as it was.

"Do you live here, Mabel?"

The little girl shook her head, then nodded. "Now I do."

"And how long have you been here?"

"Since this morning."

"Ah." It was a syllable that meant understanding, but Lilian had no understanding of whom the child belonged to or why she was here. Perhaps she was a niece? She really didn't know the Dunford family well enough to know whether she could be or not. Then she decided not. The child looked rather like a ragamuffin, with a drab, ill-fitting dress, soft brown hair that needed a good combing, and a general air of neglect. She'd seen children in London, hands held out for coins, who looked much like this little girl.

Mabel took a few steps toward her, eyes wide, clutching something with her little fists. Lilian patted the bed and said, "Come on up so I can braid your hair."

Mabel smiled and, with a bit of assistance, climbed up and knelt beside Lilian. She was a pretty child, with big hazel eyes below a wispy fringe of bangs.

"Who is that?" Lilian asked, indicating the bit of cloth in Mabel's hands.

"It's my dolly."

Though Lilian's heart clenched a bit, she smiled. "Does she have a name?"

"Alice, after the princess."

"A lovely name. And what color hair does she have?"

That question seemed to tickle Mabel, for the stocking obviously didn't have any hair at all. Then she looked at the sad bit of cloth thoughtfully and said, "Yellow. And she has blue eyes and is wearing a pretty blue dress. With lace."

"With lace? What a grand doll you have."

Mabel's eyes twinkled and Lilian was completely charmed. It didn't matter whom she belonged to, for she was a pure delight.

"The man said she was a stocking," Mabel said, a bit of challenge in her tone. Odd that she called his lordship "the man" as if she herself didn't know her connection to the Dunfords.

"A stocking? Anyone with any sense can see she is a doll."

And of course, when Lilian looked up, the man with no sense was standing there, one brow raised, as he looked at the two of them.

Mabel turned about on the bed to face Lord Granton, and Lilian immediately began braiding the girl's hair. It was thick for a young child's and a bit matted, making the task difficult. "Do you have a comb or brush I can use to untangle Miss Mabel's hair?" Lilian asked, not looking up from her task.

Without a word, Lord Granton laid a robe at the foot of the bed, then walked to a set of drawers, producing a comb and a brush. "Mind you get all that hair out of my things when you're finished," he said, handing them over so Lilian could begin her task.

"Ow," Mabel said, turning to give Lilian a scowl, and Lilian pulled in her lips so she wouldn't smile.

"I'm sorry, Mabel, your hair is very tangled. I will try not to pull so hard."

Mabel turned back around and placed two hands atop her head. "This helps," she said. "Laura always started on the bottom."

"I shall do that, then," Lilian said, smiling at the way the little girl was ordering her about.

"You shall address the lady as my lady or Lady Lilian," Lord Granton said. "And you may call me sir, my lord, or Lord Granton. Do you think you can remember that?"

"No, sir," Mabel said.

Lord Granton narrowed his eyes, but Lilian saw a small smile on his lips before he turned to leave.

"Good day, ladies," he called, as he walked out the door.

After he'd gone, Lilian's curiosity only grew. The girl, as sweet as she was, clearly had not been properly cared for. Her dress, so clearly a hand-me-down, was faded from hundreds of washings, and her hair had a chopped look to it, as if in the recent past someone had hacked it off with little care. "Who is Laura?" Lilian asked, and immediately wished she hadn't, for the little thing burst into tears, covering her face with her hands.

"I don't want to live here," she cried plaintively. "I want Laura. I want to go home."

Feeling terribly helpless, Lilian was tempted to call Lord Granton back, but it seemed that was unnecessary, for the man returned, carrying a ribbon in his hand. As soon as he saw Mabel was crying, he hesitated, looking as if he were about to flee the room.

Lilian pulled Mabel to her, looking helplessly over her head to where Lord Granton stood, frowning. "I know it's frightening to be away from everyone and in a new house," Lilian said, trying to soothe the little thing but not knowing how. "Look, Lord Granton has brought you a pretty ribbon for your hair."

"I don't want a ribbon," she cried. "I want Laura."

"Who is this Laura person?" Granton said, as if he could somehow magically conjure her here.

"My sister," Mabel said, sounding terribly sad.

"She has no sister," Granton said, and Lilian immediately and frantically shook her head.

It was too late, of course, because following Granton's pronouncement, Mabel cried even harder, prompting his lordship to pull out a handkerchief and hand it to Lilian.

"She needs a glass of water," he said, obviously wanting to do something to stop the girl's tears. He walked over to the nightstand and poured a glass, then held it out for Lilian to take. She had little faith that a glass of water would stop the tears, and so was surprised when Mabel pulled back and took the glass, her crying for the moment interrupted.

"Did Laura take care of you?" Lilian asked.

Mabel nodded.

"You shall have Lord Granton to take care of you now," Lilian said. Mabel turned, giving his lordship a dubious look.

"Do you know how to play Squeak Piggy Squeak?" she asked, her voice thick from crying.

"Indeed I do," Granton said solemnly. "My brothers and sister played it often when they were young."

"You did not?" Lilian asked.

"My father forbade it."

He said it simply enough, and Lilian sensed no underlying hurt. But how could it not hurt as a child to see your siblings playing when you could not? Her own life had been filled with all sorts of games, for their mother, before she'd fallen ill, had been a lively wonderful parent who had found joy in nearly everything, particularly in preparing Lilian for her one and only season. Because it had given her mother such happiness, Lilian had never complained until the duke turned his sights toward her little sister.

"Do you know how to play Hide the Button?"

Mabel was directing all her questions to his lordship, so Lilian remained silent, watching the interplay between the pair with interest. She still had no idea of their relationship, though clearly there was one, as Mabel had been introduced as a Dunford.

"I do not."

"I can show you. It's an easy game and you don't even have to have a button, though it's better if you do. You can hide anything. Shall I tell you how it's done?"

"If you insist." Granton's eyes met Lilian's, and she felt her cheeks flush—why, she couldn't say. Perhaps it was the unusual shade of his light brown eyes, the way he seemed to study her, as if trying to read her thoughts. He was handsome, in a fierce, masculine way that made her uncomfortable, and she'd be glad when she could leave, even though she hadn't a clear idea where she was going. Just that fleeting thought had her stomach churning. What was she going to do?

She forced herself to listen to the simple rules of the game as she braided the little girl's hair. "The ribbon, if you please," she said, holding her hand out. She took the ribbon from his large hand, thinking he had the hands of a working man, broad and strong. Capable. His Grace's hands had been soft, almost delicate, an incongruous feature on a man who had been so large. Lilian forced thoughts of the dead duke out of her mind, for every time she thought of him, she would see him in his bed, his face spattered grotesquely with blood. After tying the ribbon with hands that slightly shook, she pronounced Mabel beautiful.

"I've never worn a ribbon," Mabel said, pulling her braid over her shoulder and touching the bit of cloth reverently.

Lilian wasn't certain, but she thought she heard a sound very much like a growl emanating from his lordship.

"My lady, may I have a private conversation with you? The child may stay here. Perhaps take a nap."

"I'm not at all tired."

"Lie down and see what happens," he said, and Lilian hid another smile. He might feign lack of interest in the girl, but he had taken the time to fetch a ribbon for her hair and had the patience to listen to a little girl list the rules of Find the Button, rules Lilian had a feeling she had been making up on the spot.

Granton walked from the room, and Lilian, her legs still a bit wobbly, pulled on the robe and followed him, trying not to notice the scent that was suddenly wrapped around her, a combination of cigar and some other pleasant smell that instantly reminded her of her childhood. Perhaps her father had worn a similar cologne; she couldn't be certain, for he had died when she was about the same age as Mabel and all his belongings remained at their former estate, now taken over by her cousin.

She found Granton standing not far from the bedroom door, and when he saw her, he moved further down the hall, down a small set of stairs, and into a study that smelled very much like the robe she wore. The walls were lined with high bookshelves, filled with tomes of all sizes, a collection that must have taken generations to accumulate. A large, ornately carved desk, with huge eagle's talons wrapped around smooth spheres, dominated the small room, which held only a leather sofa and a wing-backed chair of the same dark and well-worn leather. Heavy velvet curtains were pulled closed against the sun, though a sharp shard of light dissected the thick carpet beneath her feet.

Granton moved behind his desk and waited for her to sit before taking his place, his hands folding loosely on the smooth, well-polished mahogany. "The girl is my wife's daughter," he said without preamble. "Until today, I had no idea of her existence. Indeed, I have no idea who does know of the girl's existence other than the awful woman who brought her here today. I don't know what to do with her. I thought perhaps, given you are a woman, you could be of some assistance in the matter."

"I?"

"Yes. I thought you could recommend a school, perhaps."

"School, sir? She seems awfully young. I believe most schools do not accept children under the age of seven."

"Certainly they have schools that take younger children."

"Unwanted children, you mean." Lilian could not help herself. She couldn't imagine little Mabel living in a cold school, with no one to tuck her in or read her a story at night. She was practically a baby.

"Of course she is unwanted," Granton said brutally. "When I say she is my wife's child, does it escape you, my lady, how such a child could have been conceived without my knowledge?"

Lilian blushed. She hadn't actually thought it through, not wanting to dwell on the idea of conception and all that meant. And, of course, it would have been painful for him to discover the full extent of his wife's betrayal. But no matter how the child had come into the world, she was here and a darling little thing, and Lilian felt the need to defend her. "It is not the child's fault."

"And sending her off to school is not a punishment," he said, with no small amount of exasperation. "Does this household look to be a good place for a child? If she was in a school, she would have other children to play with. Here, she will be entirely alone. I certainly am not equipped to deal with a small child." He took a breath as if to calm himself. "I apologize. This has nothing to do with you, other than I thought, as a woman, you might have advice."

Lilian relented. After all, she did not know this man, and in a few short days, she would leave, never to see Mabel again—a thought that produced a sharp twinge in her chest. One of her largest weaknesses was that she could become instantly attached to things and people. She couldn't simply pet a kitten. As soon as she touched it, felt its soft fur, it claimed a piece of her heart. She'd once found a pretty rock on a walk along a lake, picking it up, liking the smooth, cool surface. She held it for a short while and was about to throw it into the lake, but couldn't. She had become *attached.* So she'd tucked that rock into her pocket, ridiculously thinking the rock would be somehow offended if she were to toss it away without a thought. She knew a rock didn't have feelings; she wasn't *that* batty. But she'd kept the darned thing anyway. It currently sat on a shelf in her room back at Mount Carlyle, and even now the thought of it there, that a maid might throw it away, bothered her to a ridiculous degree.

If she felt that way about a rock, how would she feel about little Mabel when it came time to say good-bye?

"Perhaps you could secure a kindly nanny, one who would keep the child away from you," Lilian suggested, keeping her tone level and her face bland, but his eyes narrowed slightly and she couldn't stop the small blush that tinged her cheeks.

He stared at her, his unusual-colored eyes unwavering, as if determining whether she was being critical, until Lilian felt like squirming in her seat. She did not, for she was far too disciplined to allow him to see how he disconcerted her.

"You, my lady, are a mystery," he said, apparently deciding to ignore her small jibe and change the subject entirely. "I don't care for mysteries." He said the words slowly, as if he was analyzing each word's effect on her as he spoke them.

"I'm afraid I don't understand," Lilian said, lying through her teeth. She knew full well what he'd meant.

"I think you do," he replied after a long, excruciating pause. "I find you wandering the moors, without funds, half starved, with nothing except a torn dress and battered slippers. A mystery, indeed."

"I believe I told you I had a falling-out with my sister," Lilian said, trying to maintain her calm.

"And left in so much haste you didn't take a valise? Or funds?"

"I had some funds, which I used for a train. I'm afraid it wasn't enough to get me to Scotland and my uncle."

"Strange, I thought you said you were visiting a family friend," he murmured, steepling his fingers in front of his mouth.

"We called him uncle even though he was not a relation," she answered.

"If you have no funds, how do you expect to travel the rest of the way?"

"I need only have my bank wire me money, I assure you, my lord." That was a blatant lie, for it would still be three years before she could access the kinds of funds that would allow her to live on her own. In any case, that did not seem to satisfy him, for his dark brows drew together as he considered her words. Lilian wondered if he already knew of her troubles and was simply being cruel, then immediately dismissed that thought. Granton struck her as a man who would have called the local magistrate immediately if he knew he was harboring a suspected murderer.

"I wonder why you haven't already done that?" he asked.

Because I don't have any money, and even if I did, contacting a bank would give away my location and I would surely be arrested for the murder of the Duke of Weston. She almost wished she could say that aloud, for the weight of all she carried was beginning to wear her down.

"As I said, I left in haste and was quite upset at the time. Not thinking clearly." He surely would think her a complete dolt or a liar. "I thought I would wire my uncle," she said, thinking quickly. The man would not be happy to hear from her, that was for certain. He hadn't seen her in years, not since her mother's funeral, and no doubt hadn't spared her a thought in the interval. It was a sad state of affairs, indeed, that she had nowhere else to turn.

"It would be ungentlemanly for me to express doubt in your story,

so for now I will accept you on your word. Sadie will bring a seamstress from Whitby on the morrow, and then you can continue your
journey to Scotland."

On that final note, a deep depression settled over Lilian. She was
not going to Scotland. It had been a foolish, and completely unrealis-
tic notion, the frantic plan of a woman who'd had no other choice.
She was quite certain that even should she wire her uncle, it was unlikely he would invite her to live with him. Her cousin, who'd taken
the title when her father had died, was an onerous man, a skinflint
and religious fanatic whom Lilian loathed. His mother, Lilian's aunt,
lived with him in the home Lilian had grown up in. They were a
strange pair with whom Lilian had always felt uncomfortable. The
thought of living with her cousin and aunt was worse than wandering
the moors until she starved to death.

As Lilian made her way back to the room, a small laugh escaped
her on that thought. It didn't matter; she was fairly certain that no one
would want to harbor a woman who was accused of murdering a
peer. She had little doubt that eventually she would be found, that
Lord Granton would learn of the murder, that he would turn her in to
the authorities, and that, after a quick trial, she would be hanged for a
crime she hadn't committed.

She stopped dead in the hallway, fighting down a sob that threatened to erupt from her burning throat. She didn't want to die, and
certainly not on a hangman's noose. She fisted her hands by her sides
and swallowed heavily, pushing down the terror she felt, pushing
down the panic that was growing in her chest. She was only safe until
Lord Granton learned what had happened, and then she was doomed.

Chapter 5

Marcus watched Lady Lilian walk hurriedly down the hall and then stop abruptly, her entire body taut, hands fisted. Her shoulders heaved as if she was taking long, deep breaths, the kind of breaths one took to stem the tide of some great emotion. He narrowed his eyes, fighting the urge to go to her and try to offer some comfort. Clearly, she was struggling with some sort of demon. No high-born lady of her ilk would run away from a comfortable home unless something frightening had happened. She didn't strike him as a woman who wept easily or became hysterical over nothing. After a few moments, she lifted her head and, no doubt stiffening her upper lip, continued down the hall toward his bedroom and Mabel. She stopped at the doorway, and he could see that she was smiling. It was difficult not to smile at Mabel. He'd always wanted children, which was perhaps the great irony of his wife being impregnated by another man and leaving Marcus with his by-blow. Mabel was legally his daughter, and whether he liked that fact or not, he was responsible for her. Who her true father was didn't matter. Hell, it could have been any number of men, some of whom he'd thought were his friends.

He felt the familiar wash of humiliation he experienced whenever he thought of Eleanor's dalliances, and closed his eyes against it. When his wife had first died, he had been tortured by the knowledge of her betrayal, and felt foolish for caring even a little that she was dead. He'd thought he wanted her dead. God, the pity he'd seen in the eyes of his brothers when he'd stood at her graveside and wept. Just the thought of it made his stomach churn.

He needed to ride. Nothing helped clear his mind better than taking his beloved gelding, Chief, and riding hell-bent on the beach, letting the ice-cold water splash around him, feeling the sharp sea air cleanse him. He stalked toward his room to grab his coat, stopping suddenly at the door. He kept forgetting his room was no longer his.

She was there, sitting in his bed, reading his book, wearing his robe. And Mabel, who had protested that she wasn't at all sleepy, lay next to her looking like a ragged little angel, fast asleep. It was wrong, all wrong, but for some reason, his immediate thought was, *Yes, this is right.* He liked seeing a woman in his bed, a child fast asleep, as if God were cruelly showing him what might have been had Eleanor been the sort of wife he'd thought he was marrying. But Lady Lilian was not his wife and Mabel not truly his child, and so that image mocked him for a stupid sentimental fool. Perhaps he was sentimental after all.

"Are you enjoying my book?" he asked softly, not wanting to awaken the child.

"It's wonderfully gruesome, isn't it?" she asked, smiling at him. "I read most of these stories when I was younger but had forgotten how much I enjoyed them."

"My favorite of his is 'The Tell-Tale Heart,'" Marcus said, walking over to a small desk and opening a drawer. "You might like this when you've finished. Have you read 'The Pit and the Pendulum'?"

Lady Lilian looked at the small orange-bound book and shook her head. "Perhaps, given that I am staying in a haunted house, I shouldn't read such fare." She looked at the book as if he were holding out a tempting treat. "But I can always stop reading if it's too frightening." She took it from him and smiled, looking impossibly adorable sitting in his bed, smothered by his large burgundy robe. She was pretty, a bit of femininity in this otherwise dark and dreary home, and it was a nice change, he supposed.

"I see Sadie has been talking to you about our ghost. No doubt the footsteps she hears are my own."

"You wander around the attic at night, my lord?"

"No, but I have been known to frequent the tower on clear evenings. I have an interest in astronomy. My grandfather was a founding member of the Royal Astronomical Society and passed his love of the science to me. It's one of the reasons I like it here; the stars are easier to view." Marcus realized, with no small amount of surprise, that this was the longest conversation he'd had with another person in nearly a year, and it wasn't entirely unpleasant. He'd come to the conclusion upon his wife's death that he held no interest in society, in chatting about mundane topics with mundane people. He'd been so sick of trying to pretend his life was as it should be, that he was, if not happy, at least content. He dreaded the thought of walking into a ballroom, of seeing the same faces he'd been seeing since he'd reached his majority, the endless talking and questions about how he was faring, the thought that his mother would begin matchmaking.

For some reason, this winsome girl had him talking like a veritable magpie. He realized she'd offered no condolences on the death of his wife, no questions, as if she instinctively knew not to talk about his personal life. Either that or she was completely uninterested. Not a welcome thought, that.

"So you have no belief in ghosts?" Her eyes danced with amusement, and Marcus nearly smiled.

"None at all. I put ghosts in the same category as nymphs, fairies, and trolls."

"Never say you do not believe in fairies, sir. How else to explain how a room is kept clean?"

"Servants?"

She let out a light laugh. "My nanny told me fairies did all the work, and I believed her for far too long."

Mabel stirred, stretching her little body and rubbing her eyes, her nap over.

"You will join me for dinner this evening?" he asked, suddenly wanting company. Lady Lilian would be gone soon enough, and he'd be alone again, so he might as well be a proper host while she was here.

"I can hardly sit at a dining table wearing only a robe."

"Of course you can." When she made to protest, he said, "I would like the company, my lady." He didn't realize he was holding his breath until she nodded, and he let it out, slowly, so as not to call attention to his apprehension. Why the hell was he apprehensive? Maybe he had been living alone for far too long.

"Then, yes, I would enjoy sitting at a table and eating for a change. It feels like months since I have done so. And Sadie is a capable cook. I shall look forward to it."

Marcus looked down at her and tried not to be affected by the fact a beautiful woman, wearing hardly anything at all, was sitting in his bed smiling up at him. "I shall look forward to hearing your opinion on Weston."

For some reason, his words startled her, made her face heat instantly, and he felt a surge of some emotion he couldn't quite name. Just hearing Weston's name caused the lady to blush, and he couldn't help but wonder why.

"I fear such a discussion might spoil my appetite," she said tightly.

When Marcus chuckled, she seemed to relax. "At least I know you share my enmity toward the man. I shall look forward to dinner, my lady." He gave a small bow, grabbed his coat, and headed out the door, trying to stop himself from whistling.

One of the challenges of living in a large home with only two servants was that Marcus was called upon to do certain chores that a man of his standing should never be expected to do. He was used to finding flaws and telling a servant to correct them. Living at Merdunoir, he'd become far more independent. Doing even the smallest chores, such as driving a nail in the wall to hang a picture, he found ridiculously satisfying. His ride on the beach was precisely what he'd needed, a mindless, physical activity that drove thoughts of his dead wife and her child out of his mind and let him forget that a beautiful and nearly naked woman was at that moment lying in his bed.

He returned to an empty stable as the sun was dipping toward the horizon. Palmer was off doing something else, and it was left to him to brush down his horse, a task he quite enjoyed. He tossed Chief some fresh hay, gave him an affectionate slap on his shoulder, and walked to the house, a sense of calm steeling over him as he looked up at it. Merdunoir was a monstrosity of a house, but he loved it. A second-story shutter was askew, and an attic window broken, no doubt letting in some creature that sounded like a ghost walking about at night. He made a mental note to fix the shutter and block off the window on the morrow. Perhaps the attic had bats. Despite its flaws, Marcus liked the old place and decided it might be time to give her a bit of attention. He paused on the low stone step that led to the kitchen and stamped his boots, loosening a small bit of sand that clung to them. He opened the door, frowning at how the doorknob jiggled, as if it was close to falling off. Bending over, he peered at the knob and tested it, realizing it needed only a bit of tightening. Back home, he would have immediately told a footman, who would have told someone, who would have fixed the door. Here, he would either have to wait for Palmer to be available or do it himself. Tightening a screw was certainly on the list of easy repairs that he could manage.

Marcus headed directly to the kitchen's large L-shaped pantry, where he, much to Sadie's dismay, had reserved one shelf for the tools he used most—hammer, nails, screwdrivers, etc. The high windows of the pantry let in a soft, peachy-yellow light from the setting sun. It was a homey place, with smooth brick floors and wooden shelving stocked with all manner of food, pots and pans, and dishes. If Sadie never washed a plate, he could eat for a month and not run out of plates. He couldn't recall any party ever being held at Merdunoir and wondered why such a large set of dishes was needed in this remote estate.

Marcus strode to his shelf, looking at his small array of tools, then froze. He'd heard a sound, a soft drop of water, a distinctive drop, such as one heard during a bath. And he knew, without a doubt, who it was taking a bath in the pantry, most likely frozen in horror at the sight of him.

"Lady Lilian?"

A long silence, so long he began to think he'd imagined that sound.

"Yes, my lord."

For some reason, Marcus found himself smiling as he looked at his tools and pictured Lady Lilian, eyes wide, completely still, mortified that he might . . .

"It seems I have a moral dilemma," he said finally.

"You do not, sir. As a gentleman, you have only one course of action."

He chuckled softly. "I am a gentleman, you are correct, my lady. But I am also a man, a man who has not had the pleasure of watching a lady in her bath in too many years to count."

"Sir." She sounded quite angry, which made Marcus smile even more. Feeling absurdly mischievous, Marcus spun around.

The lady gasped, immediately lifting her knees up and wrapping her pale arms around them, completely shielding anything worth looking at from view. Her expression was one of disbelief tinged with anger, and perhaps, though he might have been imagining it, amusement.

Then the oddest thing happened. He could see nothing but her pink knees, her slim arms, her creamy shoulders, her riot of hair, still wet and curling around her. And, of course, her face, looking ethereally lovely in the last of the day's light. It hit him, unexpectedly, a raw wave of lust so intense, he nearly staggered from it. Marcus spun around, praying she hadn't seen it in his face, horrified that his body had, for lack of a better term, sprung to life in a way that hadn't happened since he was a teenager.

"I do beg your pardon," he said, grabbing the screwdriver and hastening out of her line of sight. He stopped, caught his breath, and adjusted himself to ease some of the ache. "Until this evening, my lady." He didn't want her to think she could use this encounter as an excuse to avoid dinner.

Lilian let out a slow breath, listening intently as his steps receded. "Of all the . . ." What kind of a man *did* that sort of thing? She let out a soft laugh. It was odd; if she had been in the same situation and the Duke of Weston had walked in on her, she would have been terrified. She would have shrunk beneath his gaze, felt sickened by his actions. For some reason she could not explain, Lord Grafton's actions left her more amused than anything. The dickens. She could comfort herself in the knowledge that he hadn't truly seen anything other than her knees, arms, and face. He'd seemed rather amused himself, unmoved by her state of undress. Before he'd spun back around, she'd seen something else in his enigmatic eyes, something dark and slightly disturbing, but nothing that gave her an ounce of fear. Still, that she had been alone in a room, unclothed, with an unmarried man . . . it didn't bear thinking about. Women had been forced to marry for far less than that. In fact, her presence in his home alone was quite scandalous, but there was nothing to do for it now.

Then again, she was already ruined beyond redemption. The article in the *Times* had, in one instant, made her a societal outcast. How much worse could her reputation get, after all?

Lilian completed her bath, then stood and grabbed up the towel, shivering and wrapping it around her. Such luxuries as a bath would be few and far between now. Once she left Merdunoir, she would be quite alone. Perhaps she could travel to America. Perhaps she could hide somewhere until she was twenty-five, then go to her bank, remove her funds, and escape the country before anyone was the wiser.

It was a foolish thought, for she had the fear that the moment she tried to remove her money, someone would sound an alarm and she'd be dragged away by a constable. In chains. With people throwing rotten vegetables at her. As an heiress, she was well-known at her bank and now, no doubt, a notorious figure.

Once she was dry, Lilian put on his lordship's robe, holding the material to her nose and breathing in his scent before she realized what she was doing. Immediately, she thrust the material down and wrinkled her nose at her own behavior. Then she drew it back up, slowly, a little guiltily, and inhaled again, feeling a sudden and unexplainable sense of longing. Shaking her head, she tightened the tie and tugged on a thick pair of woolen stockings Sadie had given her. They were warm and much appreciated, particularly on the cold brick of the pantry and kitchen.

Lilian made her way back to her room and on the way ran into a frazzled-looking Sadie, who must be hurrying to the kitchen to cook a hasty meal. She paused just long enough to dip a quick curtsy and moved down the hall muttering something about how one person could only do so much. Indeed, poor Sadie seemed terribly overworked, especially with two additional mouths to feed. No wonder only a handful of rooms were opened.

"Would you like to play a game?" Mabel asked.

Poor little thing must feel a bit lost being in this big, dark house with no one to talk to except her sock doll. Lilian smiled. "Hide the Button?"

Lilian couldn't remember being so nervous before attending a dinner, which made no sense at all. Perhaps, she thought, it was because earlier that day, the man she would be dining with had come upon her naked in her bath. It didn't matter at all that he hadn't actually seen anything. She still did not understand why she wasn't livid; she ought to be. But the only emotion she could conjure up was one of mortification, which no doubt explained her nerves. She descended the stairs, her wool stockings making her approach quite silent. Yet when she entered the dining hall, Granton, who appeared to be going through his correspondence, lifted his head and immediately stood.

"My lady, thank you for joining me," he said formally. "Please forgive my casual appearance, but I do not have a valet here with me."

Lilian looked closely at him to see if he was jesting, for she was standing in front of him wearing nothing but a robe and her shift, still damp from a hasty washing. He, on the other hand, was the epitome of a country gentleman, wearing a brown wool jacket over a green silk vest and dark trousers. His whiskey-colored eyes might have shown the slightest bit of amusement, but Lilian didn't know him well enough to be certain. Lilian did not meet his eyes for long, unable to hold his gaze for more than a few seconds, but she could feel his stare just the same.

As she walked toward the setting that had been placed to his right, he pulled out her chair and sat back down. Lilian, in her man's robe and woolen socks, tried to maintain her dignity, but the situation was so odd that she let out a small, sharp laugh. "I've never dined in a robe," she said in an attempt to explain her nervous laughter. In truth, she'd never dined alone with a gentleman; it was decidedly foreign and completely scandalous. One month ago, she never would have considered such a thing, but now it didn't seem to matter at all.

"Actually, that's not true," she amended. "I've often dined in my dressing gown in my room. In private. In fact, that is how I spent most evenings when visiting my sister." Lilian liked to use the term "visit" rather than live, even though her visit had lasted three years. "I had a lovely room overlooking the garden, in an entirely different wing of the house from Their Graces. It was almost as if I were living alone."

"And did you enjoy living at Mount Carlyle?"

"Not in the least." Lilian decided not to elaborate. What would she say to him? That she'd had no choice but to live with a man she loathed and a sister who loathed her? They'd only tolerated her out of a sense of duty and the censure they would receive should they make her leave—at least that's what Theresa, ever the martyr, had told her on more than one occasion. Lilian and her sister had been close when they were young, but all that had changed, seemingly overnight, when Terri married the duke. Once Theresa realized what her marriage to Weston would be like, she'd grown to resent Lilian her freedom. Theresa conveniently forgot how Lilian had begged their mother not to allow the marriage. But her sister had been so swept up in the attention she received, the dreams of Worth gowns and being a duchess, she'd refused to listen. Weston had been a monumental mistake, something Theresa had likely realized quickly in her marriage. As an unmarried woman, Lilian could hardly live on her own, not when she had family willing to take her in. She had no elderly aunt to live with and had wanted to avoid any hint of scandal, still hoping that she might someday marry. Now, she had more scandal tied to her good name than she knew what to do with, and marriage to even the lowest peer would be out of the question.

Sadie entered, carrying a large tureen of what turned out to be a rather wonderful potato soup, and Granton turned the conversation away from Weston.

"How is the child?"

"Mabel is fast asleep. I think the events of the day have worn her out. We were playing Hide the Button and she fell asleep waiting for me to hide it." Lilian prattled on for a while, keenly aware of his unrelenting gaze as she spoke, while she mostly looked down at her bowl. He listened, but never interjected a comment, leaving her voice to trail off into an uncomfortable silence. She let out a small sigh and turned her full attention to the soup. Clearly, Granton was not a conversationalist, which made her wonder why he'd asked her to dinner in the first place. When he finally did deign to speak, Lilian wished he'd remained silent.

"How is Weston?"

The question took her off guard, and instantly she could hear her blood pounding in her ears. "When I last saw him, you mean?" she asked, picturing His Grace's blood-stained chest.

"I daresay I realize you cannot know how he is at this very moment." His lips lifted a bit. "I meant the last time you saw him, of course."

Panic flooded Lilian; she'd barely heard his words. As she stared down at the delicate gold flowers painted on the rim of her bowl, she wondered briefly whether his lordship would change the subject if she remained silent. But he continued to stare at her politely, waiting for her answer.

"He was unwell," she said, trying desperately not to lie. But it was a lie, and she loathed lying, so she laid down her spoon and looked up at him. "His Grace is dead. He was found murdered in his bed." The inadvertent rhyme struck her as impossibly funny at the moment, and she let out a laugh, mortified that she was laughing about the dead duke but unable to stop herself.

Granton laid down his spoon as well and took up a letter that lay on top of his correspondence. For some reason, the deliberate way he made the motion filled Lilian with a terrible dread, and she could feel her entire body begin to tremble. "Ah," he said, his gaze unwavering, and Lilian had to look down. "I enjoy poetry as well. Perhaps I can add to your rhyme." He looked at her, his whiskey eyes level. "The lady panicked and ran away, thinking she would have to pay." Lilian gasped. *Oh God.* "But then a local man admitted, that he's the one who really did it."

Lilian's blood roared in her ears ever louder, making it difficult to hear, and it took several moments for her to understand the last line in their ridiculous poem. She snapped her head up. "What did you say?"

"They caught the man who murdered His Grace, my lady," he said blandly, indicating the missive. "My brother writes to me regularly and this was rather an exciting story in our sleepy little county. Apparently, His Grace got one of the maids with child. She was fourteen and her father decided Weston deserved to die. I completely concur. Sadly, the gentleman took his own life, but before he did, he left a detailed letter admitting his guilt."

Lilian sat back, the relief she felt profound, making her almost lightheaded. "I can't believe it," she said, looking with wonder at Granton. "Are you certain?"

"The magistrate has closed the case." He set the letter aside and pierced her with a searching look. "Why did you not tell me? I might have helped."

"I could hardly introduce myself in that manner. 'Hello, I am Lilian Martin and everyone believes I've murdered the Duke of Weston.'" She drew a still-shaking hand over her brow, as if the motion might help her brain accept what she had just heard. She was exonerated. Free. "Oh my God. You have no idea how frightened I was. I could picture myself, walking up to the gallows, some horrid man standing there grinning at me, ready to put that . . ."

"Blindfold? Hood?" he supplied.

"Yes, blindfold."

"I think they use blindfolds for firing squads."

"Then a hood," she said impatiently, allowing a small amount of exasperation into her voice. He was so blasé, as if they were discussing the weather, for goodness sake, not her execution.

"How is it that they believed you were the murderer?"

"I found him. I was on my way to my room from the library when I heard a strange sound and investigated. I saw his door was ajar and I could see from the door that his hand was dangling from his bed and so I called to him. When he didn't answer, I entered the room and kicked an object on the floor. It was a small pistol. I remember thinking it was such a curious thing to find on his bedroom floor, so I picked it up. Then I walked further into the room and saw that he'd been shot. And that's the very moment my sister's maid and later my sister came into the room. I suppose I did look rather guilty, standing over him holding a pistol. Like a scene out of a bad dramatic play. I can hardly blame them for jumping to such a conclusion."

"And so you ran."

"I grabbed what I could and left immediately. My sister was hysterical, screaming that I murdered her husband when, all along, I thought she'd done it. She had enough reason," Lilian finished darkly.

"Weston had his share of enemies. My only wish is that the gentleman hadn't committed suicide, for I would have liked to have shaken his hand."

Lilian could feel tears pressing against her eyes; the emotions swirling through her were nearly overwhelming. She rarely cried and never in front of another person, so she set her emotions as straight as her back and pushed the tears aside. Granton was looking at her with concern and so she forced a smile. It did no good to think about how lost she'd been, how lost she still was. She was free to go anywhere, but the sad truth was, she had no place to go. Lilian had little desire to live with a sister who had accused her of murder.

"Do you really have a friend in Scotland?" Granton asked, then took a sip of wine, as if this were everyday dinner conversation.

"I do, but I doubt he would welcome me."

Sadie entered with a pie, smiling brightly at the pair of them. "Some nice pork pie for you," she said, setting the plate down. "My mother's recipe and the best pork pie in Yorkshire, if I do say so myself."

"Thank you, Sadie," Granton said, as Sadie cut into the steaming meat pie and gave each of them a large portion. "It is true I have never eaten better in all of England."

"Cinnamon is the secret, you see," she said with a nod, and by the indulgent smile on Granton's lips, Lilian suspected this was something he'd heard many times.

"Palmer is going to town tomorrow to recruit some servants, and I would like you to go with him, Sadie, so you may interview any prospects. I ask that you be silent on the subject of ghosts and perhaps reassure anyone who asks."

"I dare not lie," Sadie said, looking at the ceiling as if the ghost might hear the conversation. Lilian shot Granton an amused look, and he shook his head slightly, silently imploring her to indulge his servant. It was oddly intimate, that look, and for some reason, Lilian flushed and looked down at her plate.

"Have you ever seen this ghost?" Granton asked Sadie.

"No, sir, but as I've said, I've heard him plenty. All that moaning and walking, back and forth, back and forth. All sorts of noises in the night."

"If someone asks about a ghost, you can honestly say you have never seen one and leave it at that."

"I suppose that would do," she said, sounding uncertain.

"Thank you, Sadie. This seamstress, she works quickly, I hope. I am certain Lady Lilian is anxious to return home."

Sadie started slightly, as if word that Lilian was leaving was unexpected, and for some reason, Lilian found that statement rather jarring as well. Yes, she was feeling much better and could most certainly travel, but she realized she was in no real hurry to rush off. Strange that she shouldn't want to, but there it was.

"Why, then, we'll have you on your way before the week is out," Sadie said, an odd note in her voice. "Where is your home, my lady?"

Marcus turned his attention to his pie, but raised his head when he heard nothing but silence following his housekeeper's question. Lady Lilian's cheeks were flushed becomingly, and she opened her mouth as if to speak, then closed it without uttering a sound.

"I'm sorry, miss. I didn't mean to pry," Sadie said, hastily gathering up the soup bowls.

"Oh, no, Sadie, you were not prying, so no apology is necessary." Lady Lilian looked up at him through thick, brown lashes, before fixing her gaze on her pie. "It's only that I don't actually have a home."

She said it without even a hint of self-pity. Of course, Sadie, who liked to mother everyone she came into contact with, said, "Oh, poor dear. Where will you be going then?" Sadie looked at him as if he were the reason the woman was homeless.

"I'm certain your sister will be happy to see you," Marcus said. He didn't want Sadie to get any ideas about Lady Lilian staying on at Merdunoir. He was already taking a terrible risk by allowing an unmarried woman to stay in his home without the benefit of a chaperone. As was the lady. At this point, no one knew where Lady Lilian was, and as far as he was concerned, that was the way it was going to remain. Men had been forced to marry against their will for far less a breach than this. She was not only sleeping in his bed and wearing his robe, he'd also seen her naked in her bath. Not nearly enough of her, but he had seen her. If word got out about any of this, he would be forced to marry the chit, and God above knew he'd had enough of marriage. He'd just as soon let his brother Adam take his title when he died than marry again. In short, Lady Lilian had to go, and she had to go as soon as it was physically possible for her to do so.

Lilian gave him a tight little smile. "I fear my sister will not be happy to see me, my lord, but see me she will as I have nowhere else to go."

"Have you no aunts or uncles? What about Redding?" Granton asked, referring to the loathsome cousin who had inherited her father's title.

Lilian actually shuddered. "Have you met Lord Redding?"

"Indeed I have." Marcus remembered a reed-thin man who barely topped five feet tall and spouted Scripture at the least provocation. Within five minutes of meeting the man, he'd quoted Proverbs: *Everyone who is arrogant in heart is an abomination to the Lord; be assured, he will not go unpunished.* To which, Marcus had laughed, much to the man's disgust. "I see your point."

"I have thought about setting up my own house, hiring a companion."

"There you go. Capital idea." Marcus turned his attention back to his pie.

Sadie, who was still in the room on the pretense of cleaning the side table but was most likely shamelessly eavesdropping, let out a small snort.

"You don't agree, Sadie?"

The older woman's cheeks turned ruddy. "If she were on the shelf with no prospects, I'd say she should. But she's practically a girl. No one will want to marry a young girl who lives by herself, companion or no. Unless you don't want to marry?"

Lilian was clearly embarrassed by the conversation, but gamely answered. "I have not gone out into society for three years. My mother died shortly after my sister's wedding, so I was in mourning for a year. Weston disliked society and rarely went to London, much to my sister's dismay, and he saw no need for me to have a second season, given, as he put it, I had a man to care for me. Instead, we stayed in the country no matter how much Her Grace complained."

"You dislike the country?" Marcus asked, praying she was longing for London. She was far too tempting sitting there, her hair barely tamed, the robe showing tantalizing glimpses of her creamy skin. It was all he could do to concentrate on his meal; he found himself staring at her, feeling almost drugged by lust. It was not a state he found at all enjoyable.

Lilian shook her head. "I'm happy anywhere."

"And how do you like our lovely moors?" Sadie asked, impertinent woman. Marcus had suspected the older woman of matchmaking when she'd burned Lady Lilian's dress, and now he was quite certain of it. Did she not know that as a servant she should not be inserting herself into the conversation? Then again, he had invited her response.

"I do not know the moors well enough to form an opinion. When I was wandering about, I hardly had time to appreciate their beauty."

"Poor lass," Sadie said, clucking her tongue. Marcus controlled the urge to roll his eyes.

"Perhaps, when you are feeling better, his lordship can show you about. Or perhaps you can tour the secret tunnel."

"Sadie, thank you," Marcus said, dismissing the servant.

Sadie looked at him, seeming slightly annoyed, but made her way out of the room.

"Tunnel?" Lady Lilian asked.

Marcus let out a sigh. No doubt when he told her about the tunnel, she would want to explore it, and he could hardly send her down by herself. That meant she would need clothes and shoes, which meant when she should be in a carriage on her way to London, she would be with him, exploring the tunnels. "For smugglers. Brandy, mostly, during the Napoleonic Wars."

Her eyes widened with excitement and Marcus couldn't help but be charmed. He remembered with fondness exploring the tunnels with his brothers. Only during their summers at Merdunoir had he been sometimes allowed to have fun and engage in activities his father normally prohibited.

"Secret tunnels? How exciting. I would like to explore them. Perhaps Mabel can come along if it's not too dangerous."

"It's only dangerous at high tide, and I will be sure not to show them to you then. It is rather an ingenious system. There are a series of caves, some of which are completely submerged at high tide and others that stay dry, and they are all connected via a tunnel to the basement. My brothers found out the hard way to watch the tide. They got stuck in a dry cave overnight, unable to leave. Worse, they had let my sister tag along with them. She was six at the time."

"Your parents must have been terrified," Lady Lilian said. She took a bite of her pie and smiled. "It is quite good. Go on with your story."

He hadn't talked to anyone about his childhood in years, and he hadn't a clue why he was sharing such stories with this girl. Perhaps it was because he would never see her again, or maybe that she actually seemed interested in what he had to say. Or maybe he knew that if he kept their conversation going, their time together would be extended before he went off on his own to spend the night in his study. Alone. "My father was in London, thank God, but my mother was here. My brothers and sister were laughing when they walked up the stairs, full of themselves and the adventure. She stood there holding a switch, so angry she couldn't even yell at them properly. And then she started crying and hugging them. I think they all felt worse about making her cry than if she'd struck them with the switch." Marcus smiled at the memory.

"Why weren't you with them?"

His smile slowly faded and he could feel that old resentment churning in his stomach. He'd been sixteen, and his mother had had a list of duties he was to perform while his father was in London, duties that did not allow for him to be with his siblings on that day. It was just as well. Had he been with them, the blame would have fallen squarely on his shoulders. Even as it was, his father hadn't been angry at Adam, but at him for allowing them down too close to high tide.

"I'd grown bored with the tunnels by that time," he said, the enjoyment of the conversation gone. It was almost as if his father were there, frowning and shaking his head that he was having too grand a time with his lady guest.

"Or are you afraid of the dark? Mabel can hold your hand." She lifted one brow, clearly teasing him, and he found himself smiling, his dark thoughts swept away with a speed that was stunning.

"Do you really want to see them?" For some reason, he began hoping that she truly did. What would it harm to have her stay one extra day? Or two? That was a dangerous thought, intoxicating, and he pushed it solidly away.

She smiled, a full smile that lit her face, that made her look even more stunningly beautiful and terribly young. "I do. I love exploring ruins and such. I'm afraid I'm a bit of a bluestocking when it comes to history."

"What an old-fashioned turn of phrase. Bluestocking, indeed."

"I'm a bit old-fashioned, I suppose."

Marcus studied her face as she turned her attention to her pie. Her nose was straight, with a slight uptilt, just enough to make her look a bit impertinent, her mouth soft and pink and . . . He tore his gaze away and shifted uncomfortably in his seat, hating the hot wave of lust that consumed him. "How old are you, my lady?"

She looked up, swallowed, and even that filled him with desire. God, he was depraved. "Twenty-two."

He'd thought her younger. She looked younger. He'd wanted her to be younger so she would be unsuitable, so he could banish completely the lust he felt when he looked at her. He wished she were seventeen so he could pat her on the head and shove her up into his carriage and be rid of her. But she was twenty-two, only six years younger than he, an age that made her perfectly suitable to be a man's wife. Some other man. But her being twenty-two and not seventeen made her, if not available, then damn more tempting than she'd been not two minutes prior.

"And how old are you?" she asked, looking mischievous.

"Twenty-eight."

"I thought you much older." She said the words casually, but he could hear the teasing in them. He knew for certain when she darted a look at him and her lips tightened a bit as she tried not to smile.

"How old did you think I was?"

"I was thinking closer to thirty-five. Perhaps older?"

Now that was a stunner. "You did not."

She grinned. "No, I did not."

He let out a sound that might or might not have been a laugh. He wasn't quite sure, and he could see she wasn't either, for she looked at him cautiously. His eyes drifted to her mouth and she stilled. If he leaned a bit, he could place his hand behind her head and draw her to him, and kiss her. He wondered what she would do. It was a useless thought, for he'd never do such a thing. But, he realized grimly, it was rather a nice thought. She swallowed, and his gaze dropped to her throat, creamy and smooth, and trailed downward to the V in his robe, that dark shadow that prevented him from seeing the curve of her breasts. How easy it would be to pull apart the edges of her borrowed robe and see what lay beneath. Would she be completely naked? Or was she wearing some undergarment? God above, he was tempted to find out.

"Oh, I'm sorry. I'm getting your robe full of crumbs." She hastily batted at them, rubbing the velvet material where indeed some crumbs had fallen, and he jerked his head back, stunned by where his thoughts had gone.

Marcus let out another short laugh and forced his attention back to his meal. She'd thought he was staring at her chest because of a few errant crumbs? Good God, she was more innocent than he'd thought.

When Granton finally lowered his eyes to his meal, where they belonged, Lilian glared at the impertinent man. Really! Staring at her chest. She fought the urge to pull the robe tighter and thanked goodness she was at least wearing her shift beneath. The way he'd been looking at her it was as if he could see right through the thick velvet material. Rogue.

Lilian had once been an innocent girl, but she could hardly have remained so living in the same house as the Duke of Weston. He had cornered her more than once and tried to molest her, pawing at her and pressing his stiff thing against her. Lilian had done her best to avoid ever being alone with the man, but it had been a nearly impossible task. At first she thought it strange that whenever she had been cornered by His Grace, a footman would happen by or a maid would suddenly get the urge to dust or stir the fire. After some time, though, Lilian became aware that she had several protectors in the house, led by Weston's butler, a stern man whom Lilian had at first disliked.

Mr. Dawson was as stiff and proper as a man could be, but he ran the house like clockwork and Lilian had never seen a more proficient nor hardworking staff. A year into her stay, she came to realize that no female servant was ever alone. They moved in pairs, ever watchful, and a footman was almost always nearby. At some point, they had collectively taken Lilian under their wing, though no words had been exchanged. Lilian had simply become aware that she had protectors in that house, who made it their mission to stop anything untoward from happening to her.

Once it had become clear what was happening, Lilian had approached the stalwart Mr. Dawson and thanked him. "It has not escaped my notice that the staff is watching out for me. It means more to me than you could ever know, Mr. Dawson. Please convey my thanks to the staff."

Mr. Dawson had lifted his chin and drawled, "I am afraid I do not understand what you are referring to, my lady."

"Thank you just the same, Mr. Dawson." He'd finally looked down and, still frowning heavily, winked.

Nothing else was ever said, but Lilian adored each and every one of the staff. It was odd, though. Here she was, sitting at a table with a virtual stranger, a stranger who had seen her naked, who stared at her chest like some lecher, and she not only wasn't offended, she was, if she were perfectly honest, vaguely intrigued. Which was quite shocking.

As it was quite clear his lordship wanted her gone from his home at the soonest possible moment, she decided to push any warm feelings she might or might not be feeling to the furthest recesses of her mind.

"My lord, I was wondering something." He lifted his head in inquiry. "You've seen Mabel's doll."

"The stocking, you mean?"

"That's just the point. I was wondering if when Sadie goes into the village tomorrow, she might purchase a real doll."

He was silent for a long moment, chewing thoughtfully. "No. It is not necessary."

Lilian was outraged, but remained outwardly calm. "She's a little girl, and little girls need toys. I understand the situation, but certainly you cannot deny a child just a little enjoyment. The sins of the father, or in this case the mother, should not be visited upon the child. It seems to me—"

He halted her in midsentence with his flint-like stare, and Lilian could feel her face heat. "You misunderstand," he said, his voice frigid. "If the child asked for a doll, I would not hesitate to buy her one. But she has a doll."

Lilian was feeling either very brave or very foolish, because she went on, even though it was obvious she had angered Granton. "As you have pointed out, it is merely a stocking."

"But to her it is a doll."

Lilian thought that was the end of the conversation and decided not to argue the point. Before she left to go home, she intended to buy Mabel a doll and Granton be damned. She only prayed he would allow her to accept it. She could understand why Granton did not want to care for the child given the circumstances of her birth, but denying Mabel toys seemed almost cruel.

"You think me harsh when I am only thinking of the girl's best interests."

"Not at all," Lilian said stiffly.

Granton let out a long breath, as if trying to control his temper. "When I was a lad, I wanted tin soldiers more than anything in the world, in the way only a child can want something. My father forbade it. And so I created my own little army with clay and sticks. In my mind, they were infantry, cavalry, officers. They had names and uniforms and would live or die depending upon whether they were French or English. To anyone else, they were simply sticks and clay. I don't think I would have liked a real set of tin soldiers; it would have been a betrayal of sorts to my men."

"You are sentimental," Lilian said, smiling at him, her heart breaking a little bit for that boy who'd wanted tin soldiers but made do with sticks. Lilian must have attended functions with Granton's father, the Earl of Chesterfield, but she could remember nothing of the man. Still, she was growing to dislike the earl immensely.

He frowned, obviously not liking the term "sentimental" to describe him. "I am not. I am and was practical. Having a vivid imagination does not mean I am sentimental."

"I still say you are sentimental."

"Call it what you will, but I will not have the child feel ashamed of her stocking by presenting her with a real doll."

"Can I say you are kind without your biting my head off?"

A smile curved on his lips just before he scooped up the last bite of pie. "You cannot."

Chapter 6

L ilian awoke feeling so rested the next day, she could hardly recall how very weak she'd been not two days prior. She spent the
day exploring the upper floors of Merdunoir with Mabel, for there
was no one else to watch over the child and Granton was nowhere to
be found.

"Is this where the ghost lives?" Mabel asked as they trudged up
the wooden stairs to the third story.

Since she didn't sound at all frightened, simply curious, Lilian said,
"I don't think so. In fact, I don't think there is a ghost at all. I think
Lord Granton walks about at night and that's what Sadie hears. But
you never do know, do you?"

"I should like to see a ghost," Mabel said thoughtfully. "I should
like to say boo." And then she giggled, tickled with herself.

"Perhaps we could rattle chains and moan and scare that ghost
right back."

The two reached the landing, and it was immediately apparent to
Lilian that this floor was reserved for low-born guests, children, and,
on the east wing, servants, for the floors were not carpeted and the
stairs were worn smooth by decades of footsteps. "Which way shall
we go? Left or right?" Lilian asked, pointing to help Mabel understand the difference.

"Left," she said, peering down a sunlit, dusty hall. Cobwebs clung to
the ceiling and glowed almost prettily in the sun, some hanging down
so low, Lilian was forced to swipe them out of the way. At the end of
the hall was a tall, multi-paned window that hadn't seen a cleaning in
years.

"Let's see if that window opens so we can take a look at the view.
I think it faces the sea." Lilian ran down the hall with Mabel shriek-

ing happily behind her, her smaller legs pumping like mad to keep up. When they reached the end of the hall, Lilian was delighted to find a small, pink shell perched on the sill, and she pictured some child leaving it there, never realizing it would gather dust for years. Lilian picked it up and wiped it on her robe, noting the shell left behind a small, dust-free area on the sill. Turning the latch, Lilian pushed the window open, gasping at the sharply cold blast of air that immediately hit them. She laughed, liking the way their hair whipped about, as if suddenly come to life. "Goodness, what a breeze."

Mabel sneezed, no doubt from all the dust the wind had just stirred up. Closing the window, Lilian said, "Let's explore, shall we? Perhaps we'll find more treasure." She held up the small pink shell for Mabel to take.

Mabel placed it in her palm and studied it. "What's it for?" she asked, rubbing her index finger over the smooth surface.

"It used to be the home of a little sea creature. We'll go down to the beach later and we can find our own." Mabel turned the shell over and peered into the shell's opening, as if trying to picture some little creature living inside, then grinned up at her, and Lilian's heart melted. Lilian opened the first door on the right and found nothing of note, just a room filled with a hodgepodge of furniture and old carpets. Lilian headed to the opposite door, pushing it open with a flourish.

"How wonderful," Lilian breathed, stepping into the large sunlit room. It was clearly the home's old nursery, for it was filled with tables and shelves and toys, long abandoned and carefully stored in wooden bins and on shelves. And there, to the side, sitting forlornly by the window, was a hobbyhorse. It was a lovely horse with real hair and a leather saddle sitting on bow rockers. Lilian looked at Mabel, who walked into the room the same way a priest would walk into the Vatican, slowly and struck with an awe that was a pure delight to see.

"It's the nursery, Mabel. It's where his lordship must have played when he was a little boy. Come see." She brought the little girl over to the hobbyhorse and lifted her up onto it. "It's been a while since he's been ridden on, but I think he'll remember how. Lean back and forward and he'll take you for a ride."

Mabel handed Lilian her dolly, then leaned forward, her eyes wide, a smile on her face as if she'd discovered the most marvelous thing. Within a few moments, she was going back and forth, her hands gripping the horse's mane. "It's lovely," she said, coming to a stop, her hazel eyes dancing as she took in the other toys in the room. Lilian helped her down, and Mabel immediately went to a low shelf with blocks, an abacus, a tiny horse and cart, and a pile of picture books. On a higher shelf was a small collection of tin soldiers, and Lilian frowned as she walked over to the shelf and picked up one impressive-looking fellow. Had Granton been lying about his sticks and clay simply to make a point?

"They were my brothers'."

Lilian whirled around to find Granton studying her from the door. "I don't understand. Were you not allowed to play with them?"

"I am the heir. My father thought toys would distract me from learning my duties. He was correct; they did." He walked over and picked up one of the soldiers, examining it before placing it back down on the shelf, standing close enough that Lilian could tell he'd just come in from the outdoors, for he carried with him the distinctive smell of the sea. He was still wearing his coat, and his dark hair was tousled and windswept, making him look almost boyish. Lilian reminded herself that he was a relatively young man, only six years her senior, though he seemed older. "My grandfather, Thomas Dunford, was a frivolous man, you see, with a penchant for ignoring his duties. He died when my father was young, leaving my father to flounder on his own. It was difficult for him, and he made certain that should the same befall him, his son would be prepared to take on his duties."

"And are you?"

"I was ready when I was a lad, but am happy to wait another twenty-eight years to assume the responsibility." Granton said this without self-pity, giving Lilian a greater insight into his childhood and into the man he'd become. As he spoke, he examined a few of the soldiers, picking up an odd one before placing it back down. "I'd forgotten these were here," he said absently, almost to himself, before plucking one from the shelf and placing it in his pocket. "When the new servants have the main rooms settled, I'll have them come up and clean the place." He turned to survey the room, his eyes resting on Mabel, who had discovered a wooden doll wearing a plaid dress. He did not smile, but Lilian was certain his eyes softened a bit. Mabel's stocking lay forgotten by her side as she peeked up the doll's dress to see what lay underneath.

"That was my sister Rose's doll," he said to Mabel, who looked up before she placed the doll carefully back on the shelf. "You may have it if you like. My sister is quite grown now and has little use for dolls, you see."

Mabel stared at the doll a long moment before shaking her head. "I'll let her live here," she said. "She'd miss her friends." Then she stood and ran back to the hobbyhorse, climbed up on it, and began to rock as if she'd grown up with such a lavish toy.

"Was this your sister's too?" Mabel asked.

"Indeed it was. She adored horses. She still does." He frowned, his dark brows coming together, almost as if he were angry.

"And this upsets you, your sister's love of horses?" Lilian asked lightly, almost teasingly.

"Certainly you've heard the scandal, my lady. My sister married our former head groom. My mother nearly died of the horror." He chuckled, as if the thought of his mother dying of such a thing were somehow amusing. He must have noticed Lilian's confusion, for he added, "You have to know my mother. There has never been a more ambitious woman on this planet. Rose, as you know, was engaged to Weston. And now she is married to a former servant. You can imagine my mother's disappointment."

"Indeed, I can. I did know your sister was once engaged to Weston, but I thought she married an American politician."

"She did. But the fellow died not two years ago and she married the man she'd loved all along, our groom."

"I suppose that must have been quite a shock for your mother. I cannot say I blame her," Lilian said. "If I were to have married one of our servants, I think it would have most certainly killed my mother."

"Charlie is a good man and wealthy beyond measure now. And he loves her."

"And she loves him?"

He frowned again, making his words seem incongruous. "With all her heart."

Lilian watched, troubled by the subtle shift in his expression, for he clenched his jaw, as if saying such a thing physically hurt.

"I didn't come here to reminisce or discuss the appropriateness of my sister's marriage. The seamstress is here, as are several servants. Sadie is busy directing the maids and Palmer is helping prepare Mabel's room and a guest room for you, so she asked me to fetch you for the seamstress." He gave a small bow and waved a hand, indicating that she should precede him out of the room.

"Come, Mabel. Don't forget your dolly." Mabel whirled around and grabbed her sock, holding it against her tightly as if in apology for nearly forgetting her. "Perhaps we can have the seamstress make something for Mabel, as well. Would that be all right?" Lilian asked, fearing she'd stepped out of bounds.

"Of course," he said, sounding slightly testy. "I've already instructed the woman to do so."

Lilian smiled at his surly response, which only caused his frown to deepen. She didn't care what the man said: he was nice, whether he liked it or not.

Chapter 7

That evening, when Marcus arrived for dinner, he fully expected Lady Lilian to again be in her robe. In fact, he'd been looking forward to it. Instead, he found her in a severely cut dove-gray dress with long sleeves and a high collar that would have looked quite fine on an old maid or stern governess. Marcus hated it on sight and wished he could command her to remove it and put the robe back on. She looked exactly like what she was: an unmarried, untouchable young woman. He didn't know why that bothered him, because that was what Lady Lilian was, but it did bother him. Tonight, she would sleep in her own room and he would sleep in his, and within a day, she would be gone forever. He should have felt like celebrating, but instead fought a wave of depression such as he hadn't felt since first discovering his wife's infidelity.

"How is it that the seamstress managed to dress you so quickly and in something so ugly?" Marcus asked as he sat, knowing he sounded surly.

"You think this dress ugly?" Lilian asked, as she looked down at the dress, but not before he saw a distinctive twinkle in her eye.

"Not quite the height of fashion, no."

"It suits me well, my lord, I assure you."

"How on earth did she sew it so quickly?" Marcus asked. Why he should care was beyond him. He should be celebrating, for the lady was dressed and could now leave.

"She happened to have this dress on hand and, fortunately, it required very few alterations. I'm quite grateful, actually."

"Hmm. And what about shoes?"

She thrust one foot up and showed him a pair of shoes that appeared to be just slightly overlarge.

"I suppose you'll want to go to the train station tomorrow and be on your way."

"Of course," she said readily, and something in his chest gave an odd pull. "Except I promised Mabel the adventure of the tunnels. I do hope you don't mind if my departure is delayed one day. Mabel would be so disappointed."

"I can show the child the tunnels," Marcus said, forcing himself to sound dismissive while at the same time he found himself hoping she would stay. At least another day. The truth was, he liked her. He'd found himself looking forward to dinner far too much, and the thought of eating alone again, even though he'd only had company two nights, seemed untenable. A ridiculous thought and one he didn't like, not one bit. Best to have her go on her way and get on with his solitude. It wouldn't do to become too used to company.

She was silent for a long moment, twisting her napkin on her lap as she looked down at her bowl of mushroom soup. Suddenly, Marcus noted with some irritation, Sadie had decided it was time to serve multicourse meals when not a few days ago she'd been more than happy to place a large, steaming bowl of stew in front of him and be done with it. "I was looking forward to seeing the tunnels, but if you think it's best for me to go—"

"I suppose you could stay." Marcus took a spoonful, hating that his cheeks were slightly ruddy, as if he'd asked to court her. It had been a long time since he'd been alone with any woman other than Eleanor, and it felt strange, almost as if he were doing something immoral, like being unfaithful to his wife. "The girl is a bit shy around me, and she might not want to go without you at any rate."

"I was thinking the same thing, my lord. I do hope she is not becoming too attached. I fear I am a lost cause where she is concerned. I adore her."

"The thought had occurred to me that if a woman had to faint in front of my carriage, it would have been much more convenient if she were a woman of lower birth, who could have been a nursemaid," Marcus said blandly, then looked up in surprise when Lady Lilian laughed.

"I have to admit, the thought of being Mabel's nursemaid isn't altogether unpleasant, but I fear my mother would be so vexed at me that she'd find a way to complain even from the grave. I'm very much afraid I'm going to have to seek out Her Grace and resume my life as the unwanted sister."

When Sadie arrived carrying a tray with a course of trout, Marcus raised his brow in question. He hadn't been fishing and he knew for certain Palmer hadn't had a chance, not with helping to move furniture and open rooms for unexpected guests.

"I sent one of the new boys to the lake to fish," Sadie said as she dished out the trout. "Your menu should expand considerably now that we have more staff on hand, my lord, and it's a pleasure to cook for company." She beamed a smile at Lady Lilian, and Marcus could almost see the wheels whirring in her head, no doubt imagining what it would be like to serve an entire dinner party. Even before Eleanor's death he hadn't been one for balls and dinners, much to his young bride's dismay. A quiet evening at home reading before the fire or atop the roof gazing at the stars and planets suited him just fine.

Marcus was tempted to say these changes were temporary, in place just long enough to set the house a bit more in order, but he found he couldn't dash the older woman's hopes just yet. He'd no intention of hiring on a permanent staff. It was bad enough that his home had been invaded with half a dozen people, talking, disrupting his day, asking questions. When his temporary servants climbed aboard the wagon at six o'clock to return to the village, he'd watched from his room, relieved that he would finally get some peace and quiet.

"How many courses this evening, Sadie?"

"Just three more. One of the maids is quite handy in the kitchen, my lord. A blessing, she was."

"I wonder if his lordship could convince any of them to live in?" Lilian said. "I can't imagine having your brother go to the village every day is ideal."

"He doesn't mind, my lady. He's got a sweetheart in Whitby and jumps at every chance to see her. Going to town twice a day is like winning the Scorton Silver Arrow, he's just that pleased."

Sadie hurried off to fetch yet another course, leaving Marcus feeling slightly off-kilter. Palmer had a sweetheart? Did that mean he'd want to marry her soon? And bring her here? Or would his new wife want to start a life together somewhere else? And why the hell did Palmer have a sweetheart?

In the back of his mind, Marcus knew he could not stay at Merdunoir forever. His siblings would make certain of that. He was half surprised more of them hadn't shown up to drag him back to London. Just the thought of going back to London, visiting his clubs, hearing the whispers and seeing the smirks, was enough to keep him at Merdunoir forever. He hated the idea of being the object of ridicule. His father had said he had too much pride, and he supposed it was true. He'd married Eleanor because of his damned pride, because she'd come from a family with a fine pedigree and everyone had told him she'd be the perfect wife. Eleanor had been the perfect fiancée, the perfect bride, and he'd fooled himself into thinking he actually might be happy with her.

As he took the last bite of his very finely cooked trout, he realized he'd been silent for several minutes, and looked up to see his guest sitting politely, her plate clean, her hands folded neatly on her lap, watching him. Her cheeks instantly reddened, and she looked down as if embarrassed to be caught staring.

"You'll have to forgive my lack of dinner conversation," Marcus said. "I am unused to company."

"You did seem very deep in thought, and I didn't want to interrupt you," she said, meeting his gaze and smiling. Nearly everything she said was tinged with teasing, almost flirtation, and he wondered if she even realized it. In the candlelight, her beautiful eyes seemed to glow from within, as if some tiny lamplighter were holding up a flame. Marcus tore his gaze away from her, horrified by his ridiculous thoughts. Tiny lamplighter indeed. He blinked and turned toward the entrance, where he hoped to see Sadie bringing in the next course. The entrance remained depressingly empty.

"You don't have to converse if you don't want to," she said. "I know you did not plan to have a guest, and I am very grateful for your hospitality." She bit her lip briefly, and he couldn't help but watch, fascinated by her soft mouth. "I have imposed on your hospitality too long as it is. I think it would be best, after all, for me to leave in the morning. Palmer can bring me to Whitby when he fetches the day staff."

What the hell was she going on about? Leave? Tomorrow? "No. Mabel will be disappointed if we do not explore the tunnels."

She looked down at her lap, obviously trying to suppress a smile.

"Why are you smiling?" he demanded.

"Because even though you sound angry, you are being kind. To both me and Mabel. And that is the first time you called her Mabel instead of 'the child.'"

"I fail to see why that is amusing."

She looked at him, her eyes sparkling, her pink lips curved up slightly, and something about that look caused a sudden rush of heat to his groin. He shifted uncomfortably in his seat. He should have found a woman to tup while he was in London; he'd never gotten achingly hard because a woman looked at him before. "It's not amusing, my lord. It's heartwarming."

He shook his head and scowled just as Sadie walked into the room carrying a large silver platter filled with roasted potatoes and what looked like duck. His mouth watered, and he realized he'd become rather sick of simple country fare.

"Excellent, Sadie. I do hope we can continue showing off your culinary skills when our guest is gone."

"Gone, sir?"

He very nearly barked out a laugh. "Lady Lilian's visit is drawing to a close, I fear. She is leaving the day after tomorrow."

"The day after tomorrow," Sadie repeated, putting a curious emphasis at the word *after*. "I shall do my best to serve you adequate meals." Somehow, Marcus suspected that meant he'd be eating stews, soups, and cold ham sandwiches again.

Yorkshire's coastline, with its plethora of caves, had been a favorite among smugglers sailing from the Continent to sell their wares, tax free, to those British subjects with enough money to buy them. And Marcus's grandfather not only had the money, he'd rather enjoyed the idea of making money—at least until his untimely death at the age of sixty-two, when Marcus's father was just twenty-two. Indeed, Thomas Dunford had been so busy accumulating wealth and playing the smuggler, he'd quite forgotten the rest of his duties, leaving his son to carry on with little training and even less experience. When he was a lad, his grandfather—or rather the idea of him, as he'd died long before Marcus was born—had been a bit of a hero. A brave rascal who defied his aristocratic birth to thumb his nose at society and its strict rules of conduct. Now, though, he recognized him for what he'd been—a selfish, reckless man.

His grandfather's smuggling was the not-so-secret family secret that Marcus's father was deeply ashamed of. Marcus and his brothers, on the other hand, had found the idea quite exciting and, unbeknownst to their father, used to play Smuggler.

Before his father decided Marcus was too old for such nonsense as playing in the caves and tunnels that led to Merdunoir's lower levels, he'd spent untold hours exploring with his brothers. The caves were a series of connected rooms, some accessed only on one's hands and knees, and some that, at low tide, were dry and at high tide were completely under water. As a boy, Marcus had enjoyed the rather gruesome story of a smuggler who had been caught stealing and had been chained to one of the caves that was submerged at high tide. His grandfather reportedly found the poor soul, still chained and drowned, two days after his scallywag of a partner departed back to the Continent, never to be seen again. It was the sort of tale that drove a young boy's imagination, and Marcus had spent many an hour thinking about that man, how he must have struggled knowing the tide was coming in, how his black soul might very well be haunting the labyrinth of caves along the shore.

He figured Mabel was too young to hear such a gruesome tale, so as Marcus led the girl and Lady Lilian down the hidden, rough-stone staircase to the secret tunnel that accessed the first of the caves, he kept his comments to the less sensational history.

Marcus, holding a lantern above his head, moved down the stairs, cautioning the two to watch their steps.

"Go slowly, now," Lilian said to Mabel, her voice echoing softly in the passageway. The walls, carved a century ago, were rough and shining with moisture. Marcus knew this passage like the back of his hand, but he moved slowly, intensely aware of the lady walking behind him. Her skirt rustled softly and he could smell her light floral scent even as the air grew musty and thick. He heard a gasp and a hand landed heavily and almost painfully on his shoulder as she lost her footing momentarily.

"Goodness, it's quite slippery, isn't it? It's these shoes, I think."

"Put one hand on my shoulder if you think that would help. I don't want to have to carry you back if you break an ankle."

She let out a small sound, of protest or amusement, he couldn't tell, but then he felt a warm and tentative touch on his shoulder. He found himself smiling, liking her hand there, and immediately wished she would remove it. To be touched by a woman, particularly this woman, did things to him he didn't like. Or rather, liked too much.

"Are there ghosts down here?" Mabel asked, sounding completely unconcerned.

"Perhaps," Marcus said.

"Oh, I think it's much too damp for a ghost," Lilian said. "Ghosts don't like cold, damp places."

When they reached the bottom of the long, stone stairway, they encountered a thick metal door. Marcus turned and held the lantern up high. "Are you certain you're brave enough?" he asked Mabel. Her eyes were wide, but he saw little fear in them and he suppressed a smile. She really was a darling girl, and something in his chest hurt to think she might have been his if Eleanor hadn't been so free with her favors.

"I'm quite brave," Mabel said solemnly, and Marcus found himself hoping she'd never had cause for fear. How would a little girl know if she was brave or not?

"When I open this door, you will feel a blast of air. My brother Adam always said it was the devil's breath."

The little girl smiled, a completely unexpected reaction to his rather ominous words.

Marcus bent down to the girl and said, "I think we shall get on quite well."

When he straightened, he saw that Lady Lilian was smiling, her eyes almost misting, and he scowled. Couldn't a man be nice to a little girl without Lady Lilian noting it with that smile of hers? He turned and grasped the cold metal of the handle, looking forward to the cold blast of air, as if it would purge that knowing smile from his mind. Did she think he would be cruel to the child just because of her birth? Truth be told, he hadn't wanted Mabel, but he wasn't such an ogre that he would be cruel to her.

He pulled at the door and the wind whistled past the opening, bringing with it the smell of dampness and the sea.

"Oh," Lilian said as the wind buffeted her face and pulled a few strands of her thick hair from their moorings. Then she laughed and closed her eyes as if relishing the feel of the wind on her skin, and Marcus realized with no small amount of disgust, that if they'd been alone, if Mabel hadn't been standing there blinking against the wind, he might have kissed Lilian, might have pulled her into his arms and pressed his mouth against hers.

Marcus turned toward the blackness that marked the entry to the first cave, his jaw clenched tightly. What the hell was wrong with him? She was an innocent, and all he could think about was bedding her. And if he bedded her, he'd be stuck with her, stuck with another woman who would find herself married and wishing she was not. Marcus had quickly learned the misery of being married to a woman who'd been forced into a union against her will.

He walked quickly ahead, not realizing he was leaving the other two in the dark until Lilian cried out, still laughing, and he stopped and took a breath. "Sorry," he mumbled, waiting for them to catch up to him. He continued down the passage, which was now covered with fine sand, wishing she was gone. If she was gone, he wouldn't have to torment himself with thoughts of how she would taste. God, it had been far too long since he'd had a woman; he was going mad.

"I think you should leave this evening when Palmer brings the day servants to the village. Now that you've recovered, I see no need for you to remain. I . . . I miss my solitude." He knew his voice was tinged with an odd desperation, but he found he did not care.

She was silent behind him, and he wished he could see her expression. Relief? Anger? Dismay?

"Of course. I didn't realize."

"I've no wish to entertain guests. I thought I'd made myself quite clear."

Silence.

"Am I to go too?" The sound of Mabel's soft question made Marcus pause.

"No. You are to stay here. With me. At least for the time being."

"Oh." The word sounded small and sad, and Marcus briefly closed his eyes.

"I shall hire you a nanny and she will care for you. And play your button game if you like." He couldn't bring himself to turn and look at them, for he couldn't face Lady Lilian's censure, her disappointment that perhaps he was not as kind as she had imagined.

"Yes, sir."

The small group walked on in silence, the day ruined by his foul mood. As they walked from one cave to the next, he offered some commentary about the smugglers. His two charges remained silent, Lady Lilian nodding once in a while, her face set. It wasn't until they entered the largest room that she showed any interest at all. The main room was a stunning example of Yorkshire caves, complete with stalagmites and stalactites.

"This is astounding," she breathed, touching one of the stalagmites that hung from the limestone ceiling. "I've never seen anything more beautiful. What fun it must have been exploring when you were a boy."

She stood and turned in a circle, looking about her with complete wonder.

"My brothers and I spent countless hours here. We always hoped we'd find something the smugglers left behind, but we never did. I have a feeling my father or my grandfather cleaned out the caves long before we came along."

"It's dripping," Mabel said, looking up at the rock formation.

"That's how it grows," Marcus explained. "It's a bit like a rock icicle, but it grows far more slowly. Here." He lifted Mabel up with one arm and held the lantern with the other so she could get a closer look at the glistening water and he was struck by how very small she was. "Go ahead and touch it." He was watching Mabel touch the rock when his eyes drifted to where Lady Lilian stood, her incredible eyes seeming to glow almost ethereally in the soft light. She was a lovely girl, tall and lithe, and in the lantern's light she looked particularly beautiful. Marcus let out a long breath and set Mabel back on the ground, feeling unaccountably irritated, mostly with himself. He should have insisted Lady Lilian leave as soon as she had clothes on her back and shoes on her feet. For some reason, his legendary control was slipping.

"May I go over there?" Mabel asked, pointing to a rock shelf where his brothers had stored a collection of rocks safe above the high water mark.

Lilian forced a smile as she watched Mabel run over to the shelf and successfully navigate some makeshift stone steps that led up to the ledge. Sunlight streamed into the cavern from high above through a wide crevice, giving the cave an almost magical glow. Beneath her feet, the floor was covered with a wet layer of sand, and she could feel the dampness seeping in through the soles of her shoes. When she was in London, the first thing she would purchase was a pair of sturdy boots.

Despite her wet feet, she was glad she had stayed to tour the caves, no matter that Granton seemed unduly annoyed by her presence. Though she hardly knew the man and realized she was being foolish, his words *had* hurt her—far more than she would ever admit aloud. Lilian had never thought of herself as an overly sensitive woman, so she didn't understand why his words had cut her. It wasn't as if they were friends; they were simply two people forced together by a rather bizarre situation. After she was gone, she wouldn't spare him a thought. Perhaps one thought, she admitted, looking up at him through her lashes. It would be rather difficult to put a man such as Lord Granton completely from her mind.

She walked away from where he stood and moved into the soft beam of light created by the sun, imaging what it must have been like to be a young child discovering it for the first time. She couldn't picture Granton as a boy. He was too large, too stern, too everything, now that she thought about it. She wondered if he'd ever felt the joy of discovery or if he'd always kept his emotions at bay. Perhaps he didn't feel emotions beyond irritation. *I've no wish to entertain guests. I thought I'd made myself quite clear.*

She'd wanted to say, *No, you have not made yourself clear. Not when you invited me to dinner, not when you spied me in my bath.* The truth was, she didn't want to leave. She felt safe and comfortable. She liked Granton's company, even though apparently he'd had enough of hers.

Other than her father and Weston, Lilian hadn't much experience with men. Her season had been cut short by her sister's wedding and then her mother's death. She knew little of the opposite sex, and what she had known, she hadn't much liked. Granton wasn't like the other men she'd known, who were full of false flattery, who treated her as if she had a pea for a brain.

Something about Granton was pleasing, and it was more than just his handsome face, though he certainly *was* handsome. Breathtakingly so, if she was completely honest. In her limited experience, it was easy to tell if a man was interested in her or not. With Granton, she couldn't tell if he liked her, was bored by her, or wished her to perdition. Then again, he *had* asked her to leave as soon as it was physically possible for her to do so. More than once. Still, she had a feeling it wasn't she he disliked as much as having a stranger in his home.

And then there was Mabel.

It had only been a few days since they'd been introduced, but she adored the little girl and had grown rather attached to her. They spent nearly every minute of the day together, and Lilian had surprised herself by her patience. She'd never thought of herself as a woman who enjoyed children, perhaps because she'd never actually spent any time with them since becoming an adult. But she liked spending time with Mabel. She liked playing games she hadn't played since she was a little girl, seeing everything fresh and new through her eyes. She'd forgotten how much fun it was to pretend. Saying good-bye in a few short hours would be terribly difficult.

"You are quiet." It was so strange, how his deep voice stirred something inside her. When she didn't respond, he walked toward her. "I fear I have hurt your feelings by asking you to leave."

Lilian immediately protested, even though he had hurt her. But to admit such a thing would never do, for it made no sense, not even to her. "Oh, no. It's just that I am not particularly eager to resume my life or see my sister again. We're no longer close, you see, and now that she is a widow, I fear she will be even more insufferably smug about her position. I think I shall begin searching for a home in London." And live there alone for the rest of her days. Alone. Goodness, it was a depressing thought. But she had a feeling few people in society would welcome her back into their homes, not with such a scandal attached to her name. Here, she could pretend none of it mattered, not the murder, not her sister's accusations, not the fact she was truly, completely alone. The only thing that gave her comfort was knowing that one day soon she would have enough funds to live quite well for the rest of her life.

Lilian looked away, not wanting Granton to see how very terrified she was at the thought of leaving and facing society.

"Where is the opening to the sea?" she asked, hoping to change the subject. "Is it far?"

"I'm afraid it's been blocked off by a rock fall. You will live alone?"

Lilian turned back to him and allowed herself a small smile. "For someone who enjoys his solitude as much as you do, I would think you'd understand."

"I am alone because that is what I choose. I could go home and be with my family, my brothers. You are alone because you have no one, and that is a far different thing."

Lilian laughed. "You make my situation seem so tragic. I assure you, I will quite look forward to my own company. It is far better than spending time with someone who wishes me gone with such ferocity." His eyes sharpened, and she felt her face heat, immediately regretting her words. In fact, she could hardly believe she'd uttered them. "Oh, goodness, please do accept my apologies. I can offer no excuse other than I think I'd rather be anywhere but with my sister."

"How can I take affront when you were simply being honest?"

"Tact is something I fear I'm still learning," Lilian said, feeling a bit sheepish. "I do realize I should have left as soon as possible. I have no excuse other than the complete terror I feel when I think about seeing anyone I know. They will not be able to look at me without thinking about the duke's murder. It matters not that I am innocent. I wish I had my own Merdunoir so I could hide there forever."

"I am not hiding," he stated flatly.

"Aren't you? Again, I apologize." What was *wrong* with her? Suddenly, she felt like weeping, for she'd never been so rude in her entire life, and she certainly had no reason to be angry with Granton, who'd saved her life, fed and clothed her, and asked nothing in return but that she join him for dinner. "Lord Granton," she said, pushing her words past a closed throat. "You must think me the most ungrateful and shrewish sort of woman. I am not. I don't know why—"

He held up a hand, stopping her midsentence. "You are forgiven, my lady, and I took no affront. Shall we go? The tide will be coming in soon, and I have no wish to get my boots wet."

"Of course. Come along, Mabel. I'm sure his lordship can bring you down another time." Even as she said the words, she could hardly picture Granton coming down to the caves alone with Mabel.

Mabel scrambled down from her perch and ran over to her, a small shell in her hand. "Look, miss, I found a seashell like the one in the house."

"My lady," Granton corrected.

"Look, my lady, I found a seashell," she repeated.

"Oh, it's lovely," Lilian said, bending over to get a better look.

"Look in the center, how pink it is. I believe that's my favorite color."

Mabel beamed, her hazel eyes turning to half-moons, then tucked the shell into her pocket before running to where Granton stood holding the lamp. She grabbed his hand as if it were something she'd done a hundred times, and Lilian couldn't help but smile at the confused look on the man's face before he turned toward the tunnel, Mabel's hand firmly grasped in his.

Marcus walked ahead of them, holding the lamp high, as they made their way back toward the house. When they reached the steps, he handed the lamp to Lady Lilian, then picked up Mabel, who wrapped her arms tightly around his neck. "Do you mean to strangle me?" he asked, raising one brow as he leaned back so he could see her face.

She immediately giggled and loosened her hold. "I shouldn't like to strangle you, sir." Then she did something much worse; she laid her head against his shoulder, her soft curls touching his cheek. He suspected, without turning around to verify, that Lady Lilian would be smiling at him, as if carrying a child were some sort of heroic deed. The truth was, he wanted to be up the stairs and into the house as soon as possible, and carrying Mabel made their trip shorter.

They reached the main level of Merdunoir, and Marcus put the girl down and turned toward Lady Lilian, steeling himself against his reaction, reminding himself again that it was good she was leaving. Pulling out his watch, he said, "I daresay you don't have much to pack. Palmer should be leaving shortly and I'll bid you good-bye now." He gave her a small bow, ignoring the odd tightness he felt in his chest at the thought of never seeing her again.

She curtsied and smiled, as if she knew what was going on behind his carefully dispassionate expression, and he had the oddest thought: *I shall never kiss her.*

It seemed important that he amend this and just as important that he never act on such an impulse.

"I bid you a good journey home," he said, stepping back, sealing his decision.

"Thank you. For saving me from the moors, for allowing me to stay. Perhaps if you go home to Cannock, we will meet again?"

"I spend most of my time in London, and I believe I shall stay on here for a while." He looked around at the library where they stood and noted the cobwebs floating from the ceiling and the thick covering of dust on the furniture and books. "I think I might try to bring the old girl back to life."

"That's wonderful. Merdunoir is such a lovely home. Even with its ghost." She pressed her lips together to hide her mirth.

"He and I get on quite well," Marcus said. "We keep the same hours." Mabel leaned against Lady Lilian, looking very much like she might fall asleep standing up, and the tightness in his chest grew stronger. "I think my charge is in great need of a nap. Good day and Godspeed, my lady."

Marcus left the two there, standing in the library. No doubt Lady Lilian watched his hasty departure with a mix of dismay and bemusement. He'd produced that very expression on enough faces to suspect it was there. He planned to take a long ride on the moors to clear his head of beautiful women with creamy skin and eyes the color of butterflies. He planned not to return until Mr. Palmer and the carriage and the lady were long gone. And then, when he came back to his nearly empty house, he could pretend she'd never been in his home, or tempted him with her soft lips and her untamable hair.

He rode hard and fast away from the sea, streaking across the moors, lush and green from the recent rain, blind to the beauty of his surroundings until he crested a hill and looked down at a valley dotted with farms, the sheep small bits of cotton in the distance. "Sorry, old man," Marcus said, patting his horse, which heaved great lungfuls of air after the bracing run. He rode down the hill at a slower pace, aware that the sun was moving lower, painting a golden light on the grasslands.

She'd be gone soon and he was glad of it. He didn't need the distraction of her presence, the uncomfortable and powerful lust he felt for her. If he felt a bit lonely sitting at his table this evening, then so be it. He would get used to Sadie's simpler fare, the quiet, endless nights, the absolute silence that permeated the old house. Mabel would be there, of course, at least until he could find her a good boarding school. And he wouldn't feel guilty about it. Certainly he was in no position to offer a small child what she needed, other than a bed and food. That duty would go to either a nanny or a schoolmistress. She would be far better off in school than with him. Perhaps he would find her real father and give him the responsibility of raising the child.

Such thoughts battered his conscience, try though he might to push them away. He knew better than most what it was like to grow up without affection, to have only teachers and tutors to guide him. When he was seven years old, his father had sent him to a school, one known for its strict discipline, one, it turned out, that was run by a sadistic headmaster who seemed to loathe his charges as much as they feared him. His only respite had been Christmas and a few precious weeks in the summer, when he would return home to his rambunctious brothers. He'd hardly spent any time with them growing up; his father had seen to that. All his life, he had been kept separate; he didn't even know why they cared a fig about him and was quietly surprised when they showed him affection. He'd been set apart, as if not even a member of the same family, better, special, and so damned lonely it didn't bear thinking about. It had been a kind of torment, those awkward moments when he'd returned home, so happy, so glad to be away from school. It always took weeks for Marcus to relax enough to have fun with his siblings, and by the time that happened, it was time to return to school.

Marcus let out a curse, hating that his heart was so soft, that he longed for something that could never be. He'd be damned if he sent Mabel off to live in a school alone. Shaking his head with no small amount of disgust for his changeable mind, he turned Chief around and made his way slowly back to Merdunoir, his gut churning until he saw that the carriage and the day servants had departed. He told himself he was glad, but for some reason, the house didn't seem quite as welcoming as it had just one day ago.

"Bloody hell, Marcus," he muttered as he eased himself off the horse. After taking care of his gelding and making certain Chief was settled for the night and was well fed, Marcus headed to the house, bracing himself for the complete emptiness of the place. When he realized what he was doing, he shook his head—hard—as if he could rid himself of her image, her scent.

God, he wished he'd kissed her. Just once.

Chapter 8

"Mister?"

Marcus was in his room, flipping through his copy of Edgar Allen Poe stories and trying not to picture what Lilian looked like in his bed, when he heard Mabel's soft voice calling to him from outside his door. Heaving a sigh, he placed the book aside and stood to go to the door. Opening it, he peered down and down, slightly surprised at how very little Mabel looked peering back up at him. She was dressed in a nightgown, her long hair a tangled mess.

"How may I help you?"

She worried her hands in the soft cotton of her nightgown and bit her lip. "Where is the lady?"

"She's gone. Did she not say good-bye?"

Mabel shook her head, her big eyes shining with unshed tears. Marcus hunkered down to her level, hoping the little thing wouldn't burst into tears and force him to give her a hug. "I'm certain she meant to say good-bye. She was likely just excited to be on her way."

"But . . ." She looked past him as if Lady Lilian might be hiding behind him. "Did she give you my dolly?"

Marcus furrowed his brow. "Your stocking? No, she did not."

"I don't know where dolly is. The lady said she was getting her."

Something cold blossomed in the pit of his stomach. "Where was she going, Mabel?"

"To get dolly. But she didn't come back." It was obvious she was trying her damndest not to cry.

Marcus's heart seemed to stop at that moment, then beat painfully, almost sickeningly in his chest. "Where is dolly?" he asked, trying with all his might to sound calm.

"The cave."

* * *

Lilian gave her lamp a worried look and realized, with no small amount of dread, that the oil would be gone before the tide was out enough for her to leave her safe haven. She knew, in a short time, she would be alone in utter blackness and completely helpless even when the tide was low, for the idea of feeling her way toward the main cavern was completely unthinkable.

When she'd returned to the caves to retrieve Mabel's doll, she hadn't thought twice about what she was doing. It wasn't a very complex route, a straight path directly to the main cavern, where Mabel had no doubt left her doll on the rock shelf where she'd been playing. At that time, there hadn't even been a hint of an incoming tide, and Lilian thought she'd have hours to complete her task. Just the thought of poor Mabel doing without her doll and falling asleep with empty arms was enough to drive Lilian down into the caves. She hadn't been afraid; indeed, she'd thought of the task as a bit of an adventure. She'd always had an adventurous spirit when she was young. When she was a child, she had lived in Cornwall, a rugged and isolated part of England, and had spent many happy hours outdoors, exploring. She was no frail miss, afraid of spiders.

But she did have a wee bit of fear of the dark.

Unfortunate, that, because she was about to be thrown into complete darkness with only the eerie sound of sea water moving in the cave for company.

It was her adventurous spirit that had gotten her into trouble. When she'd returned to the cave, she'd taken a bit more time to explore without the distraction of Lord Granton's brooding gaze. The cavern, with the sun still streaming weakly through the crevice above, was a purely wonderful place. She'd never seen anything quite like it, and she found herself wishing she could take hours to explore rather than a few spare minutes. As she moved around the perimeter of the cave, she noticed a large pile of heavy boulders, as if long ago a rock fall had covered up an entrance. Moving to the wall of boulders, she could feel a bit of air seeping through and she smiled. Indeed it was likely there was another room beyond the rock fall. It seemed a silly thing to do in hindsight, for what were the chances that she would be able to move even one heavy stone away, never mind an entire wall? But it so happened, the one rock she pulled had acted as a keystone, and removing that rock caused the entire wall to tumble down. If not for her quick feet, she might have been crushed, but Lilian was too excited to dwell overlong on how lucky she'd been to escape injury.

Holding her lantern up high, she looked past the fallen boulders to see a low, narrow passageway. With a game smile, she clambered over the boulders and, holding the lantern in front of her, moved along the rock corridor, silently praying it wouldn't take too long to discover where it went. The path moved upwards, and for a time Lilian wondered if this was some sort of secret entrance into the caves. The ceiling got suddenly higher, and Lilian found herself at the entrance to a large chamber. She let out a small, happy gasp, for before her were dozens of crates. It was like finding a treasure, long hidden, and Lilian grinned. Walking to the first of the crates, she put the lantern aside to try to pry it open, surprising herself at how easy it was to lift the lid.

There she found dark bottles neatly stored in sawdust. Lifting one she read, "BOUTELLEAU FIL 1795." Brandy. "Oh, my." Lilian grinned. She imagined the smugglers returning to the cave only to find that their treasure was completely covered in boulders—or so they must have thought. Lilian opened a few more crates and found more of the same. It was a bit disappointing. While it was exciting to find anything in the cavern, it would have been much more exciting if it had been fine porcelain or gold or silver. Still, brandy from nearly a century ago was a bit fun. She couldn't wait to tell . . .

And then she felt a small piercing of disappointment. She would tell no one, except perhaps Sadie or Mr. Palmer. No doubt Marcus would not appear to say good-bye; he'd already said it, after all. With one last look at the brandy, Lilian headed for the passageway, then laughed aloud when she realized she'd forgotten, on one of the crates, Mabel's dolly, the whole reason she'd been in the caves in the first place. She was very near the main cavern when she stepped into water. Sea water.

"Oh, no," she said, lowering the lantern so she could see proof of what she felt. "Oh, drat." Water lapped up into the passageway, deepening toward the tumbled boulders that had given Lilian access to the secret room. She looked with disbelief at the water that now nearly covered the entirety of the boulders that had fallen and knew with a sense of inevitability that she was trapped until the tide went out. The water would nearly be above her head and she couldn't swim. That she was safe gave her some comfort, but she immediately thought about Mabel, who would be worried, and Lord Granton, who would be angry she'd delayed her departure yet again. She hadn't even told Sadie that she would be leaving that afternoon, so she wouldn't be missed when Palmer headed to Whitby with the day servants.

"You stupid girl," she said, almost in awe of how foolish she'd been to allow the tide to rise and block her way. It had been surprising, though, how very quickly the chamber had filled. She'd obviously been exploring longer than she'd realized.

With a sound of disgust, Lilian turned around and headed back to the chamber, wondering idly what brandy tasted like.

Marcus felt fingers of cold fear trying to take control of him, but he pushed them away. It wouldn't do to show how very worried he was in front of Mabel. "I'll go get her, shall I?" he said to Mabel, who looked at him with those solemn eyes that so much resembled Eleanor's.

"And dolly?"

"Of course. Now, back to bed with you. I'll bring you your stocking when I get back."

Mabel giggled. "It's a dolly."

Marcus watched the little girl head back to her room, then took a deep, bracing breath, refusing to allow the fear back. Had he told Lady Lilian about the dangers of the caves at high tide? If she'd gone exploring, she might have gotten lost. She might have ended up in one of the chambers that was completely submerged at high tide. He briefly squeezed his eyes shut, trying not to imagine Lilian struggling as the water grew ever higher; it would not be a pleasant way to die.

Throwing on a pair of old boots, Marcus headed to the caves, silently praying he would meet the lady as she was heading back to the house. But the further he got, the more worried he became, and when he hadn't run into her by the time he came to where the tide had reached, a terrible sense of dread washed over him. It was a full moon and the tide was unusually high. Where he stood, with water lapping gently at his feet, was normally dry. "Lilian," he called, peering into the darkness in front of him. He listened intently for a reply, and cursed aloud when there was none.

He stepped into the water, grimacing slightly at the cold temperature. The North Sea was never a very warm body of water, even in

July. As he sloshed through toward the main chamber, the water edged up higher and higher, until he had to hold the lantern above his head to keep it dry.

"Lilian," he called, stopping briefly. He was about to take another step, but froze. Had he heard something? "Lilian!"

"In here." Her voice, sounding as if she were standing quite near. Fierce joy nearly felled him, and he swung the lantern toward the sound of her lovely voice only to find himself quite alone in the chamber. The light from his lantern was illuminating nothing but rock walls and boulders piled high from a long ago fall.

"Where are you?" he called out, frustrated and confused that he could see nothing but could hear her voice quite clearly. Unless he was going insane.

"In here. A secret chamber. Behind the boulders. It's marvelous, though a bit dark, and I'm so glad you're here. I've found brandy."

And been imbibing a bit, Marcus thought, from the sound of her overly cheerful voice. "Can you get to me?" Marcus asked as he moved quickly toward the boulders. His left foot jammed into an unseen stalagmite and he found himself falling helplessly forward with no way to brace himself. Thrusting the lantern as high as he could, Marcus struggled to keep the flame above the water, but the splash from his impact sloshed up and over the lamp, dousing the flame and leaving him in utter blackness.

Marcus was not a man who swore often, but the words that erupted from his mouth at that moment would have done a seasoned sailor proud.

"I take it you've doused the lamp," came her disembodied voice, sounding entirely too cheerful.

"Yes, my lady, and I do apologize for my language." Marcus threw the lamp as hard as he could across the chamber and heard a gratifying sound of breaking glass. He was wet and cold and bloody angry that this woman had been foolish enough to get herself trapped at high tide. And he'd been a bloody idiot to worry himself sick about her. Now they were both in the dark, but she was high and dry and probably a bit tipsy from drinking what was likely one of the finest brandies ever created. While he stood shivering and wet and probably more in need of saving than she was.

"I thought I'd wait until the tide went back out. I don't know how to swim, and the water looks rather cold."

Shivering, Marcus glared toward where the lady likely stood, warm as toast. But not for long if it were up to him. And it was.

"No worries, my lady. The water isn't over your head, and if you have any difficulties, I will try very hard not to let you drown."

A long silence ensued. "You are angry."

"Angry? I? Not at all. I quite enjoy slogging through ice-cold sea water at nine o'clock at night to rescue a woman who apparently doesn't require rescuing and who was stupid enough to put her very life in danger. Do you know there are chambers in these caves that are completely submerged at high tide? And do you know that people have died?"

Another silence. "You were worried." She sounded entirely too happy about the prospect.

"You're goddamn right I was worried. Do you realize how maddening it is to nearly die from worry, only to find you not only well, but dry and partaking of my brandy?"

"You wanted me to die?" It was obviously a rhetorical question, but Marcus answered it anyway.

"No, I did not. Now, however, is a different matter entirely."

To his surprise, he heard her giggle. Giggle. Then he heard the obvious sounds of her moving through the water toward the fallen boulders. With a sigh of resignation, he moved carefully in her direction until he felt the first boulder at his feet.

"Would you mind talking to me? I'm quite afraid of the dark, and if you are silent I'll let my imagination run amok and picture you eaten by some cave-dwelling sea monster who is lying in wait for me as well." She paused to take a breath. "It's quite large, you see, with sharp, pointed fangs and great slimy scales and soulless eyes that . . . oh!"

While she'd been talking, Marcus had climbed the boulders and followed the sound of her voice until it was clear she was just inches away. "I've got you, my lady," he said softly, and indeed he was grasping one of her forearms, frail and icy beneath his large hand.

"So you do." He smiled at the false bravado in her voice.

"I'll pull gently to guide you over the wall."

"H-how deep is the water?"

"It's only chest high. Chin high for you. I'll carry you, if I must."

"I think you must. I've never been in water deeper than a bath."

Of course, now all he could picture was her in her bath, her skin soft and rosy. He said a silent little prayer that the frigid water would cool his ardor. Marcus eased her over the boulders, wondering how such a massive amount of weight could have been moved by one small woman. "How did you manage to tumble this wall? I remember my brothers and I trying to remove the rocks. They were all far too heavy for us."

"I felt a breeze and pushed at the smallest of the boulders, and down everything came."

"My God, you could have been crushed." He pushed down stark fear—and anger that she had put herself in such a position.

"I'm quite nimble," she said as she pushed her way over the wall. "Ouch. I struck my knee. Blasted stone."

Marcus chuckled and pulled her over the top and directly into his arms. She did the most surprising thing. Instead of going rigid, she folded herself against him, wrapping her arms gently around his neck and laying her head on one shoulder. He breathed in her floral scent and pressed her tightly against his chest, allowing himself the pleasure of holding her against him.

"T-the water is f-frigid," she said, her teeth chattering near his ear.

"Is it? I hadn't noticed whilst standing several minutes in it. And I certainly didn't notice the temperature when I fell in over my head and doused the lamp." He could almost picture the face she was probably making, her nose scrunching up adorably.

That was precisely what Lilian was doing. Despite the fact he'd been in the water for several long minutes, his body felt so warm compared to the frigid seawater. "Are you very angry with me?"

"Yes." But his hold on her tightened infinitesimally.

"I'm sorry I worried you."

He grunted, then said, "After all this, I do hope you found Mabel's stocking and remembered to bring it with you."

She pushed the soft cloth against his cheek as proof that she had at least accomplished her task. "I couldn't let her go without her dolly. And I pictured it down here, cold, abandoned."

"It's a stocking."

"I know you do not believe that any more than Mabel does. Why do you insist on pretending you are horrid when you are not?"

"I am not pretending," he said, sounding as if he was talking through gritted teeth. He hoisted her up higher, and Lilian draped herself over one solid shoulder, liking the feel of his powerful body beneath her. In her experience, men of the aristocracy were, if not delicate creatures, then certainly nothing like the large and muscular man now holding her. He smelled of the sea and clean hay—not unpleasant smells, to be honest—and Lilian smiled. Never in her life had she been held by a man, and even though Lord Granton acted as if it were a great chore, Lilian decided she would enjoy it. When would she ever be held this way again? Beneath her, he shivered, and she felt a sharp pang of guilt.

"I am sorry for putting you through this," she said softly, her mouth nearly touching his ear, and he took a sharp breath, as if he'd stepped on something painful. "Are you injured?"

"I'll live," he said, again shifting her in his arms.

"Am I too heavy? With my wet skirts I must weigh ten stone."

He let out a laugh. "If you weigh ten stone, I weigh twenty. And I do not weigh twenty."

"Still, perhaps you should put me down," she said, even as she tightened her grip around his neck and allowed herself to press her cheek against the warm crook of his neck. She was just being polite, after all; she truly didn't want him to lower her to the water. Firstly, it was terribly cold, and secondly, she was rather enjoying the novelty of being held in the arms of a man—even if he did so begrudgingly.

"Yes, I should put you down," he said, and to her surprise, he dropped her, right there, into the cold seawater. She was only up to her waist, but still. It was cold. And he was the most insufferable man she'd ever met in her life. He gripped her arm firmly and pulled her along until she could tell they had entered the tunnel that connected the caves to the house. Up ahead, she could see the dim outline of the metal door that separated the house from the tunnel. Within minutes, they were walking on dry ground, and Lilian's great adventure was over.

"I imagine Mr. Palmer has already left for Whitby."

"Yes."

Lilian lifted her soggy skirts and attempted to keep up with him. "I do hope my shoes and dress dry in time—"

He spun around so quickly, Lilian let out a small cry. "You are leaving, Lady Lilian, if I have to drive you to Whitby myself."

He turned and continued walking toward the staircase, his boots leaving well-defined wet prints on the floor. Lilian felt unaccountably hurt. What was it about her that made Lord Granton dislike her so? She did have a habit of getting herself into trouble; it was her cursed sense of adventure. Her years living with Weston had been dreary beyond words because His Grace kept a tight rein on the two sisters. Lilian had never complained because she'd feared angering the duke nearly as much as she'd loathed him. What would she have done, where would she have gone, if Weston had forced her out? Her three years at Mount Carlyle had been spent in bored misery, a boredom that was only interrupted by feelings of disgust and terror when Weston showed interest in her. He took a sick pleasure in trying to make his young wife jealous and would constantly compare the two women, with her sister nearly always coming up short.

As cranky as Granton was, he was far more pleasant to be around than Weston, God rest his rotten soul.

Lilian lifted her sodden skirts, taking care not to get Mabel's dolly too wet in the process. Her shoes squelched with each step, and when she reached the staircase, she realized they were covered in sand. Knocking her shoes against the first step to rid them of the sand, Lilian followed Granton up to the house, grateful that the higher she climbed, the warmer the temperature got. When she reached the top, Granton was there, scowling at her, his arms crossed. As he stood there, his body convulsed with a violent shiver, and Lilian felt another stab of guilt—one she had no idea of letting Granton know about.

"I apologize for being curt," he nearly growled.

Lilian lifted her chin. "Apology accepted." Then she brushed by him, her shoes still making soft wet sounds and leaving behind small footprints in her wake.

Chapter 9

It was to be her last day at Merdunoir. For some reason, Granton had let her sleep, so she'd missed Palmer's trip to town to collect the servants. It was just as well; her dress and shoes were likely still damp, but as she had nothing else to wear, she would have to make do. When Lilian awoke to the furtive sounds of Mabel entering her room on tiptoe, the sun was quite high.

"Are you awake?"

Lilian smiled at the silly question, for her eyes were wide open. "No," she said, closing her eyes, "I'm quite sound asleep, but I'm having the most wonderful dream about a pretty little girl coming in to my room to wake me up."

Mabel giggled and climbed up on to her bed. "Thank you for getting dolly. I woke up, and there she was, in my arms."

"She had quite an adventure, but she was very brave, even in the dark."

"Dolly isn't afraid of the dark."

"I am," Lilian admitted.

"Me too."

"What adventure can we have today? Shall we go down to the beach and hunt for treasure?"

Mabel's eyes lit up. "Could we?"

"Yes. Absolutely. Let me get dressed and have a bit of breakfast, and we can head right down to the beach."

The previous night, Sadie had knocked on her door quite late and handed her Granton's robe and asked for her dress so that she could bring it to the kitchen, where it might dry a bit more quickly. After Sadie had left, Lilian had wrapped the soft robe around her and held it against her nose, taking a long breath. It smelled of Granton, and she smiled. Now her dress, looking freshly pressed, lay on the end of her bed, but her shoes were nowhere in sight. They must be still in the kitchen, drying.

Lilian pulled on her dress and grimaced. She was deathly sick of the plain garment, but the seamstress had promised she would have more dresses ready when it was time for Lilian to depart. She need only stop by the woman's shop in Whitby to collect them. And then she could go . . . somewhere. Soon after she'd received news that the true murderer had been found, Lilian had written her sister, but it was far too soon to expect an answer. Still, she couldn't help thinking that she would not be welcomed back in her sister's home; she'd never truly felt welcome there at all.

Theresa had more than once reminded Lilian that she was at Mount Carlyle only thanks to her charity. Lilian had remained only because the alternatives were even more unpalatable, and at that time she'd still hoped that she could marry well. Now, though, that hope was dashed. The scandal surrounding the duke's murder would follow her to her grave. She must become resigned to the fact that she would never marry, never have children. But at least she could live where and how she pleased. She was truly lost to society now.

Perhaps that's why she viewed her departure from Merdunoir with such dread. It had nothing, she told herself, to do with a certain man with golden-brown eyes. Or a little girl with a stocking for a dolly.

Marcus was returning from a ride when he spied Lady Lilian and Mabel walking across the lawn toward the sea. Her hair whipped back in the wind, and her dress was pressed against her slim form, leaving little to the imagination. At least not his imagination. With a determined step, he continued walking toward the house, but he could not ignore her completely when she called out to him.

"Lord Granton, would you care to join us? We're searching for treasure on the beach."

No. No no no no no no. "Of course." Damn, what the hell was wrong with him? He was just a few short hours away from being free from temptation, and there he was, walking headlong into it. The pair waited for him, both smiling, as if his presence were some great gift.

"I thought I saw a set of stairs from my room that leads down. Are they safe?"

Were they? He had no idea, as he hadn't used them in years. "Let me go in front of you to make certain," he said, and he couldn't help but see, with the wind buffeting her dress, that she wasn't wearing any shoes. Instead, her feet were encased in a pair of woolen socks that looked extremely familiar.

"Those are my socks."

She looked down, as if she were surprised to find them on her feet. "Oh, yes. My shoes are still a bit damp. I hope you don't mind."

Yes, he did mind. Because from now on, every time he donned that pair of socks he would think of her and her untamed hair and her plush pink lips and her extraordinary eyes. "I suppose it's fine."

"Come along, then. I'd hate to dally and miss Mr. Palmer again. Really, going back and forth each day must be quite wearing. Aren't the servants yet convinced the house is not haunted?"

"As a matter of fact, one of the footmen has asked if he might stay overnight. I suppose once he does that without a ghostly incident, others will follow." He let out an unhappy sigh. "Before I know it, I'll have a house full of servants and my mother will insist on visiting." He gave a mock shudder.

"Relatives can be trying, can they not? While it can be convenient to have them, it's rather nice to have few, as is the case with me."

When they reached the top of the stairs, Marcus looked down and was pleasantly surprised to see the steps appeared to be in good order. In fact, it appeared as if someone had made a recent repair— Palmer, no doubt.

"Here, I'll carry the child." Mabel immediately lifted her arms, and her instant trust in him, that he would not drop her, that he would keep her safe, made his heart give a now familiar lurch. She clung to him much as she had when they were climbing the stairs from the cave, her weight so slight Marcus made a silent promise to make certain the little girl had more than enough to eat.

It was a glorious day, the sort of day that seemed so rare—warm and clear with puffy white clouds dotting the horizon and nothing but blue sky overhead. Kittiwakes nesting in the cliff nearly drowned out the sound of the sea with their chatter as the three of them made their way down to the beach. Marcus breathed in deeply, surveying the scene before him. He'd been living in Merdunoir for months and yet hadn't ventured down to the beach; he hadn't bothered really looking at the sea that had once drawn him as a boy. Strange that something that had held such a place in his heart had gone practically unnoticed until this day.

"It's so beautiful," Lady Lilian breathed, stopping behind him on the steps where he had paused to survey the scene as if he'd never viewed it before. "It makes me wonder why anyone would live anywhere else in the world."

"Summer is lovely, but winter can be rather bleak here."

"I should think winter would hold its own kind of beauty," she said, a wistful note in her voice.

He continued down the steps until they reached the golden sand that made up the rock-strewn beach. The tide was going out, leaving behind a narrow strip of wet sand and exposing the shells Mabel was so fascinated by. When he was a lad, his brothers and sister would come down and look for the treasure that came to shore each day. They would always find something, be it a fisherman's net or a piece of a ship long gone from this world. It was something he missed when his duties became too numerous for him to spend time at play.

"If you're very lucky, you may find a fossil," Marcus said, placing Mabel down on the soft sand.

"What's a fossil?"

"An impression of an animal that lived thousands of years ago. Have you ever put a fingerprint in dough?" The little girl nodded. "A fossil is very much like the mark that is left in the dough when you lift up your finger. It shows the shape of the animal that died all those years ago. When I was a lad, we found an ammonite. That's a creature that lived in a spiral-shaped shell. It was quite an exciting find."

"Can we find an ammo . . . ammonanite?"

"Ammonite. We can certainly try. But I think we'll have more success just looking for ordinary shells."

"Like this," Lady Lilian said, walking up to the pair, her palm filled with a large, sun-bleached shell.

"May I go treasure hunting?" Mabel asked, stepping from foot to foot as if she could hardly stand still from the excitement.

"Stay where I can see you. Off you go," Marcus said, and found himself smiling as she skipped away.

"Are you very certain you want to send her away to school?" Lady Lilian asked, clearly teasing him.

"Very," he said dryly, but he really wasn't certain. Surely he could find a nanny and later a governess who could care for the child.

It wasn't quite as imperative that he have her removed from his home as it had been just a few short days ago. She was a quiet child, and she didn't take up too much space or make too many demands.

They stood watching Mabel skip down the beach, and Marcus had the distinctly uncomfortable feeling that the earth's axis had shifted subtly, lifting him out of his perpetually black mood. It was difficult to scowl watching the girl and standing next to a woman as lovely as Lady Lilian. Her hair, never fully tamed, whipped about her head in the wind, the strands seemingly participating in a wild dance. No matter how many times she pulled it back in an attempt to refasten it to the loose bun at the back of her head, strands continued to break free, and he was tempted to try to tame one particular strand that kept brushing her pink lips. Every time it sprang loose from its anchor, his eyes were drawn to the soft pillow of her lower lip, and no matter how many times he told himself to stop looking, it seemed he could not. She stood not three feet away, watching Mabel as she ran from one shell to the next, gathering them in her pockets. While she watched Mabel, he watched her and wondered what madness was taking him over. Tonight, the house would be empty, or nearly so. Tonight he could relax. Tonight, perhaps, his dreams would not be filled with tantalizing images of her. He really should never have looked at her in her bath, for now he was tortured by the memory.

Without realizing what he was doing, he took a step closer and lifted his hand. It seemed to happen slowly, as if he were moving in some sort of thick molasses that prevented normal movements. He lifted his hand and touched that strand of hair, the one brushing against her lips, and allowed himself to graze that soft, soft skin. She inhaled sharply and turned her gaze to him, a question in her eyes that seemed to say, *Are you going to kiss me?*

"Lady Lilian, I should very much like to . . ." *Kiss you. Everywhere. Hold you against me, feel your heat around me, press myself inside you. Make you cry out in ecstasy.* ". . . correspond with you after you leave." He closed his eyes briefly, allowing that idiotic sentence to settle in before he stepped back and forced himself to look out at the sea.

"Of course." She cleared her throat. "I don't have many people to write to, and I would be happy to exchange letters with you. Perhaps when you are back home, you can visit."

No. He would not. For if he visited, he would begin courting her, and if he began courting her, inevitably he would have to ask her to marry him, and he'd decided that one terrible marriage was enough. He planned to find a like-minded widow, someone he would not fall in love with. Someone who didn't hold enough power over him to destroy his life, to humiliate him beyond reason. If he ever did marry, it would be to a quiet mouse of a woman who was content to stay at home and read. Or knit. Not one who was young and beautiful and who would cause men's heads to turn the moment she walked in the room. Not one who would cause his heart to ache every time he looked at her or make him think of murder if someone dared touch her.

"This is my home," he said finally, meaning every syllable. He did not want to return to his boyhood home, nor his townhouse in London. At least not for a long while.

She looked away. "I expect I shall be quite busy setting up my house. Perhaps I'll find a lovely cottage in Whitby. I've heard it's a charming village." He knew she was teasing him, but he wasn't particularly amused. And she could tell, for she laughed. "Have no fear, sir. Once I have removed myself from Yorkshire, I daresay I will never return. Not even to visit a brooding lord living in a haunted house."

"I am not brooding." She raised one eyebrow as if challenging his assessment of himself. "Do you truly think I am brooding?"

"Most darkly."

"Hmm. Perhaps I am brooding." He took a deep, bracing breath. "Though it is difficult to remain disagreeable on such a pretty day so I will endeavor to lighten the mood. Have you ever waded in the sea, my lady?"

"No," Lilian said cautiously, thinking he might be planning to throw her into the water. For a few wonderfully tense moments, she'd actually thought he was going to kiss her, and she idly wondered what she would have done. Kiss him back, no doubt. Perhaps it was just her imagination or wishful thinking. Really, he was more likely to throw her into the sea than kiss her, though she very much doubted he would do either. If he were to do so, she'd have to remain at Merdunoir until her dress dried and she knew that would not go well with him. For some reason, the thought of staying one more day was a rather happy one. She was so dreading going back to Mount Carlyle and her sister.

He surprised her by shucking off his boots and stockings and rolling up his pants. "Come on," he called, already jogging to the water's edge, a boyish grin on his face. Suddenly, he was no brooding lord, but a stunningly handsome young man with a penchant for mischief. She knew instinctively that this was a rare thing indeed, for him to actually play, so she bent down and removed her, or rather his, warm stockings and followed him, stopping just at the edge of where the waves sank into the sand. The sand beneath her feet was cold and she curled her toes into it, laughing at how the sand began to swallow up her entire foot.

"You'd better lift your skirt, madam, or else your dress will get soaked. I promise not to look at your pretty ankles."

She made a face at him, but relented, lifting up the material just high enough so her hem would remain dry.

"Very pretty indeed," Granton said, leaning back so he might get a better view of her ankles. What a flirt. Lilian had never given that part of her body much thought, and couldn't imagine what a man would find fascinating about ankles. She ignored him and took a tentative step into the icy water.

"Oh, it's so cold."

"It's quite warm, actually. You get used to it. My brothers and I used to swim here in early June and come out with blue lips every time."

"Yes, that does seem appealing."

He chuckled before bending down and picking something up from the surf. "Look here," he said, showing her a small porcelain bird. It was hopelessly chipped and missing its tail, but it had once been a darling little piece and somehow held even more charm having survived the sea.

"My gift to you, my lady," he said, bowing formally.

"I daren't accept such a gift from a gentleman to whom I have not been properly introduced," Lilian said, playing along.

"Very well." He turned and drew his arm back as if to throw the bird back into the sea.

"Don't you dare," she shouted, grabbing hold of his arm. She looked up to find him grinning down at her, and she had that wonderful feeling again in the pit of her stomach. *He is going to kiss me. He is.*

His smile slowly faded and Lilian found herself inexorably drawn closer to him. She swallowed thickly and her eyes fluttered closed. And then she felt something hard and cold pressed into her hand, and she opened her eyes to find the little bird in her palm and Granton standing straight, gazing out to the sea.

She closed her eyes briefly again, this time in humiliation. She'd thought she was fairly good at reading whether a man wanted to kiss her or not, but Granton did not look like a man who was tortured with longing. He looked annoyed, and Lilian had to stop herself from apologizing. What would she say? Sorry I desperately wanted you to kiss me? He wanted to correspond with her, not kiss her. She could feel her cheeks heating with embarrassment.

"It's just as well you are leaving today," he said, drawing her from her self-flagellation. He continued to look at the horizon. "I don't think I could resist kissing you if you were to stay."

Lilian immediately pressed her lips together to stop them from blossoming into a full smile. "Oh," she managed after a time. "Perhaps you may kiss me good-bye."

He turned his head sharply to look at her and gave her a grim smile. "I plan to be out riding when you depart, my lady."

Just as well. It would have only made leaving more difficult, but at least she would have had the memory of his kiss. She cleared her throat. "You don't really want to correspond with me, do you?"

He shook his head, his brown-gold eyes steady on hers. "No. I don't." Then he smiled and her heart did a little flip. "But I shall."

"Perhaps I will not write back," she said saucily, but ended up grinning back at him. "Thank you for the gift." Still smiling softly, she looked down at the small blue porcelain bird sans tail feathers, poor thing. She knew, even years from now, she would look at that bird and remember Merdunoir and Mabel and standing in the cold water of the North Sea beside Lord Granton. At that moment, a larger wave hit them, and wet the bottom of her skirt, breaking the spell. She let out a small shriek and ran from the water, shaking out her skirts.

"It's not completely ruined, my lord," she called out. "It should only take a day or so to dry."

He let out a small laugh and joined her on the beach, then called out for Mabel, who had gotten quite a distance away from them. Mabel lifted her head and immediately started running toward them, and even from a distance, it was easy to tell her pockets were stuffed full of shells.

"Did you find a lot of treasure?"

"Oh, yes," she said, out of breath. "All sorts of shells. And pretty rocks. And a tooth." She held it up for him to see.

"A tooth?" Granton asked, bending down so he could see what was clearly a large shark's tooth. "Are you certain that's not your tooth?" He peered into her mouth as if it might have fallen from it. Mabel giggled and put the tooth back into her skirts.

Lilian looked up the steps, which seemed rather daunting now that they were on the beach.

"Can you make it up the steps, my lady?" he asked, obviously seeing her reticence.

"Sir, I practically walked here from London. I most certainly can manage a short set of stairs."

"Let's race, then. From here to the front door."

He'd surprised her again. It was such a silly thing for a serious-minded man to propose, and it was for that reason Lilian found she couldn't resist. This man who had not been allowed to play when he was a boy would be allowed now, if she had any say. "All right, but you should make some accommodation for my skirts. And what about Mabel?"

"I'll carry her. That will be my handicap. I shall even give you a head start. I won't start running until you reach the bottom step."

Lilian eyed the distance between them and the first step. His legs were long and he would no doubt be able to take two steps at a time, but she was nimble and young. "All right." And then, without another word, she took off, laughing as she ran. The minute her foot hit the step, she realized she'd forgotten her stockings, and so she called back, already out of breath, for Granton to pick them up.

"I already have them," he called, far closer than she would have imagined, and she let out another laughing squeal as she picked up her skirts a bit and ran up the steps as quickly as she could. She could hear him pounding up the steps right behind her as Mabel urged him on, the little traitor.

"You've lovely ankles," he said, and she could hear the smile in his voice. Letting out a small growl of mock anger, she was tempted to let her skirts drop and allow him to win. Instead, grinning, she picked up her pace. When Lilian reached the soft grass, she sprinted forward toward the house and the front entrance. The drive was gravel and the stones were sharp beneath her feet, but Lilian didn't care. She hadn't had such fun in years. He was right behind her now, seemingly jogging easily while her lungs were about to burst and her legs to give out.

"Give up?" he called.

"Never!"

She rounded the corner of the house and threw herself up the steps, barely getting through the threshold before he tumbled in behind her, both laughing and out of breath.

Lilian was still laughing, still trying to catch her breath, when she looked up and into three pairs of horrified eyes. Next to her, Granton had gone abruptly silent and still.

"Mother, this is unexpected," he said.

Chapter 10

"What is the meaning of this?" His mother stood stone-faced and stared at her oldest son before moving her cold eyes first to Mabel and then, scathingly, to Lilian. Beside her stood his brother, Adam, and his sister-in-law, Georgette, who both looked as shocked as his mother. He wondered sardonically if it was because he was dressed so casually or that he actually seemed to be enjoying himself for the first time in memory.

Marcus set Mabel down, and the little girl immediately grasped his hand, as if she were comforting him and not the other way around, so he gave her hand a little squeeze of reassurance. *I'm fine.* "Mother, I was not expecting you. Obviously. May I please introduce—"

His mother took a sharp gasp. "You may *not*," she said. "How could you think to introduce such a woman to me?" She looked at Adam and Georgette, who remained mute, apparently as stunned as his mother. Marcus could feel himself heat from anger but took a calming breath.

"This woman, Mother, is Lady Lilian Martin."

Once this information settled into his mother's rattled brain, she grew quite pale and actually staggered back a step.

"I do believe she might faint," Adam said, moving behind his mother apparently to catch her fall.

"I am not going to faint," she said testily. "But this is perhaps the most shocking news of all. Not only are you here with a woman when we all thought you were despondent and alone in your misery, but we find you are cohabiting with a murderess."

Lady Lilian let out a sound and looked ready to defend herself, but Marcus held out a hand, forestalling her. The last thing he needed at the moment was his mother and Lady Lilian arguing.

"She is innocent and you know it, Mother. And we are not cohabiting. The story of why she is here can wait, but please be assured that nothing untoward has occurred."

Lucille's mouth was set, her hands in front of her clenching her reticule tightly, as if she could hardly contain her anger. "Nothing *untoward?* You cannot be so obtuse as not to recognize the full implications of—" She stopped abruptly and pointed a finger at Mabel, who still clutched his hand. "What is that?" his mother asked.

Marcus looked down at the wind-mussed head of Mabel and was about to dismiss his mother's question, when the little mite looked up at him, her hazel eyes wide and trusting. Bloody hell, he was going to regret this, he was certain. "She is my daughter."

From the corner of his eye, he saw Lady Lilian turn her head and smile. "Don't," he snapped, but the lady kept smiling at him anyway. He couldn't help but notice Georgette and Adam exchange curious glances. Suddenly, Marcus wanted to scream for them all to leave. What were they doing here, invading his privacy, disturbing the one time he'd felt happy in memory? "Mabel, you should curtsy when you are introduced. You practiced that, did you not, with Lady Lilian?"

Mabel nodded and dropped his hand, then stepped up and curtsied rather inexpertly to his mother, who looked down at the little girl with clear distaste.

"You would introduce me to your bast—"

Marcus felt a surge of rage, one that must have immediately shown, for his mother stopped talking midword, apparently rather terrified by the look of pure fury in his eyes. "Lady Lilian," he said with measured calmness, trying to ignore the way her eyes smiled at him, "would you mind taking Mabel to the nursery? I shall be up once I have spoken with my mother." Lady Lilian held out her hand to Mabel and gave Marcus a grateful look, no doubt wishing she could run from the room. Marcus wished he could leave as well instead of dealing with his relatives.

"Shall we go into my study? I can expound on my current situation much more comfortably from there." As they walked to his study, Marcus spied a maid and called her over. "Will you please tell Sadie that I need two more rooms made up and to expect three guests for dinner?" God above knew he hated saying those words, but he could hardly throw his relatives out after they'd traveled so far.

"Yes, sir," the maid said, bobbing a curtsy.

"Why are your servants not in uniform?" Lucille asked.

"Because I didn't want servants permanently and didn't see a reason for the expense," Marcus responded impatiently, almost angrily.

"Do not use that tone with me. It matters not that you are a grown man. Certainly you can understand a mother's concern for her son. Not only had you disappeared for months without a word, not one single word, but when I do find you, you are frolicking about with a woman and holding a strange child in your arms. What mother wouldn't be concerned? I asked only why your servants don't have uniforms."

"I apologize for my tone, Mother."

Mollified, she continued walking, and Marcus followed, trailed by his brother and sister-in-law. A deep sense of dread filled him as he walked into the room where, as a boy, he'd spent so many long hours with his father learning how to manage their estates. When they were all seated, Marcus calmly explained who Mabel was, how Lady Lilian had ended up in his home, and that she was leaving, unscathed, to return to her sister.

"I'm afraid that's not possible," Adam said.

"What do you mean?"

Adam nearly squirmed beneath his brother's hard gaze. "It's not a secret that you have a woman here. We were only in Whitby for a few hours and we started hearing things about how you were keeping a woman at Merdunoir. They know her name, Marcus, if not her lineage. But it will only be a matter of time before it reaches London, and then she'll be ruined."

"She's already ruined," Marcus said coldly. He knew what his brother was hinting at and he wanted none of it.

"She is the daughter of an earl, Marcus, not some commoner we can pay off. Oh, my God, he must *marry* the girl," his mother said, clearly horrified by the idea. "My son will be married to an accused murderess." She pulled a handkerchief from her sleeve and dabbed at the real tears forming in her eyes. Marcus loved his mother and didn't want to upset her, but he was not marrying anyone.

"The murderer confessed and killed himself," he said reasonably

For some reason, his brother Adam looked exceedingly uncomfortable. "It's not as cut-and-dried as one might think. Some say the gent was only being chivalrous."

"Are you saying a man confessed to a murder he didn't commit,

then killed himself all to save Lady Lilian?" Marcus asked incredu-
lously.

"The staff at Mount Carlyle is fiercely loyal to the lady," Georgette said softly. "People actually do believe that, Marcus."

"And there is also a question of whether the man killed himself
at all."

"But that's absurd. What man would write a confession for a crime
he didn't commit? Anyone who believes that belongs in Bedlam."

"I'm afraid that particular rumor is being perpetuated by her sister," Adam said.

"Her sister," Marcus said with clear disgust. "So Lady Lilian cannot return there."

"And she cannot stay here," his mother said. "Now that you have
ruined her, you have an obligation to marry the girl. Oh, this is a
nightmare."

Marcus felt nauseous. He looked at his family and knew, he *knew*
what he had to do. But he wasn't going to. He didn't want to be married and certainly not again to a woman who didn't love him. And
one he didn't love. He would not. He would do all he could to protect
her reputation, short of marrying her. He would hire the best lawyer
in Britain if it came to that, but he would not marry her. Good God!
The walls of the room seemed to be coming closer, the air thicker. He
could hardly breathe.

"You are past your mourning period," Georgette said gently.

Marcus snapped his head toward his sister-in-law, who actually
flinched beneath his gaze. And his brother tensed as if ready to
launch himself at Marcus to protect his wife. Bloody hell, had the
world gone mad? He was *not* marrying Lilian. He wanted them gone.
He wanted everyone out of his house and out of his life.

"Let me tell you all something," he began quietly, with barely
suppressed fury. "I am not going to *bloody hell marry anyone!*" This
last ended on a roar, the type that caused windows to shake and
nearby birds to take flight. And a woman, who was calmly walking
up a set of stairs, to freeze in shock.

Yes, Marcus looked up to see Lady Lilian, her face pale, staring
at him from the stairs, holding her shoes in her hand. Damnation!

Marcus tore his gaze away from Lilian, but from the corner of his
eye, he saw her hurry up the stairs and out of sight. He would have to
go to her later, he knew that, but for now he simply wanted to dis-

pense with this torturous interview with his family. "You may all leave me now," he said, staring at the floor, for he could not bear to look at them and their pity any longer.

"I'd like to stay, if you will allow it." His brother, brave man that he was, stood to escort the ladies from the room, then calmly shut the door behind them. After they'd gone, he turned. "Is it too early for brandy?"

Marcus let out a humorless laugh. "Is it ever?"

"Actually, yes." But his brother made his way over to the sideboard, where he poured two glasses. Taking a sip, he said, "This is damn fine brandy."

"You should see what Lady Lilian found in the caves. I haven't had any yet, but I suspect it's even finer," Marcus said, taking a proffered snifter from his brother's hand.

"She found brandy?" Adam asked, seeming delighted.

"Yes. After she was trapped there by the high tide. Now that was a bit of a scare."

Adam looked at his brother thoughtfully. "Do you care for her?"

"I like her well enough."

His brother chuckled. "That's not what I mean. Do you love her? I thought I detected something . . . more."

Marcus shook his head. "No. I hardly know her. She's only been here a few days and would have left immediately if Sadie hadn't burned her dress, leaving her literally without a thing on her back."

"If you're certain."

"I am," Marcus said evenly, and though he believed it, something in his heart rebelled at those two words.

"Then again, how would anyone know? It's not as if you go around with your heart on your sleeve."

Marcus felt himself bristle unaccountably at his brother's light words. "I'm not certain I know what you mean."

"You're not a man given to large emotions, Marcus. Hell, on your wedding day, you looked *bored*, as if you were attending some endless soiree, not your own wedding and looking forward to your wedding night."

"I wasn't overmuch, as a matter of fact." But that was a lie. He had very much been looking forward to bedding his lively new wife, but he simply hadn't seen the point of letting everyone in the room know it.

Adam shook his head. "My God, Marcus, when Jupiter died in that fire, you didn't shed a tear. *I* cried, for God's sake, but you stood there as if nothing had happened."

Marcus calmly placed his snifter down and his brother eyed him warily. "Just because I didn't become a blubbering idiot does not mean I did not hurt. My God, Adam, didn't anyone notice I didn't ride for two *years?* Two years, I could not bring myself to ride another horse because it hurt so damn much." He closed his eyes briefly. He hated this . . . *feeling.*

"We didn't know. How could we? You never show what you're thinking. You're always even, Marcus. No matter what happens, you are calm, reserved, so damned cold. It's almost as if you feel no joy, no sorrow. No love. It was damned frightening to see you rush into the house laughing. I can't remember the last time I saw you laugh. Didn't know you were even capable of it."

Marcus gave his younger brother a withering look. "I haven't had much to laugh about lately, Adam." It wasn't that he didn't feel; it was that he felt too damned much. Always had. "Do you blame me for what Eleanor did to me? Do you?"

"No, of course not."

"You sound unconvinced."

Adam gave a helpless gesture. "It's just that if you did love Eleanor, how would the lady have known?"

Marcus sat down heavily. "The worst part about caring for Eleanor was even after I'd discovered what I thought was her first infidelity, I still admired her, still liked her. I couldn't help it. It was humiliating and God, it nearly killed me. By the third time, I had managed to feel nothing. Most days."

"If you do marry again, Marcus, try to let the lady know you love her if you do. Wives like to know they are loved."

"Georgette must be giddy with happiness, then," he joked.

Adam grinned. "She is, actually." He took a sip of brandy and looked contemplatively at Marcus. "You never loved Eleanor, did you?"

"Perhaps. In the beginning. Before we were married." He took a long breath. "I have no wish to marry again. Obviously," he said on a laugh.

"I'm afraid you don't have much choice. You must have known the consequences of allowing her to stay."

Marcus stared gloomily at the floor. "I kept telling her to leave. As soon as she regained consciousness. I expected every day here would be her last, but it always seemed something got in the way of her leaving. You have to remember, it was only me and two servants here. It wasn't as if I had a wardrobe of female clothes I could have put on her. Should I have cast her out with only my robe on her back? Besides, Sadie was here."

"Servants don't count. You know that."

"I suppose I thought no one would find out." Marcus buried his head in his hands, his elbows resting on his thighs. "I don't want to marry anyone."

"If you must marry someone, at least Lady Lilian is pretty. She has remarkable eyes."

"Like a butterfly's wings," Marcus said, before looking up at his brother.

Adam raised one eyebrow.

"Sod off, Adam. They're the same color as a morpho butterfly. I wasn't waxing poetic."

The two brothers were silent for a long stretch.

"She made you laugh, Marcus."

Yes, she did that.

Lilian watched Mabel on the rocking horse, trying not to think about Lord Granton or how adamant he'd sounded when he'd shouted he didn't want to marry her. *I am not going to bloody hell marry anyone!* There was certainly nothing ambiguous about that sentence. It was the strangest thing. She didn't want to marry him, hadn't even given the smallest thought to it, but the fact that he was so opposed . . . well, it *hurt*. It shouldn't, of course. She hardly knew the man, after all. And she didn't even really like him most of the time. But the thought that he'd be so stunningly opposed to marrying her made her feel unexpectedly awful. It was almost as if she was unsuitable. Which she most certainly was not. Except, of course, for the whole wanted murderess scandal. Lilian knew it would be years, if ever, before that gossip died. For the rest of her life, if she was part of society, she knew people would whisper behind her back. Lilian had had enough time to think about the scandal to realize she would never marry, unless she traveled to America or Canada. Perhaps, she thought with a giggle, she should go to Australia. It might not be a penal colony any longer, but she would certainly fit in better there than in England.

"I should like a real horse when I grow up," Mabel announced.

"I'm sure Lord Granton will give you one," Lilian said distractedly. Downstairs, Granton's family was no doubt plying him with questions and making plans for a hasty wedding. Of course she would not agree to such a thing, and she had no one on her side of the family who would press the issue. She would simply refuse to marry, Granton could let out a sigh of relief, and she would go on her merry way.

Her merry way!

"Oh, my goodness. I've forgotten that I need to be in the carriage today," she said, rushing over to the still-rocking Mabel to kiss her on the cheek. "I've got to go, but I'll write to you and when you learn how, you can write back. I shall miss you, Mabel."

Mabel stopped rocking and stared at her, her expression solemn. "Do you truly have to go?"

"I truly do," Lilian said, forcing a smile even though her throat closed up a bit. She had the urgent need to escape before Granton took up the notion that his mother was right. If she left immediately, he wouldn't know how to find her and this mad idea that they should marry would blow over. "Give me a hug. I expect the next time I see you you'll have grown a foot." Lilian gave her another quick kiss, then turned quickly and headed for the nursery door, praying the tears she was about to shed would wait until she was over the threshold. With her head down, she opened the door and rushed into the hall, only to run directly into Lord Granton, who grasped her upper arms gently to steady her.

"Where are you going in such a hurry?" he asked, dropping his hands.

Lilian lifted her chin, deciding to pretend she hadn't overheard him as she walked up the stairs. "I believe I have a carriage to catch," she said, and went to make her way around him.

"We need to talk." His tone brooked no argument, but Lilian decided to argue anyway.

"We have nothing to discuss, Lord Granton," she said, her voice clipped. "I planned to leave today and so I shall. If you will excuse me, sir."

"I will not," he said, his tone matching hers but somehow much more authoritative, likely due to his father's expert tutelage. "It has come to my attention, Lady Lilian, that your presence at Merdunoir has been noted by more than one individual. While I had hoped to avoid such a complication, and while this gives me great pain to say, I believe we have both been rather foolish in allowing you to stay here unchaperoned."

Lilian held up one hand, stopping him. "I know what you are going to say and I would like to spare you the task of uttering the words. I am leaving, sir. I am leaving today, and you shall likely never see me again and good riddance. I hope that ends any foolishness, either on your part or mine. I have no wish to marry you, and I'm quite certain you have no wish to marry me."

Granton peered down at her as if her words had made him angry, though Lilian could hardly say why, as she'd been quite certain it was what he would want to hear. "That is where you are wrong," he said in a dangerous tone, and Lilian furrowed her brow in confusion.

"I am not deaf, my lord." There, she'd just admitted she'd been eavesdropping, though one would have to be deaf not to have heard his angry words.

"I've changed my mind. I think we would suit." Lilian nearly snorted, but her expression must have conveyed her thoughts. "Fine. Let's be honest, shall we? As a man of honor, I cannot allow you to face society without my protection. I knew the consequences of allowing you to stay here unchaperoned, and I ignored them. I am entirely at fault, and now I must make amends."

"Make amends? So marrying me would be making amends?" she asked, incredulous.

"Yes," he said. "As you might expect, I have no wish to marry, but if I am forced to marry someone, you are not at all disagreeable."

"How lovely that I'm not disagreeable." A smile tugged at his lips, and Lilian nearly found herself grinning up at him. "I'm so sorry, Granton, that my presence here has put you in this situation. You must know I would have left with just my shift on if I'd known this would happen. I was ruined long before I arrived on your doorstep, sir, so you have no obligation to save my reputation. It was in tatters the moment I panicked and fled Mount Carlyle."

"A man confessed to the murder. You are as much a victim of that night as he was, except that you were an innocent victim." He let out a hard puff of breath. "I cannot stand by and allow your name to be sullied, my lady. What kind of a man would I be if I allowed such a thing?" He looked away toward the nursery door. "And she needs a mother."

"As well as a father."

"I have laid claim to her, it seems. Much to my mother's horror. I set about trying to find her father, you know. Wrote to my wife's maid to find him. I don't know what I will do in the remote possibility the man stakes a claim to her, and I have no idea how I will explain her presence. She's not legally a bastard, and yet she's not mine." He let out a sigh. "I suppose she is mine now. And yours, if you'll agree to marry me."

Lilian looked at the door to where Mabel still played. It was tempting to say yes. She adored Mabel and enjoyed Granton's company. Perhaps they could grow to care for one another. She'd thought she would never marry, and so the prospect of marrying and having children was slightly intoxicating.

"What if we grow to hate one another?" she asked, her voice small.

"What if we grow to tolerate one another?"

Lilian looked up at him and laughed. "Tolerate? You will make me swoon with your romantic nature, Lord Granton," she said, holding one hand over her heart.

"I think we could suit. In time." He looked at her, assessing. "I would dearly like to see your hair down." He reached up and tucked one tendril behind her ear. "I do find it intriguing."

Lilian felt that odd heaviness in her limbs and a sense that he was pulling her toward him even though he wasn't touching her. His eyes became hooded and he leaned toward her, just a bit, just enough to make her heart beat like mad in her chest, just enough to make her believe that this time he would, indeed, kiss her. She realized she wanted him to. Rather desperately, actually.

"I've been resisting kissing you for days now," he said, his voice low. "Now that we are engaged—"

"We're engaged?" she asked, her voice strangely breathy.

He nodded, leaning in even closer, until she could feel his breath on her lips, until his face in front of her was nothing but a handsome blur.

And then, his lips touched hers, just a light brushing, just enough to let her know that a man was kissing her. She stood still, not breathing, and closed her eyes. Oh, this was lovely, she thought, as he moved his lips against hers. She swayed slightly and he let out a sound, deep and low, and suddenly she was in his arms, pulled hard against him, his mouth slanting on hers, his tongue sweeping over the seam of her lips. It seemed like the most natural thing in the world to open her mouth, just slightly, to let him taste her. Lilian clung to him because her knees felt strangely weak. Granton laid a hand at the back of her head, pressing her gently toward him, as his other hand snaked around her back and pulled her so that her entire body was flush against his tall, lean one. It was a bit like holding a bit of cushioned steel; his muscles were that taut. He shifted slightly and she could feel his arousal. Never in her limited experience had she been held this way by a man, felt his need. She knew instinctively what it meant, that he wanted her, and that thought shot a thrill through her, an entirely unexpected one.

"You're kissing."

They broke apart at the sound of Mabel's voice, and Lilian stepped hastily back, smoothing her skirt and wishing she could smooth her emotions as quickly. She had completely lost herself, felt a flood of sensations she'd never known in her life. With a shake of her head, she realized that she wanted more, wanted to lose herself in his kiss, his caresses. Wanted more of him. My goodness, but she could hardly breathe from the want. When she was slightly more composed, she looked from Mabel to Granton and found herself oddly disappointed by how very composed he looked. She knew her cheeks were burning, but his complexion was unchanged. If it hadn't been for the fact that she'd felt his obvious arousal, she would have thought him completely unmoved. Then again, what did she truly know of men? Perhaps it was a simple matter for their man part to come to life. That thought nearly made her giggle, but she stifled it and pressed her lips together. Unless she'd been mistaken. Perhaps he had something in his pocket? Should she ask? Lilian pressed her lips together even harder. Where on earth were these thoughts coming from?

"Why were you kissing?" Mabel asked Granton.

"Because Lady Lilian is very pretty and I like kissing pretty girls. Particularly pretty girls I am going to marry." He shot Lilian a look as if he was waiting for a challenge to his claim.

Mabel's eyes widened.

"Do you know what that means, Mabel?" Lilian asked softly,

bending down so she was at the little girl's level, and Mabel shook her head. "It means Lord Granton is going to be your papa and I am going to be your mama. Would that be agreeable?"

Mabel smiled. "Yes, my lady."

Lilian straightened and looked at Granton, who stared stonily at the wall. She felt suddenly awkward standing there in front of her future husband, a man who clearly did not want to marry her. She'd thought—foolishly, obviously—that a man who wanted to kiss a woman likely also wanted to marry her. This was not the case with Granton. "Mabel, why don't you go down to the kitchen and see if you can find Sadie? I'll bet she'll have a treat for you."

Without saying another word, Mabel hurried down that hall, her stocking flopping in her hand as she ran.

Lilian again smoothed skirts that didn't need smoothing. "Lord Granton, I am so sorry."

"As am I. But I fear we have no choice."

Lilian's heart inexplicably plummeted, and she found herself wishing she'd gotten on that carriage days ago, because she had a terrible feeling that she was not nearly as opposed to a marriage between them as he was. Under different circumstances, she might even allow herself to be happy.

"If you'll excuse me, Lady—" He stopped abruptly. "I suppose when in private, at least, we should use our given names. Mine is Marcus."

"Yes, I know, my . . . Marcus. And of course you shall call me Lilian."

"Very well, Lilian," he said, his face impassive. "I shall see you at eight at dinner. We meet just prior in the parlor." He gave her a curt bow, then headed down the hall. As Lilian watched his tall form move away, she couldn't help but wonder if she'd just made the most terrible mistake of her life.

When Lilian entered the parlor that evening, she had the distinct feeling she was in a house of mourning. Granton's brother and his wife were huddled in one corner talking quietly, as if a corpse were laid out somewhere in the room for viewing. Lady Chesterfield sat on a sofa, periodically dabbing her eyes, and Granton stood stoically by the cold fireplace, his elbow resting on the mantel, his fist against his mouth as if in deep contemplation. Or grief. A half-empty brandy sifter sat by his elbow.

Lilian paused at the threshold, uncertain of her welcome, for it was clear she was the reason for their collective dark mood. "Good evening, everyone," she said, trying not to sound too cheerful. Granton—or rather, Marcus—lifted his head and gave her something she thought was meant to be a smile.

"We'll have the wedding here," Lady Chesterfield said, still dabbing at her eyes. "Granton will obtain a special license and you will marry immediately. Under the circumstances, a small wedding seems best." The lady was barely able to get this last out before dissolving in fresh tears.

"I see no need to rush things," Lilian said, flushing when everyone but Marcus turned to stare at her. Lucille raked her eyes up and down her frame, and Lilian, who'd thought the new dress delivered by the seamstress earlier that day was quite becoming, felt conspicuously plain. "I'm sorry, but perhaps you could explain the haste."

"Tongues are already wagging and your reputation is already in tatters. The sooner you are married, the sooner Granton can offer his protection. Don't be obtuse, girl."

"She's simply concerned, my lady," Georgette said soothingly, before turning to Lilian. "I know this is difficult for you, but I agree with Lady Chesterfield. The sooner you are married, the better."

"It seems to me that if we do marry quickly, tongues will wag even more. They'll think . . . things." Her cheeks heated, but she kept her gaze direct.

"And when it is obvious there was no need for a hasty wedding, everyone will assume the two of you fell madly in love and married quickly because you simply could not wait."

Lilian let out a sharp laugh, quickly stifled by her hand, and she darted a guilty look toward Marcus. Her future husband, however, continued to stare morosely into the cold fireplace as if he hadn't heard a word.

While it rankled Lilian to have her future laid out by a virtual stranger, she was highly aware that she was the cause of all their woes. Had she not fled, had she not stayed at Merdunoir overlong, none of this would be necessary. She knew Lady Chesterfield likely expected her appreciation, and Lilian, despite her unhappiness with the situation, was able to find some of that emotion within her. "Thank you, my lady."

Georgette then came over and offered her hands. "No matter the situation, I shall be glad to have another sister," she said, and Lilian smiled in gratitude. She knew instinctively that she would have at least one ally in the Dunford family. Adam Dunford, on the other hand, remained on the other side of the room, his eyes on his older brother.

"This is just so wonderful," Marcus boomed suddenly before taking a long sip of his brandy. "The wedding plans, not this brandy. Though I must say, my future lady wife, your discovery of one of the finest brandies I've ever had the pleasure to drink is nearly as wonderful as our wonderful wedding." He took another sip.

"Marcus," Adam said, his voice laced with concern and warning.

Marcus turned his head a bit loosely, confirming what Lilian already suspected. He was drunk.

"I'm sorry, is this not a happy occasion? A wedding announcement!" He flung one hand out in a flourish, and Lilian felt her face heat with humiliation.

Adam hurried to his brother's side and whispered something in his ear, but Lilian turned away, unable to look at her future husband a minute more. She'd known he didn't want to get married. She'd *known*. But did he have to be so horrible?

"He's not used to drinking," Georgette said softly, for her ears only. "I've known Granton for years, and I've never seen him like this."

Though Lilian knew Georgette was trying to comfort her, the lady's words had the opposite effect. The thought of marrying her was so abhorrent, he'd had the need to get roaring drunk just to face her this evening.

"Why is everyone so gloomy?" Marcus asked. "Why, when you think of it, this situation is rather amusing."

"Marcus, don't be an ass," Adam whispered harshly as he darted a look toward Lilian.

"I think I shall leave you to your dinner, if you don't mind," Lilian said with as much dignity as she could. When no one argued, she turned around gracefully and left the room to calmly walk up the stairs to her bedroom. It wasn't until she softly closed the door to her own room that she let the tears she'd been holding nearly all day burst from her eyes as she flung herself down onto her bed. To stifle her sobs, she buried her head in a pillow and cried until she was exhausted. In that moment, she wished her mother were alive. She needed her. Her mother would have soothed her and told her all would be well, but mostly she would have allowed Lilian to cling to her in her misery. Instead, she hugged her soggy pillow and rocked back and forth.

After a time, she fell asleep, waking suddenly in the middle of the night, her body tense. A soft knock on her door brought her fully awake, and she slid off her bed, realizing with chagrin that she was still dressed as she had been for dinner. Palmer had returned from Whitby with two more simple dresses, and she'd happily donned a pretty blue one, glad to be rid of the gray dress she'd been wearing for days. She'd thought, when she'd put it on, that Marcus would be pleased to see her in something colorful. But he probably hadn't even noticed.

Lilian walked to the door and pressed her ear against it. "Yes?"

"It's Marcus."

Her heart jumped, but she took a deep breath. He'd sounded sober, so she opened the door a crack. He stood there in his formal attire, looking completely polished but for his hair. When she'd seen him earlier in the evening, he'd been perfection, but now he appeared a bit mussed and there were dark smudges beneath his steady gaze.

"May I speak with you?"

Lilian eyed him warily, but opened the door and let him step inside.

"I have never . . . that is . . . the man you saw this evening has never before shown himself in public, and he never shall again."

"That man was you, sir."

Indeed it was. A crazed man. A man who felt his entire life closing in on him. A man who couldn't quite comprehend that his carefully planned future had come to this: being cuckolded, having a daughter whose father was unknown, and then being forced to marry a woman he hardly knew. How had his world collapsed around him so completely? He shook his head. "I apologize. My behavior was unforgiveable."

"I accept your apology."

She'd been crying. Copious tears from the look of her red-rimmed eyes, still a bit puffy. In the lamplight, he could see the salty tracks down her cheeks. He lifted his thumb, tracing one of the salty little streaks. "I've made you cry."

"Yes."

He smiled, liking the way she never prevaricated. He dropped his hand, resisting the urge to slide it to the back of her neck and draw her close. "I *am* sorry."

"I know." She hugged herself and looked away. "It's a terrible situation, and I feel guilty having to put you through this. And I feel stupid for allowing it to happen."

"As do I."

"I suppose we can muddle through?"

"Yes. Of course." He looked past her, his eyes settling on her rumpled bed. "This doesn't have to be a conventional marriage if you'd rather it not be." God, those words were difficult to say. "Georgette said you might be frightened. That perhaps I frighten you. And it might be best to get to know one another before . . ." He looked away, frustrated with his lack of finesse. He hadn't intended for his voice to sound quite so gruff, but he was unused to talking to women. Eleanor had once joked that he barked everything.

She tilted her head. "You don't frighten me, my lord. Am I supposed to be frightened? I can act frightened if you wish."

He let out a rusty laugh. "No, I don't wish for you to be frightened. I honestly didn't think you were, but Georgette thought perhaps you might be and . . ." Dammit, all he really wanted to do was to take her in his arms and kiss her until she forgave his boorish behavior. But she'd already forgiven him, so he'd lost his excuse to ravish her.

"I suppose we could get to know one another a bit more. What is your favorite color?"

"I rather like the color of your eyes," he said before he could think better of it. She gave him a skeptical look and he shrugged. "They are your most remarkable feature. That and your ankles."

It was her turn to laugh and he found himself grinning down at her. "I was admiring your calves. They are quite shapely," she said primly.

"My calves? Not my broad shoulders or powerful thighs or chiseled jaw?" He lifted his chin so that she might get a better look.

"All fine features, I assure you. Your mouth, however, is—" She stopped and her cheeks turned ruddy.

"My mouth?" he prompted, suddenly aroused as her gaze settled on his lips. She dipped her head, no doubt mortified, and Marcus felt a surge of something undefinable. Lust, obviously, but something more he couldn't name.

"Your mouth is quite functional," she said finally, primly.

"It is, rather, isn't it?" He stepped closer, and she kept her eyes firmly on the floor, her body tense. Then he did what he'd longed to do earlier: he placed one hand gently at the back of her neck, reveling in the softness of her hair, the delicacy of her nape, and drew her toward him. He captured her lips with his, letting out a low moan of pure need. This was no tentative kiss; he'd had enough of that. He wanted to brand her, to show her how much he desired her, to make her feel one tenth of what he was feeling. She let out the softest, sweetest sound when he swept his tongue inside her hot little mouth. His heart hammered in his chest, and his cock grew painfully hard.

God, she tasted good. As inexperienced as she clearly was, she made up for it in innocent enthusiasm. Lilian wrapped her arms around his neck with pure abandon, letting out a throaty sound that nearly drove him to his knees. She was lush and soft, and she smelled like lavender. He pushed his arousal against her and could have wept when she didn't shrink away. Instead, she opened her legs slightly, instinctively, and let him press against her core so that she might feel a tiny bit of what she was doing to him. He let his mind go where it oughtn't, to a place where they were both unclothed, lying on a bed, with him moving over her. My God, he wasn't certain he'd be able to walk away from her this night. And they *were* to be married, after all. He could obtain a license in Whitby on the morrow and they could be married in days.

He moved one hand to a breast, glorying in the fullness, the way her nipple hardened beneath his caress, the way she inhaled sharply.

"Marcus," she gasped when he stroked her turgid nipple with his thumb. He longed to push her gown down, to taste that tempting bud, but he knew if he did that, he would not stop. He'd want to taste all of her; he'd want to push himself inside her and finally find his release. Instead, he slowed his kisses and dropped both hands to her waist, even though they shook with need.

"We must stop," he said, hardly recognizing his own voice.

"Yes," she breathed, still kissing him, the little temptress.

God, her mouth was so hot. He allowed himself a tantalizing fantasy of her kissing him, moving down his body, taking him in her mouth. He pushed gently away and straightened his arms rigidly to his sides. She looked drowsy with lust, and it took all his willpower not to drag her to her bed and have her.

"I do believe I shall look forward to our wedding night," Marcus said.

Lilian simply nodded. And smiled.

Chapter 11

Constable Toby Conroy lit his lamp and settled into his most comfortable chair, which had earned that title because, other than a stool by his small kitchen table, it was his only chair. He was bone tired and sick to death of investigating the Duke of Weston's murder. The case, which had seemed so cut-and-dried only days ago, had gone in circles, leaving him with more questions than answers. The chief had called him into his office earlier that day and demanded to know why the case was still open. It wasn't every day that a peer was murdered, and the fact that the murderer was likely still at large was not sitting well with anyone in the department. Nor anyone in Birmingham. He wished, not for the first time, that Cannock had its own police force so he wouldn't need to lead the investigation. Rumors were running rampant, that a mad killer was still on the loose. When Conroy had finished his explanation, the chief sat back in his chair and swore.

"And Lady Lilian is still missing? Probably with her accomplice. Hell, they could be anywhere by now. They could be in China, for God's sake. What the hell took you so long to figure this out, Conroy?"

"My apologies, sir, but it took a few days before the daughter came forward. It wasn't until she knew some of the details that she realized her father could not have been the killer."

"And you're certain?"

"As certain as I can be, sir. The fact he was shot on the right side is enough for me to at least be highly suspicious."

The chief swore again. "This is a fine mess. We have a dead duke and a member of the aristocracy as the prime suspect. It would have been better for everyone if the dead man had been the murderer. Find the lady, Conroy, or it's your job."

Conroy, his face red, left the chief's office, swearing beneath his breath. Chief Cooke had been a barrister, not a police officer, and had no idea what went into such an investigation. "'Find the lady,' he says. Why not look for a needle in a haystack? That'd be easier." After leaving the commissioner's office, he went directly home to mull over the day's events.

Lady Lilian was now back at the top of his list of suspects, though it just didn't settle right in his brain. How could a woman who was universally loved by nearly everyone he spoke with be capable of such a devious plot? Then again, like so many people who knew Weston, she had a motive. Apparently, the poor girl had lived in fear that the duke would make improper advances on her person. Every servant at Mount Carlyle had told a similar story—that they had taken it upon themselves to keep the lady safe. Which only meant that any one of the servants could also be a murderer. The more he learned about His Grace, the more he wished he could wash his hands of the investigation. Whoever had murdered the duke had apparently done the world a great favor. Instead of hanging for a crime, whoever it was should be lauded, if what he'd learned about the duke was true. But this case wasn't only about the duke, it was also about poor Silas Maine, who may or may not have killed himself.

If Lady Lilian was guilty, she'd be guilty of killing one man and conspiring to kill another, for he'd come to the conclusion that the man who'd confessed to the crime had actually been a victim, murdered to keep suspicion away from the actual killer.

Silas Maine had simply been a pawn in a larger plot to kill the duke. His daughter had, indeed, been raped by the duke, making Maine the perfect suspect. Though his daughter insisted her father would never have murdered the duke (even if he'd probably wanted to, she admitted), he would not have killed himself to avoid the hangman. Conroy had dismissed her tearful claims, for no one knew for certain what lay in the heart of a father whose daughter had been harmed. It made perfect sense—until his daughter pointed out the fact that her father had been left handed and the head wound had been on Maine's right side. Now, Conroy was no expert with a pistol, but he was fairly certain that if he was going to kill himself, he wouldn't use his weaker hand. As a right-handed man, he'd use his right hand. To test his theory, he'd asked five of his chums at the police station to simulate killing themselves, and to a man, they used their dominant hand. It wasn't proof, but it was damn telling. Mr. Maine, in Conroy's estimation, had been murdered and forced to write his own suicide note. Which left him back at square one: Lady Lilian Martin.

Chapter 12

They were married in Merdunoir's dilapidated chapel, hastily cleaned by the handful of servants who were brave enough to enter the tiny space. It was considered to be the most haunted part of Merdunoir. Lilian wore her blue dress and Granton his formal wear, which hung a bit loosely on his frame. He'd lost weight since the last time he'd been forced to wear it and expressed surprise that the trousers, once tailored to perfection, no longer fit.

Lady Chesterfield cried throughout the short ceremony, much to Lilian's despair (and irritation), while Georgette and Adam Dunford looked on solemnly. Marcus resembled a man heading to the gallows, and Lilian felt much the same. Like all young girls, she'd imagined a much different wedding from the one performed in a tiny, windowless chapel with a pair of swallows nesting in the rafters. Her sister's wedding had been a sinfully lavish affair with five hundred guests, followed by a ball that had lasted well into the early morning hours. Lilian had been her maid of honor, but only at the insistence of their dear mother. Theresa, even then, had disliked the way Weston looked at her older sister. What Theresa had never quite understood was how much Lilian had come to loathe that look of lust on the duke's face.

"My lady wife," Marcus said, bowing formally when the ceremony had concluded and kissing her hand. He then held out one arm for her to take, and they walked from the chapel, followed by his family. There had been no time to have the rest of his family make the trip to Whitby, and Lilian was honestly relieved. As for her family, she wouldn't have invited them even had her wedding been more conventional. Theresa, who had just buried her husband, would not have been expected to attend the wedding, so Lilian hadn't bothered to invite her. She would write her a letter later with the news.

Marcus had said his vows without inflection and certainly without affection, and even though Lilian knew this was not a love match, her throat closed up briefly. She'd thought, given the way he had kissed her, that he perhaps had some feeling for her, but since that night they'd hardly spoken to one another, never mind kissed. Dinners had been stilted affairs with his mother always seemingly on the verge of tears and Adam and Georgette walking as if on eggshells. The only time she'd been tempted to speak up was when the subject of where they would live following the wedding came up.

"Merdunoir is my home now," Marcus had said, brooking no argument.

His mother opened her mouth as if to argue, but wisely shut it when she saw her son's hard gaze. No one had asked her opinion. Had they, she would have told them she wanted to live in London, at least part of the year. She had friends there, friends she dearly missed and had only seen on rare occasions since her sister's wedding since Weston had refused to finance her trips. Then again, given all that had transpired surrounding Weston's murder, perhaps it was for the best. She had no idea what sort of reception she would receive and had no wish to put her friends in an awkward position.

As they left the chapel, it began to rain, heavy sheets of wind-blown drops that stung her cheeks as they hurried from the chapel back to Merdunoir. By the time they reached the entryway, Lilian's carefully coiffed hair was in ruins and her dress a wet mess. She looked down at her water-soaked slippers and couldn't help but laugh.

"Will I never be able to keep a pair of shoes dry?" she asked, looking at the watery prints she'd left on the parquet floor. She looked up, hoping to share the moment with Granton, only to be disappointed. He was already walking toward the dining room, where breakfast was being prepared by a beaming Sadie. His house-keeper/cook was the only one in the household who was excited about the marriage. Apparently no one had shared with Sadie the fact that the wedding was not a happy event. Either that or she'd chosen to completely ignore the fact that no one else wanted to celebrate; she had prepared a lavish breakfast feast. Lilian was overwhelmed by the woman's hard work, and deeply touched.

"This is wonderful, Sadie," she told the older woman. The table sparkled with the house's finest china, the cutlery had been shined, new candles stood in gleaming candelabras. And the food was exquisite: poached eggs, thick slabs of ham, devilled kidneys (not a favorite of Lilian's, but she said nary a word), strawberry scones, and an assortment of cold meats. Sadie dipped a deep curtsy, then had the audacity to give her a wink, forcing Lilian to stifle a laugh. She was a viscountess now and no doubt should frown upon servants winking at her, but Lilian found she could not bring herself to be even remotely angry.

The group ate in near silence, with Lilian sitting across from Marcus, who ate his food with unusual gusto. Only the sound of cutlery against china could be heard, something that Lilian found highly amusing. She wondered what they all would do if she let out a loud belch simply to break the silence.

"Sadie has outdone herself," she said to no one in particular. And because she'd said it to no one in particular, no one responded. It wasn't until Lady Chesterfield began dabbing at her eyes again that Lilian lost her temper.

"Marcus." He looked up from his plate as if surprised to find himself with company.

"Yes?"

"Would you please tell your mother that you have not been sentenced to death? I do believe she misunderstood the purpose of the ceremony we just participated in."

Lucille gasped in outrage, but Lilian continued to stare stonily at her new husband. The corners of his mouth curved up infinitesimally, but Lilian wasn't certain whether it was in anger or mirth. He calmly set down his fork and knife and turned toward his mother.

"I have not been sentenced to death, Mother," he said dutifully, and Lilian had to fight the urge to go over and throttle him. He gave Lilian a quick look, and this time she saw the humor in his gaze. "Indeed, Mother, I have entered into this union quite freely and look forward to a long and happy marriage."

One might have thought he had told his mother he was, indeed, heading to the gallows, for the woman burst into tears. Apparently, Lady Chesterfield had missed the lesson on keeping a stiff upper lip unless in private. Georgette, being the dutiful daughter-in-law, hurried to Lucille's side and comforted her, but spared Lilian a small smile over the older woman's head. Lilian, for her part, decided to ignore the blubbering woman and enjoy her breakfast, even though she could hardly taste it any longer.

In short order, Lady Chesterfield composed herself and apologized profusely—to her son—and then managed to eat quite a large amount of breakfast with surprising enthusiasm, given she had just been sobbing into her napkin. As they finished eating, the rain subsided, leaving behind the lovely musical sound of drops falling from the eaves.

"The rain is letting up," Marcus said. "I thought perhaps you might be trapped here for another day, but it appears you will be able to return home after all."

"What should I tell people about the child?" Lucille asked.

"I honestly don't know. It seems every story I come up with taints her, which is the last thing I want to do. In the end, it doesn't matter, for people will come to their own conclusions no matter what I say."

"They'll think she's yours, of course," Adam said. "It's unfortunate there is a certain resemblance to the family, even though she has no Dunford blood. She looks remarkably like Rose did when she was young, don't you think, Mother?"

"Not at all. She looks like Eleanor."

"True, she does," Adam said. "The eyes." Adam looked over at his brother, as if questioning whether Mabel could be his child, after all, and Marcus shook his head.

"I was in the States," he said. "I have no idea who her sire is, but you can be assured it is not I."

"I suppose you could claim she was the orphan of a friend. Do you have any dead friends?" Adam asked, clearly finding humor in the situation. Marcus was not, however, amused.

"No. I will say she is my daughter and no one will question me."

Lilian smiled, glad that Marcus was taking such a public stance on Mabel's parentage. She couldn't imagine how difficult it must be for him to accept as his own his wife's child by another man. How humiliating it must be.

"Do you know who the father is?" Lucille asked.

"I have no idea, but I did write to Eleanor's maid. If anyone knows, it would be her, as she accompanied Eleanor to Northumberland for the birth."

"And what will you do with that information?" Adam asked.

"Likely nothing. When I wrote, it was with the intention of uniting father and daughter, but that option no longer seems tenable."

"He adores Mabel," Lilian said, and was oddly gratified when Marcus scowled at her. "You do," she insisted. "I don't know why you cannot admit it."

"She is my legal responsibility," he said flatly, and Lilian nearly rolled her eyes. She had no idea why he could never admit to a tender side. She knew it was there, hidden beneath his scowls.

Following breakfast, Marcus's family readied themselves for their departure, and when they were finally gone, Lilian breathed a deep sigh of relief.

"Now you understand why I choose to live at Merdunoir," Marcus said as he watched their carriage pull away from the house. He turned to her, his expression unreadable.

"It's mostly your mother. She's rather . . ."

"Emotional? Manipulative? You did well with her, standing up to her like that." They stood side by side at the threshold of their home, not touching, staring out to the moors that surrounded the house. The heather was nearly in full bloom and quite lovely, but his mind was in too much chaos to fully appreciate the scenery.

God, he was *married*. And his wife, the wife he didn't want and who very likely didn't want him, was standing next to him looking hopeful. And frightened. Hell, if she only knew how frightened *he* was. He'd never thought he would have to deflower a virgin again. It had been damned unnerving the first time he'd done it, and it hadn't gone well. Eleanor had lain there as if awaiting her execution, rigid, hands by her sides, head turned away. Her reaction had been wholly unexpected, for during their courtship she'd been lively and almost too flirtatious. Marcus remembered looking forward to their wedding night, only to find that the girl he'd married was nothing like the girl he'd courted. He'd felt almost as if he were raping her, and it hadn't gotten much better as time passed. In the early years of their marriage, Marcus had believed Eleanor simply disliked intimacy, so it had been a double blow to realize she was lying with other men, enjoying their caresses, when she'd only barely tolerated his. It was damned unmanning, and he couldn't help but think he was somehow lacking in his bedroom skills. Now he was faced with another virgin, another wife. Another failure.

Before marrying Eleanor, he hadn't been particularly experienced in the bedroom. His chums at Oxford had purchased a whore for him and given him all kinds of tips, but by the time he'd found himself alone with the woman, he had been far into his cups and the experience wasn't altogether memorable. His father did not abide carousing, nor drinking to excess, nor whoring at all. His friends thought him cold and overly straitlaced, and he never could admit to them that he was the carefully honed product of an over-strict father whom he feared. And so, when he'd gone to his marriage bed, his experience had been limited to one drunken night with a London whore. He'd known the mechanics of it, known where he'd wanted to touch Eleanor, but wasn't certain he knew to do it at all correctly. Apparently, given that Eleanor had sought her pleasure elsewhere, he hadn't been particularly talented.

Now he was faced with another virgin, another woman who might be left wanting. Who might turn to other men to find what he could not give. In truth, Marcus wasn't at all certain he could face Lilian tonight. Part of him had almost hoped she wanted a marriage in name only, though God above knew he wanted her. Just standing next to her, breathing in her soft floral scent, made him ache for her. Pulling out his watch, he grimaced when he realized it was hours before bedtime, and he wondered how Lilian would react if he suggested consummating their marriage now simply to get the ordeal over with. He'd never made love to Eleanor during the daytime, and the thought of making love with the sun caressing Lilian's face, the sweet curve of her breasts, was enough to make him light-headed.

He thought back on his courtship with Eleanor and realized he hadn't done much more than kiss her cheek before their wedding. Although it was perfectly acceptable for engaged couples to enjoy at least some privacy, Eleanor's mother would have none of it. She'd hovered by her daughter continuously, always fearing they would get "carried away."

"Well. They are gone," he said. Indeed, the carriage had disappeared over a hill some time ago.

"Yes."

"I suppose we should go in."

She looked behind her as if reaffirming that the house still stood. "Do you suppose we should just face this head-on? Get it over with?" She swallowed and his eyes drifted to her delicate throat.

"We could. I would like that, actually." He smiled, unable to stop the sudden surge of joy he felt. It hit him hard and unexpectedly, and he frowned.

Lilian laughed. "Then why are you frowning? You are the most difficult man to understand, but I shall make it my mission to understand you." She looked up at him, her eyes particularly beautiful in the sun, as if lit from within. "I am your *wife*. I cannot fathom it. Yesterday, I was just me, Lady Lilian Martin, and today I am Viscountess Granton and someday a countess." She shook her head. "Are you very disappointed?"

He scratched his head abashedly. "I'm not certain what I feel. But I do know one thing, I would very, very much like to 'get this over with.' I've wanted to have you in my bed for quite some time, but since we weren't married, it wasn't quite the thing."

"Truly?"

He nodded. "I never should have looked at you in your bath. It was all I could think of."

"No!" she said, horrified. "Truly? All the time?"

"Most of the time." He shrugged. "You're quite pretty, you know. And there is all that hair."

She lifted a hand to her hair, suddenly seeming self-conscious. "You'll have to tell me what to do. In bed. I've never . . ."

"I know."

She gave him a tentative smile. "Shall we, my lord husband?"

Marcus grinned; he simply couldn't help himself, even though his stomach was a bundle of nerves. "Yes, we shall." As they turned to go back into the house, he said, "Georgette spoke to you last night. About tonight? She mentioned something to me to that effect."

"Yes. She did."

"So you know what to expect?"

"In a manner of speaking."

"If you'd like, we could take things slowly. Get to know one another. Wait."

"I don't think that's necessary."

"Thank God," he breathed, and Lilian laughed.

Then, without preamble, without even the glimmer of a warning, he grabbed one of her arms and spun her around so that she was facing him, and then kissed her, a long, drugging kiss that left her weak-kneed. "I've wanted to do that all day."

Lilian tilted her head and looked at him, his handsome, stern face, his golden-brown eyes, the set of his mouth, and wondered if she would ever know what was going on in his head. Had anyone asked her, she would have said Marcus was unhappy with the marriage. But would an unhappy man kiss her until her toes curled?

They walked up the stairs side by side, as if they had nothing looming in front of them, as if it were an ordinary thing to walk into a bedroom together and make love. Halfway up, Marcus shouted, "Sadie, have someone watch Mabel, will you?"

"Yes, my lord," the housekeeper called back, sounding quite happy.

Lilian stifled a giggle, then took a deep breath to calm her nerves, for she was nervous. In a few minutes, the man beside her would be putting his thing inside her and it would hurt. But Georgette had reassured her that the pain would be brief, would never happen again, and she could come to enjoy it. Based on how she felt when Marcus kissed her, she was optimistic about the future.

When they crossed the threshold to his room, Lilian said, "I daresay there are not too many brides who are intimately familiar with their husband's bedroom." She laughed, aware of how nervous she sounded. Next to her, Marcus had removed his coat and Lilian took a step away, toward the bed. Then, realizing the direction she was walking, she backed up, nearly into her new husband, who was bending over to remove his shoes. Her heart beat madly in her chest, and she suddenly didn't know what to do with her hands. Should she be getting undressed, as well? Was she supposed to take off all her clothes? From what she understood of the act, it didn't seem necessary to be completely naked.

"I don't know what to do," she whispered, her breath shallow, her stomach roiling with nerves.

Marcus snapped his head up, and for a moment, Lilian thought she saw pure anguish there before he masked it. He straightened, one shoe on, one shoe off and gave her a small helpless gesture. "I would like for you to remove your clothing."

She swallowed. "All of it?"

"Yes."

Lilian turned her back and squeezed her eyes shut. She was to be naked in front of him, completely exposed. *Oh, God, I don't think I can do it!*

Then she felt a warm hand on her shoulder, and he gently turned

her around. Lilian stared at his chest, his naked chest—oh, Lord—
and kept her hands fisted by her sides. He took one of her fisted
hands and laid it against his chest so that she could feel his beating
heart.

"I'm nervous, too, Lilian. More than you would suspect. I want
this to be good between us. I want to give you nothing but pleasure.
Please."

She looked up at his entreaty and gave him a tentative smile before looking at her fist, still pressed against his warm, lightly furred,
and gloriously muscled chest. She spread out her hand. He inhaled
sharply, and for the first time in her life she realized a strange power.
He liked that she was touching him, probably as much as she liked
being touched. Moving her hand, she explored his chest, his shoulders, his neck, finally bringing her other hand up to join the first behind his neck. He stood still, unmoving, his muscles taut beneath her
caress.

"May I help you with your dress?"

Lilian nodded, moving her hands through his short, soft hair, so
clean it was slippery beneath her fingers. She leaned forward and
kissed him in that small indent where his strong neck met his muscled chest. He was beautiful, like the statues she'd seen in museums.
She'd thought that perhaps the artists had taken liberty by creating
such perfection, but here it was in front of her, hot beneath her touch
but nearly as rigid as marble. His stomach had no hair but a thin band
that trailed from his chest to where his pants began, the first two buttons already freed from their moorings.

"You are lovely," she said, pressing her forehead against him and
smiling softly when he chuckled.

Then she straightened and, with hands that shook only slightly,
began undoing the buttons of her dress. Without a lady's maid, she
had requested that her three layers of clothing and her corset be fas-
tened in front.

"Let me, if you will," he said, his voice deep as he brushed her hands
gently away. One by one, he unfastened the buttons until her corset
cover was revealed, and then he pushed her dress from her shoulders,
down her arms, following the material with his hands, and let it drop
to the floor. She stood before him wearing a chemise, a corset, a
camisole, a crinoline, a single petticoat, and stockings. And felt completely naked.

"My God, Lilian," he breathed, looking at her with such intensity he almost seemed angry, but she knew him well enough now to know it was raw desire in his eyes.

Lilian untied the corset, followed by the crinoline, and, taking a deep breath, removed her camisole and began to work on her corset.

"Allow me. I'd no idea how many layers made up a lady's dress. Eleanor's maid always took care of things—" He stopped suddenly, as if regretting bringing up his former wife in front of his new one. "Here." He made short work of the corset, loosening it until it, too, dropped to the floor. The only thing between her and him were her chemise, drawers, and stockings.

He drew her to him and kissed her softly on her cheek, then moved his head down and nuzzled her neck, a simple enough caress, but she found herself nearly drowning in desire. "Oh," she said, moving her head a bit, loving the way he made her feel. His hands worked on the pins in her hair. One by one, each pin removed was rewarded by a kiss—on her shoulder, her neck, her chest, and finally the tip of one breast. Her breathing was becoming more and more harsh, and Lilian wasn't certain she could stand without holding on to him. Finally, her hair spilled down her back, feeling oddly sensual.

Pulling away, he drew her with him to the bed and, in one quick motion, lifted her and deposited her in the center with a little bounce.

Marcus lay next to her, one hand draped across her belly, the other bent and propping up his head so that he could look down at her. It was rather nice to have her in his bed, this time with him next to her. Her hair, a wild mass of it, was spread out on the pillow.

"We're not yet unclothed," she said softly, looking directly at him, a small smile teasing her lips.

"That will soon be amended, I assure you." He leaned down and kissed her, at first softly, gently, and then he found he couldn't stop himself from deepening the kiss. With a low moan, he pushed his tongue into her mouth, tasting her. One of her hands drifted behind his head and she relaxed beneath him as if drugged. How different was she from Eleanor, who had lain rigid, who had turned her head away when he'd tried to kiss her.

Slowly, he moved his hand from her waist, higher, to the curve of her breast, reveling in the way she arched her back, silently demanding more. He sought and found one turgid nipple, and moved his thumb back and forth until she let out a small cry.

"I should stop?" He pulled back to look at her, suddenly uncertain.

"You should never stop," she said, laughing. "It's quite lovely, actually."

Smiling, Marcus deftly untied her chemise, slowly pulling upon the four satin ribbons that held the cloth together. Each tug revealed more creamy skin, and when he was done, he pulled the cloth apart and stared down at her breasts, thanking God and all the Catholic saints for putting this woman in his path that foggy June morning on the moors. "My God, you are beautiful."

Her hands moved restlessly, as if she were contemplating covering herself, but Marcus would have none of that. "No," he murmured, right before bending his head, taking one nipple into his mouth and sucking lightly. Her gasp of breath created such a surge of lust, Marcus knew he was in danger of losing control completely, of coming before he could consummate their marriage. But she put her hand to the back of his head, keeping him there, urging him to continue, and so he did, making love to her breasts as if they had all the time in the world. His cock strained almost painfully inside his trousers, and he shifted to relieve some of the ache. If he were a bold man, he would have taken one of her hands and pressed it against him, taught her how to please him. He would guide her, down, down, until she took him into her beautiful mouth. Marcus was not a bold man in the bedroom, and so he suffered a bit, wanting release desperately, but just as desperately wanting this to last forever. So instead of guiding her hand to him, he let his own hand drift down her body until it rested at the apex of her thighs and he pressed, just slightly, just enough to show her there was more to this business of making love, that the pleasure she was feeling now was nothing compared to the pleasure he wanted to give her. She let out a small sound, of protest or pleasure, he wasn't sure, and when she spread her legs just slightly, he knew it was pleasure.

She still had on her drawers, so he found the slit in them to touch her flesh, feel her heat. He groaned when he found her slick with need.

"I want to make you come," he said, his voice gruff. "Do you understand what that means?"

She shook her head, her eyes drowsy.

"You will find your release and then I will find mine." Marcus untied her drawers and began pushing them down. Lilian lifted her bum just slightly, assisting him in his endeavor, and when he'd tugged them off her, he swallowed heavily as he looked at her dark thatch of soft curls and resisted the urge to kiss her there. Perhaps someday. He unbuttoned his trousers and slipped them and his smalls off in one deft movement, revealing his erection to her rather surprised gaze.

"There you are," she said, sounding nervous.

"Here I am. Sometime, if you'd like, you could touch me there. It would please me if you did."

She looked so doubtful, Marcus nearly laughed. Then he brought his hand to her dark, moist curls and found her small nub. She inhaled sharply and closed her eyes as he moved his hand, exploring her, tense and waiting to see if she would tell him to stop, secretly praying she would not. He slipped one finger inside, and she was so hot and wet, he groaned and his cock grew harder still.

"Marcus, what is happening?" Her hips moved slightly as he moved his finger in and out, as he moved his thumb over her, back and forth, creating a rhythm for her.

"Let go, love," he said, unaware he'd uttered that endearment, unaware of anything but how hot she was beneath his hand, how lovely she looked on the verge of her release. Suddenly, her hips began jerking wildly, and she clutched the counterpane almost desperately, and he could feel her clench around him as her body was lost in the throes of her release. With a guttural sound, she came around his finger, and Marcus felt as if he could command the earth and all the heavens.

When she was relaxed and drowsy, he kissed her softly and removed his hand.

"That was beyond lovely," she said, lifting her arms languidly and wrapping them around his neck.

Marcus positioned himself between her thighs, splayed and pliant, and brushed his cock against her curls, closing his eyes at the pleasure of this simple movement. His eyes shot open when he felt her touch him, tentative and shy, and he stifled a moan.

"There, I've done it," she said, grinning and pulling him down for a kiss.

"Very brave of you."

"Very brave," she agreed. She looked up at him and her smile faded. "It's time, Marcus."

He took himself and pressed slowly at her entrance, watching her lovely face to make certain he wasn't hurting her overmuch. Lilian shifted beneath him and opened her legs wider, never taking her eyes away from his. He felt her barrier, knew he was about to hurt her, but she felt so hot and tight and *right*, the only thing he could do was push through and make her his. And so he did, driving into her, stifling her cry with a kiss, his body taut and quivering from the effort to take things slowly when his cock screamed for him to drive into her again and again.

"Are you all right?"

She nodded and kissed his jaw, and so he pulled back slightly, then moved forward, as she tensed beneath him. Again and again, he moved, and at some point she relaxed and then she wrapped her legs around him. *The feeling of a woman's legs around a man is nothing short of miraculous*, Marcus thought, right before he lost himself to the sensation, the rhythm, the pure joy of making love to a willing woman. He came with a groan, moving his hips quickly, releasing his seed into her, and felt quite literally that he had never in his life experienced such intense pleasure.

Marcus lay on top of Lilian for so long, she thought perhaps he'd fallen asleep, even though his full weight was pressing down on her. His breathing, at first harsh and labored, finally slowed to a more natural rhythm, and still he lay there.

"Marcus?"

"Hmmm."

"I'm a bit crushed."

He rolled off her, chuckling and dragging her with him so that she lay on top of his long length. The hair on his legs tickled her feet, and it was difficult to believe that just a few moments before, she'd been quite frightened by the thought of him seeing her naked, of even touching his flesh. Now she was splayed on top of him, her hair a curtain around his head, and it felt like the most natural thing in the world. Amazing what making love could do. It was hard to believe that a pair could do it without staying in bed forever.

"Better now?"

"Much. But now I'm crushing you."

Tightening his arms around her slightly, he said, "You are not crushing me. You are keeping me warm."

"So I am nothing more than a blanket?"

"Indeed." He pulled up his head slightly and bussed her lips before rolling to the side so that they faced one another.

"I thought I wasn't crushing you," she said in mock anger.

"I lied."

She gave him a small whack on his shoulder, then nestled her head into the crook of his arm, wondering if this thing she was feeling that made her heart swell and sing was love. And she couldn't help but wonder if he was feeling anything close to what she was. Her mother had told her, long ago, when Weston had seemed to set his cap for her, that men did not see the act of making love in quite the same way as women. Men could have mistresses and wives and lovers and treat them all the same. It wasn't that the male sex was incapable of love, it was that they saw the act of making love differently. Lilian assumed her mother was warning her not to expect fidelity from her husband, but she realized, lying there next to Marcus, that she would want to die if he made love to another.

Lilian lifted her head and looked down at him. "You're very dear to me," she said in a rush, hoping she wasn't saying too much, hoping her eyes didn't say what she really longed to say. That she thought she was falling in love with him.

He said nothing, but something indefinable flickered in his eyes as he drew her back down so that when she was settled against him once more, she lay there wondering why he hadn't said anything to her. Perhaps her mother had been right.

After a time, Marcus seemed to get restless, and he sat up and swung his legs over the side of the bed. Lilian allowed herself to admire the strong expanse of his back, the wide shoulders that tapered to a muscled waist and finally to his muscular bum.

"I should like us to be happy together," he said, his words cutting through the silence in the room. Taken at face value, his statement would seem kind, but the underlying sadness Lilian thought she detected made her tense.

"I believe we shall be," she said hesitantly.

"I wouldn't want you to expect too much from me. I will be a good husband, and I will be faithful." He turned his head to look at her before turning back. "I expect the same from you, of course."

"I will never be unfaithful." She saw his shoulders lift and fall, as if her words removed some great weight from them.

"That is all I can promise now. I . . ." He stopped, and she could tell he was struggling. "I wouldn't want you to expect me to love you. That's all." With that, he stood and grabbed up his clothing, pulling his smalls and trousers on with haste, then making short work of his shirt. Taking out an informal jacket from his wardrobe, he finally turned to look at her. Lilian had snuggled beneath the covers as he'd dressed, feeling unaccountably cold even though the room was quite warm. "I'm going for a ride. Chief needs a good run."

Lilian felt like crying. Why had she told him that he was dear to her? Why hadn't she just let things go? She had no doubt if she had remained silent, they would still be in bed together. She felt his withdrawal, much like the ache that remains once a sliver is removed.

Chapter 13

Marcus rode like a madman upon the rolling hills of the moors, until Chief's sides were heaving from exertion. He pulled up where he always did, at the crest of a high hill that looked down upon the farmlands below. The heather swayed in the moist wind, an ocean of purple and green that glistened from the earlier rain beneath a weak sun.

"What the hell am I going to do, Chief?"

His horse lifted his head upon hearing his master's voice, then went back to nibbling on the sweet grass.

What the hell am I going to do? he asked himself silently. Lilian deserved better than him. He didn't want a wife, and he particularly didn't want a wife who looked at him all doe-eyed and said the sweetest things, things even the most hardened man would be hard-pressed not to revel in. *You're very dear to me.* The words were bad enough, but the look in her eyes, the love he thought he'd seen, sent such a flood of panic through him, he almost felt physically ill.

He did not want to love her. He did not want to love anything. He wasn't the sort of man who could have his heart ripped from his chest more than once. What was more difficult was knowing that even though he'd loved Eleanor, it hadn't been the all-consuming love that he had only experienced once in his life. He'd managed to hold himself in reserve, and was profoundly glad he had, given what had happened. In the end, he'd been more humiliated than hurt, and still the pain had been nearly unbearable.

Perhaps he was weak. Perhaps that was why he tried so hard to keep his emotions in check, to never let them show. Marcus looked up into the cloud-mottled sky, wondering idly if it would begin raining again. He wished it would, a hard, blinding, drenching rain that would purge all thoughts from his mind.

He didn't want to be married and he didn't want to love his wife, but he was married and he was rather terrified that he might even be in danger of falling in love with her. It would be no pallid love, he knew. It would hurt and be glorious, and it would be the kind of love that could kill him if it all went wrong.

No, for now, he would step back, gather his strength, and try not to hurt her too much.

When Marcus returned from his ride, it was nearly dark and most of the servants had departed for Whitby. With no sign of the ghost since Lilian's appearance, strangely enough, his house now had four servants who stayed overnight, including Sadie and Palmer, and another four who came daily. What he needed now more than anything was a butler who could keep things calm and steady, who would send unwanted guests away. He would have to search in London for such a man, for if one existed in Whitby, he would have already stepped forward and inquired. He headed directly to the kitchen, as he always had, expecting to find a plate set aside for him by Sadie. This time, he found nothing. He had a feeling this was Sadie's silent chastisement for abandoning his new bride for the day. With a sigh, he headed for the pantry and found some leftover ham from breakfast. Standing within the pantry, he shoved a few bites in his mouth, just to fill his belly, and looked up at the ceiling, wondering whether Lilian was in his bed or hers. It was still too early for sleeping, so perhaps she was in the parlor. He'd found her there once or twice with Mabel on her lap, reading to the child. His daughter. He supposed he would have to get used to calling her that.

The house was pitch black, so he lit a lamp, making a mental note to inquire about gaslight. Surely, in this modern age, his home should have it, as well as central heating. His townhouse in London had all the latest modern conveniences, and he had to admit lighting candles and lamps was getting a bit tiresome.

Marcus made his way to the parlor, only to find it dark and empty, then headed to the second floor, listening for the sound of voices. He thought he heard the low murmur of a feminine voice, and he couldn't help but smile, but when he reached his room, it was empty. And cold. Lilian must be with Mabel in her own room, or perhaps Mabel's. He left his lamp in his room and made his way into the hall, stopping outside Lilian's door, where a sharp line of light could be seen beneath it. He stood there, staring at that sliver of light, torn between knocking and going back to his own bedroom to read.

"My, Grandma, what large teeth you have."

Marcus grinned. Little Red Riding Hood. He could almost picture Mabel's eyes as Lilian told her the famous tale. No doubt she'd found a book of fairy tales in the nursery. He took a step back and the floor beneath his feet creaked, and he froze when the voices in the room were suddenly silent.

"Did you hear that?" he heard Lilian ask. "Do you think perhaps that is our ghost outside listening to my story?"

"I think it's the man."

"You mean his lordship, your papa? Now why would he be skulking about like a thief outside my door?" She sounded piqued, and he nearly laughed.

With a shake of his head, he relented and knocked politely on the door.

"Do ghosts knock?" he heard Lilian ask, and this time he did chuckle. "Perhaps if we ignore the ghost, he will go away."

Marcus stood staring at the door, knowing his new wife was a bit angry with him for missing dinner and, no doubt, for callously telling her not to expect him to love her—as if he could stop his heart from doing what it wanted. He heard little feet scrambling to the door, and then it swung open, revealing Mabel, dressed for bed, including a nightcap, which sat adorably askew on her little head. "It is his lordship," she called triumphantly.

"And how brave of you to come to the door, thinking you might encounter our ghost."

She wrinkled her nose, then turned and ran back to the bed, where she settled beside Lilian for the rest of the story.

Marcus walked to the bedpost and leaned against it, his arms crossed over his chest. "Do go on. It's my favorite." He gave Mabel a wink.

As Marcus listened to the story and watched Lilian and Mabel together, he couldn't stop his heart from swelling in his chest, though the Lord above knew he tried. His heart had always had a mind of its own.

When he was sixteen, Marcus had been madly and completely in love with his neighbor, Pamela Porter. No one in his family had known, but when he could, he would escape to see her and talk and walk and just glory in loving her. If someone had asked him at the time why he was keeping his love a secret, he likely wouldn't have been able to explain himself. Perhaps he knew he'd receive endless teasing from his brothers, and even from his mother and father. Perhaps he knew that had he admitted his deep and abiding love, they would have dismissed it as simply a young boy's infatuation. No matter why, he'd kept the secret as close to his heart as he had his Pamela, and to this day, no one knew.

They'd talked about marriage, about how as soon as he was finished with the university, he would return home and they could marry. They would have five children (five was Pamela's favorite number) and they'd even started naming them. They did little more than hold hands and exchange a few breathless kisses, just enough to make Marcus dream of the day they would be together forever and not have to say good-bye.

She died when she was sixteen and he was seventeen. One day she was there, laughing up into his face, and the next, she was gone. He'd waited for her at the spot where they would meet, a little shaded bend in a brook that separated their properties, each Monday and Wednesday at three o'clock. And one day, she wasn't there. That night at supper, his mother announced blithely that their neighbor's daughter had died. "The Porter girl died. Pamela was her name. I think she was just fifteen. So young." She'd tsked, and that was that. Conversation continued on another topic, and she was never mentioned again. Marcus had sat there, stunned, unmoving, afraid that if he'd taken even one bite, he would burst into tears—or worse, stand up and shout to everyone that Pamela was sixteen, not fifteen, and the loveliest girl in the world and he wanted to die just to be with her. Instead, he'd stared at his plate, his throat raw, his hands shaking, and no one had known. No one had seen. No one had comforted him, and why would they have? By that time, he'd become adept at hiding everything.

It had taken Marcus years after her death before he could even think about marrying. He was almost grateful when Eleanor came along. She had been the complete opposite of Pamela, and he'd known he would never love her the way he had loved Pamela. It was a relief. Keeping his heart in line had been more difficult than he'd thought it would be, but he'd managed not to fall over that dangerous cliff where love had the ability to destroy. The years following Pamela's death were a muddy blur in which he felt as if everything around him was dull and worthless.

And no one ever knew.

Now, looking at his new wife, her hair in one thick braid hanging across one breast, he knew he was in danger of falling off that cliff again. And still he stayed and listened to her, watched her, let his eyes feast on her lips, let his heart swell painfully in his chest, let himself dream of what it would be like to just love her without the fear of losing her.

It was a dangerous thought, that.

And so, as the story finished, he stepped back and wished them both good night and pretended he didn't see hurt in Lilian's beautiful eyes.

Chapter 14

As he nearly always did at the breakfast table, Marcus flipped through his correspondence, leaving most of the matters for another time. A week after their wedding, two letters piqued his interest and he set them aside to read immediately. One was from Kathryn Cates, his dead wife's maid. The other was from the Birmingham Town Police Department.

He opened the one from his wife's maid first, his stomach clenching nervously. He'd written to the woman almost immediately upon finding Mabel on his doorstep, demanding to know who had fathered the child. At the time, he'd been almost desperate to know and he'd had the vague idea of handing Mabel off to her true father. Now, it was a different matter entirely; he wasn't even certain he cared who her true father was. As far as he was now concerned, Mabel was his.

> *Dear Lord Granton:*
> *I would like to meet with you to discuss the matter of your inquiry. I have a position with Lady Beaumont, who resides not four miles from Hallstead Manor. When you arrive in Birmingham, I will endeavor to meet with you privately.*
> *Truly yrs,*
> *Kathryn Cates*

How very vexing, though Marcus could appreciate her discretion in not naming names in a letter. It seemed if he wanted to know who Mabel's father was, he would have to travel to Birmingham. Someday. He wasn't ready to go home as yet, not with his mother so emotional about his wedding. Marcus looked up at Lilian, but she was concentrating on her breakfast to such an extent, he knew she was still angry with him. Or hurt, which was far worse.

He was still pondering some way to make her smile when he opened the second letter that had caught his interest.

> *Dear Lord Granton:*
>
> *I am Constable Toby Conroy of the Birmingham Police Department, the lead investigator into the Duke of Weston's murder. I learned from your mother, Lady Chesterfield, that you have recently married the former Lady Lilian Martin. My felicitations on your marriage.*
>
> *As I am certain you are aware, recent questions regarding the validity of the confession to His Grace's death have been raised, requiring me to continue my investigation into that terrible night. If you are planning to return to Birmingham in the next few days, I would appreciate meeting with Lady Granton so I can interview the lady regarding the night of the murder. I can, of course, travel to Whitby and will accommodate you in whatever you choose.*
>
> *Yrs,*
> *Toby Conroy.*

When Marcus lifted his gaze from the letter, he found Lilian studying him.

"Bad news?"

"Not necessarily." He looked at the letter again. "A Constable Conroy would like to interview you regarding Weston's murder. Apparently, my brother was correct. The police are not accepting the man's confession at face value."

Lilian grew pale and set her fork down. "Am I a suspect again?" she asked.

"The letter doesn't say, but I'm certain we can straighten this out."

She looked down to her plate, her hands on her lap, no doubt clenched nervously together. "You believe me, do you not?" She lifted her head and met his eyes, a small line of worry showing between her dark brows.

"I do not believe the woman who risked her life to fetch a stocking for a little girl could be capable of murder," he said blandly.

"Thank you. But why does he want to speak with me?"

"You were there that night. Perhaps you can enlighten him on some aspects of what happened. I don't know, but I do not like this hanging over your head. I think we should travel to Birmingham and get this straightened out. I have other business I need to attend to at any rate. Perhaps we can stop in London on the way home. We could make it our wedding trip."

Lilian immediately smiled, and Marcus felt as if he'd just promised her a holiday to the Continent. "I would like that. Thank you."

Marcus put aside his correspondence. "We can leave next week if you think you'll be ready."

"Of course," she said on a laugh. "I have but three dresses here. Perhaps we can send a servant to Mount Carlyle to fetch my wardrobe. Unless my sister has burned my things. I have the loveliest riding habit." Marcus was surprised by the wistful note in her voice; he hadn't realized she liked to ride. He supposed there was a great deal he did not know about his wife.

"When we return, you can join me on my rides."

Her mouth curved up delicately. "I thought your rides were a means of escaping me."

"They are." Her smile widened. "But perhaps you can accompany me when I'm not vexed with you."

"Then I shall never ride again," she said dramatically, and laughed when he scowled at her.

"I do enjoy your company," he said, his voice low and gruffer than he'd meant, for he immediately pictured her naked and underneath him. He had tried not to indulge overmuch in his desires, but it was a difficult task given she was all he could think of. "I thought perhaps I might enjoy your company this evening." He wasn't certain she understood his not-so-hidden meaning, but he prayed she would.

Lilian blushed prettily, but lifted her chin. "I thought perhaps you would enjoy my company last evening after Mabel went to bed." *Clever girl*, he thought.

Marcus allowed his eyes to drift from her mouth to her lovely breasts. When he realized what he was doing, he forced himself to look into her eyes, which had become decidedly drowsy. He could feel himself harden, and he shifted uncomfortably in his seat. "I thought so as well but didn't want to interrupt your sleep. I did want to." *Want* was a fairly tepid word to describe how much he had needed her the previous night. He'd spent long hours staring up at his ceiling, debating with himself as to whether he should knock on her door.

She smiled, then turned her attention back to her breakfast. "I do so enjoy your company," she said, the smallest smile teasing her lips, and he nearly pushed the table aside so he could have her then and there. Good breeding—and a young footman standing by the door— stopped him. But, by God, he wanted her.

Lilian was shocked, and rather pleased, if she were honest, with how bold she had become. Flirting had never been a talent she'd thought she possessed. Indeed, she hadn't had much practice, given that her mother had died after her first season, and then she'd been isolated at Mount Carlyle. The truth was, as hurt as she'd been by Marcus's words denying any chance of love, her body had craved the release he had introduced her to. She knew nothing of marriage, of what was expected. Would he want to lie with her nightly? Weekly? Could she ever go to him, or would he find that too forward? The truth was, she'd nearly gotten out of her bed at two in the morning and gone to his room, but the thought that he might send her away had stopped her. Now, she realized, as she looked into his smoldering eyes, he likely would have welcomed her.

She toyed with a bit of egg that had long grown cold. "We are to enjoy one another's company only in the evenings from now on?" Her cheeks grew scarlet, not only from her boldness, but from where her mind had gone—directly to a sun-filled bedroom with a certain beautiful man.

He let out a harsh breath and stood almost violently, his chair tipping back precariously, and for an instant she thought she'd angered him. It was a matter of seconds before she realized she'd far from angered him.

"You are dismissed," he said, his eyes steady on her and his words for the young footman, who left the room immediately, closing the door behind him. He strode over to her, placed one hand behind her head, and heaved her up against him, covering her mouth with his. He plundered her mouth with his tongue, letting out a low moan of need that had her toes curling in her slippers. He tasted of coffee with a hint of the marmalade he'd spread on his muffin, a delicious combination.

"I would have you on this table, here, now, if I thought we would be left alone."

Lilian mewled softly as he moved one hand unerringly to her breast, teasing her nipple and making her body sing with need. He kissed her neck, something she discovered was most definitely wonderful, and she tilted her head, urging him on. If she were truly bold, she would have begun unbuttoning his shirt. Or perhaps even bolder still, pressed her hand against his rock-hard manhood. He had seemed to like it when she'd touched him before. Maybe she would, after all.

He hissed in a breath and grew still when she pressed her hand against his hard length, and Lilian smiled, liking that it was so easy to please him.

"You are a temptress," he said, then kissed her again, deep and hot and relentlessly erotic. "I think I need to show you something upstairs."

"Oh? What?" she asked, breathless.

"My bed."

Lilian giggled.

"You go first. I am in no condition to be seen at the moment." He looked down at the large and obvious bulge in his pants. Without a jacket, he had no way to hide his condition.

Lilian gave him another kiss, then turned and walked sedately out of the dining room and up the stairs. But when she reached the long hall where her bedroom lay, she picked up her skirts and ran.

The moment she entered her room, she began undressing. She started with her hair, which she had hastily put in a loose bun that morning, so it was undone and flowing down her back in seconds. She made quick work of the rest, so that when Marcus entered her bedroom, she was standing in the middle of the room in only her chemise.

The way he looked at her, his golden eyes gone dark, made her shiver with need. He made her feel beautiful, like the most desirable woman in the entire kingdom.

"You have very good ideas, my wife." His voice was low and gruff and, for some reason, made her nipples tighten with need.

Marcus literally tore off his clothes, sending at least two buttons flying through the air to land with soft *ticks* on the carpet below their feet. In short measure, he stood before her, completely naked, his manhood thrusting upward.

"Your chemise, madam. Off with it now, if you please."

"If you insist," she said saucily, and unlaced the bows that held the thin material together, then did a little shimmy and the garment fell to the floor. And then, Lilian found herself standing naked in front of her husband in broad daylight. She didn't feel nearly as bold now, standing there, completely exposed, and if it wasn't for the fact that he was naked too, and looking at her as if she'd invented naked women, she might have covered herself with her hands as best she could.

She watched as his Adam's apple did a slow dip, as he clenched his jaw, and then his fists. "Madam, I believe this was a terrible mistake."

"I-I see."

"No, I don't think you do. For now, each time I see you, at a ball, walking the moors, eating your breakfast, I shall picture you this way and be tortured by this image and want to drag you from wherever you are and bring you to the nearest bed and make love to you. Do you realize what you've done to me?"

Lilian pressed her lips together, trying not to laugh, and shook her head.

His eyes were smiling—why hadn't she noticed that he had that talent before? "I shall go around for the rest of my life trying to hide the fact that I want to make love to my wife. Perhaps I should start wearing overlong jackets."

"A kilt? Though you're not Scottish."

He smiled. "Please get in bed, my wife. I plan to show you how very much I desire you."

Lilian backed up, slowly, until she bumped into her bed. Then she sat and was about to scoot into the middle, when he said, "No. Stop there." And then he kneeled before her and lifted one foot, pressing a kiss into the delicate arch. For a moment, the pleasure of it, the pure beauty of the gesture, made it difficult to breathe. He repeated the gesture with her other foot, this time looking up at her wide-eyed gaze as if gauging whether she was enjoying his touch.

He kissed her calf, then lifted her right leg high and licked and nipped the back of her knee, making her gasp at the unexpected stab of desire that flooded her. Between her legs was aching, and she could feel herself getting wet just from his simple caress. He kissed up one thigh, coming shockingly close to the apex of her legs, then kissed his way back down the other. Feeling suddenly boneless, she fell back onto the bed, her legs shamelessly splayed, and closed her eyes to revel in the new sensations he was introducing her to. Her breath became harsh, shaking, and yet her body was more languid with every kiss. He moved back up her left leg, making small sounds, low and throaty and so incredibly erotic, Lilian felt as if he need only touch her once, lightly, between her legs and she would scream out in pleasure.

"There is something . . ." he said, softly, almost contemplatively, right before she felt his mouth on her sex. He let out a low moan, and made love to her with his mouth, his tongue, and then his fingers.

"Marcus," she moaned, moving her head back and forth, lifting her hips, clutching the counterpane with one hand and allowing the other to drift down to feel his head there, and press. And then it came, that wonderful, heart-stopping moment, when nothing mattered but the pleasure he was giving her, the flood of sensation that started at her center then moved with lightning quickness to the rest of her body, even to the tips of her toes.

Marcus kissed her soft inner thigh and thought of anything except how it would feel in about two seconds when he thrust inside her. He was afraid to move lest he lose control and spill his seed onto the floor. Never in his life had he imagined he'd become so completely aroused simply by pleasuring a woman.

"Marcus. That was . . ."

He chuckled, so pleased with himself he growled against her belly, making her giggle. Moving onto the bed, Marcus kissed her, then lifted her slightly so that she was lying on the bed properly. She was boneless, smiling up at him sleepily, draping her arms over his shoulders, her hair fanned out behind her, soft and luminous in the sunlight.

When she reached down to touch him, he stiffened and moved away slightly. "I'm afraid if you touch me right now, I'll be unable to do what I've been wanting to do since last time."

Leaning forward, he kissed one nipple, and entered her easily, and he groaned at the pleasure of how hot and wet she was. For him. Like a teenage boy, he thrust once, twice, then let out a long groan as he found his release. He pressed his head against the pillow, his mouth on her shoulder, and began laughing at himself.

"That is not what I intended," he said, still laughing.

"No?"

"No. I had the foolish thought that I would last more than ten seconds. But you are so lovely, Lilian, I'm afraid it's difficult for me to control myself. I'm not used to a woman like you."

"Like me? Am I so very different?"

"My God, yes."

She scrunched up her face adorably. "And is that a good thing, my lord?"

He kissed her softly. "A very, very good thing, my love."

And this time, when she looked at him as if he'd created the stars and the moon, he didn't even care.

On the train ride to Cannock, they had a private car. Mabel sat with Lilian, and the two played a game of Beggar My Neighbor as Marcus watched. He remembered his sister playing that very card game with his brother Stephen; the two had been inseparable as children.

"Would you like to play the winner?" Lilian asked. "It appears Mabel is going to beat me handily."

Mabel placed an ace down and clapped her hands. "Four cards, if you please."

Lilian made a face that made the little girl giggle, then handed over the last of her cards. "Indeed, you have won. Would you like to play another?"

Mabel yawned, delicately covering her mouth with a gloved hand, and Marcus felt a sharp twinge in the region of his heart. She looked so well-cared-for now compared to the pale, disheveled urchin who had arrived at his doorstep not that long ago. With her hair neatly combed and plaited, her belly full of good food, and her clothing proper, she looked like what she was—the daughter of a viscount. He just could not stop himself from loving her just a little, damn his soft heart.

"Would you like to lie down and take a nap? You could put your head on my lap," Lilian said.

"I'll use Papa's lap," Mabel said, and scooted over to Marcus's seat before he could even think to utter a protest, before he could remind her to call him sir, or your lordship, or Lord Granton. Which he would have, given the chance, if only to avoid seeing that look on his wife's face, the one that told him he had a big, soft heart no matter how much he might protest. The odd thing was, when Mabel called him Papa and then laid her head on his lap, his heart did feel rather soft. And full, almost to the point of pain. He gave Lilian a withering look, as if he felt none of these unfamiliar emotions, and awkwardly patted Mabel's shoulder.

"We should look into getting Mabel a nanny when we're in London. And a lady's maid for you. And I suppose my poor valet, Mr. Courtland, would be quite pleased if I brought him back to Merdunoir with me. He's been acting as a footman, which is quite beneath him. I suppose I'm fortunate he didn't hand in his notice in protest."

Lilian was looking at him, studying him, as if trying to see into his mind. "I believe it may be time for you to return to the world, even if that world is in Whitby."

"Perhaps." He turned to look out the window, away from Lilian's soft gaze. Every day that passed made it more and more difficult to pretend he could shield his heart from his new wife. As he sat there, feeling the slight weight of his daughter on his lap, her soft baby-fine hair brushing one hand, he knew he was losing the battle. He could feel his heart—something he hadn't been able to do in some time. He'd thought, foolishly, that though it continued to beat, he was incapable of feeling anything more than simply alive. Unaware of what he was doing, he moved his gaze from the landscape outside the train down to the downy head of the little girl sleeping on his lap.

"It's time she started calling you Papa."

Marcus snapped his head up and actually blushed. "Very well," he said, then forced himself to look out the window again.

Hallstead Manor was a grand old home, and one Lilian had seen many times, though she had never been inside. After what had happened with Marcus's sister, no Dunford had allowed anyone from the duke's household inside. This was to be a momentous and probably uncomfortable visit, Lilian realized.

Marcus had wired ahead to inform his family that he would be arriving, but Lilian had no idea what sort of reception would be had, and was frankly surprised that when their carriage pulled up in front of the house, several servants spilled out the front door, followed by his mother, father, and the rest of his family. Lilian glanced over at Marcus to see his reaction and smiled when she saw that he looked displeased.

"I'm not the prodigal son, for heaven's sake," he muttered.

"What's a pro—" Lilian placed a gentle hand on Mabel's arm, stopping her words and shaking her head, silently telling Mabel that this was not the time for her questions.

The steps were lowered, and the door opened, revealing a liveried footman wearing Chesterfield gold and blue, and Marcus's curious family standing on the marble steps. Lilian handed down Mabel first, her stomach in knots, then followed and stood awkwardly waiting for Marcus to step down. He did so with ease, though Lilian knew he must feel a bit uncertain as to his reception—particularly from his father. Mabel immediately went to Marcus and took up one of his hands, a gesture that was followed with obvious disapproval by Lady Chesterfield.

Lord Chesterfield, who oddly looked nothing at all like Marcus except for his brownish gold eyes, stepped forward. "Welcome home, Granton." Though he showed little outward emotion, something in the older man's eyes and the way he said those three words seemed to hold far more weight, and Lilian realized Marcus had more in common with his father than she'd first realized. Lord Chesterfield turned to her and gave a small bow. "Welcome to Hallstead Manor, Lady Granton."

Lilian curtsied and, beside her, Mabel did her best to emulate her. "This is Miss Mabel Dunford."

Lord Chesterfield looked down at Mabel, and while most small children would have shrunk away from such a stern countenance, Mabel simply looked up at her grandfather with curiosity. "Miss Dunford," Chesterfield said, and Mabel's brows immediately came together. She looked up at Marcus, no doubt wondering why on earth this old man was calling her Miss Dunford instead of her given name. Marcus looked down at her and gave her a quick wink.

Then a young man Lilian didn't recognize but immediately realized must be Marcus's youngest brother, Stephen, came forward, hunkered down to Mabel's level, and said, "I am your Uncle Stephen. A pleasure to meet you."

"You look like his lordship," Mabel said, looking from the younger version of Marcus to the man himself.

"I'm taller," Marcus said.

"And I'm smarter," his brother said without missing a beat.

Then Stephen stood and gave his brother a hearty embrace. "It is so good to see you, Marcus. I only wish Rose were here, too. She's been so worried about you."

"No thanks to you, I am certain," Marcus said darkly. "I shall have to write to her to dispel any rumors that I'm living in a cave with a beard down to my knees."

Stephen laughed, and Marcus nearly smiled.

Lady Chesterfield clapped her hands, and the family and servants moved into the home, with quite a few of the servants welcoming his lordship home. Clearly, Marcus was well-liked by both his family and the staff.

As they went in, Lilian hurried her steps until she was even with Lady Chesterfield. "Thank you for that wonderful greeting," she said. "I know Marcus was moved by the gesture."

The older woman looked at Lilian curiously as if she hadn't any idea what she meant—or who she was for that matter. "Chesterfields always do their duty."

Now that was a bit of a cold bath, Lilian thought as she let the other woman proceed ahead of her.

"What was that about?" Marcus asked, coming up beside her.

"I thanked your mother for the warm reception," Lilian said, her eyes on Lady Chesterfield's small frame. If she'd had any notion that she would be a welcome part of this family, Lady Chesterfield had disabused her of that idea.

Lilian's rooms were vast and beautifully appointed, with white-washed walls and gold trim, and a thick Aubusson carpet beneath her feet, but she missed the intimacy of Merdunoir more than she would have thought possible. Her suite adjoined her husband's, but they were separated by two sitting rooms, one for each of them. The suites were mirror images of one another, though Marcus's rooms were quite a bit larger than hers, but such comparisons concerning rooms as large as theirs held little meaning. Her suite was larger and grander than her duchess sister's, and part of Lilian wished she could invite her sister for a visit just to show her. It wasn't a very charitable thought, but Lilian could not help but think it.

Her letters to her sister had gone unanswered, and Lilian wondered if Theresa actually thought she'd had anything to do with Weston's murder. Despite her accusation the night of the murder, it seemed impossible that she would think that, but the fact Theresa hadn't written, hadn't responded at all, was quite telling. And Lilian knew the lack of response had nothing to do with the fact her sister was in deep mourning; she was certain Theresa had probably danced on her husband's grave. More than once.

Theresa had confided to Lilian many times in the past three years that she was terribly unhappy. She would cry on Lilian's shoulder one day, then rant that her misery was all Lilian's fault the next. At times, Lilian wondered if her sister was a bit unstable, driven that way by the cruelty of Weston.

A tall bank of windows, their heavy gold velvet curtains pulled back to allow in the day's bright sun, beckoned her and she let out a delighted gasp when she realized they were not windows, but doors that led out to a narrow balcony overlooking one of the most beautiful gardens she'd ever seen. In the distance, a small pond, complete with two swans, was surrounded by a lawn of emerald green, and leading to the pond was a pebbled path lined with riotously blooming roses.

A soft sound behind her made her smile, for she knew, without turning, that her husband had joined her on the balcony.

"Those roses," he said, a small amount of humor in his voice. "They were planted when my sister was born. Poor mother had suffered through three boys and was so delighted to finally have a girl, she planted a garden of roses in her honor."

"For Rose. I see."

"Yes. The irony is, Rose doesn't care for her namesake flower, though every suitor she ever had sent her dozens of the things."

He moved behind her and wrapped his arms around her waist, resting his chin on her shoulder. It was such a husbandly gesture, marking them completely as a couple, that Lilian couldn't help the way her heart melted. She loved him. It was as simple as that. Placing her hands against his, she hugged him to her and leaned against him.

"The sun is out," he whispered next to her ear.

A slow smile spread on her face. "Indeed it is."

"For some reason"—he kissed her neck softly and moved a hand up to cup one breast, causing her to stop breathing for a moment—"every time the sun is shining, I think of you, naked. Strange thought, yes?"

"Very strange," she said, then turned in his arms so she might kiss him. "Very strange indeed." And, feeling shamelessly bold, she dropped her hand to the top button on his trousers and undid it.

Chapter 15

Constable Toby Conroy took off his top hat and rested it on his desk next to an impressive pile of paper that represented the investigation into the Duke of Weston's murder. With no small amount of relish, he grabbed up a large stamp and pressed it into his ink pad, and was about to thump it down when he paused, just a moment, before slamming it with vigor on the top of the stack.

CLOSED.

"Smithers," he called, ignoring the small doubt in his mind. "File this when you can, will you, chap?"

Smithers, who was otherwise occupied, waved a hand of acknowledgement. He didn't know why a case that was so obviously closed would continue to bother him. He usually liked it when murders were easily solved. Take the Whitson case. Man killed another man over a cow. Whitson had walked into the police station holding a bloody axe and announced he'd just killed his neighbor. Other than dealing with the hysterical wife of the dead man and the equally hysterical wife of the murderer, the case had been a pure joy. Open and closed before he'd even known there was a case.

But this one, involving a peer of the realm and a father getting revenge for his daughter, well, this case had been a nightmare from the beginning. And now it was closed. *Closed*. He set the stack of papers away from him. Snapping open his watch, Conroy noted that Viscount and Viscountess Granton would be at the station momentarily, something that was wholly unnecessary now. If things had been different, Conroy would gladly have traveled to Hallstead Manor, but as the case had just that day been turned on end, he'd had no time to send a note.

Those thoughts were still bouncing around in his head when he heard a deep voice request his attention, and Conroy stood.

"My lord," Conroy said, bowing slightly. "My lady. Please sit down."

While they sat, he fetched the register that all visitors signed when they entered the police department on business. "If you would sign here, please," he said, laying the register on the desk in front of the couple. Lord Granton signed first, then handed the pen over to Lady Granton, something Conroy noted only because it was a rare man indeed who allowed his wife to sign for herself.

The lady looked nervous and Conroy couldn't say he blamed her. Having a murder charge hanging over one's head was no laughing matter.

His lordship looked about to make an impassioned speech defending his lady, but the constable forestalled him by raising one hand. "The case has been solved," he said, and the viscount snapped his mouth closed.

"Thank God," Lady Granton said feelingly. "Who . . . ?"

"The same man who confessed." Conroy passed a weary hand over his brow. "They're Catholic, and the daughter, the one who was the center of all this, couldn't bear the thought of her father, who died for her, you see, to be buried in unconsecrated ground. Suicide, you know. And murder. It was just too much for the poor girl. And so she made up the whole thing about her father being left-handed. She was clever to claim that, she was. She wanted her father to have a proper burial and be laid to rest in consecrated ground. Her mother just left, not twenty minutes ago, with her daughter in tow, having explained the whole thing. We're not pressing charges." He waited to see if the pair would become incensed by this last, and he was ready to defend his decision. The poor girl had been beside herself, fearing the church would dig up her father and remove him from the cemetery where he now lay. She'd begged him not to say a thing. It had been one of the most wrenching scenes Conroy had ever been a part of, and so he'd promised to do what he could so that her father could stay where he was. Still, something niggled at his brain, as if he were forgetting an important detail. His unease made no sense and so he dismissed it. The man had confessed, the daughter admitted her lie. Case closed.

"So it's over." Lady Granton's eyes were suspiciously shiny, but she did not cry. Hell, Conroy wasn't certain he could take it if another pretty lady burst into tears in front of him.

"This is the case?" Lord Granton asked, eying the bound stack of papers. Beside it was a smooth stone, which Granton picked up. "A worry stone, Constable?"

Conroy chuckled. "Not mine, though this case did cause me no amount of worry. I thought it might be a clue of some sort. I found it next to Mr. Maine, you see, and his wife couldn't recall the gentleman having one."

"If it had nothing to do with this case, then perhaps you can benefit from it in the future," Lord Granton said, placing the stone back on his desk.

"Yes." He sounded entirely convinced. "I will inform Her Grace of this development. I fear she still retains some doubts. In fact, I will inform Her Grace that if she continues to disparage your character, she will face charges."

Lady Granton's eyes grew wide. "Will she?"

Conroy smiled. "No, but it won't hurt to let her think so, will it now?"

Lady Granton smiled, and Conroy felt the impact of that smile like a small blow to his head. "Thank you, Constable."

"You are more than welcome, my lady. And may I congratulate you in person on your recent nuptials." He darted a look to Granton, who scowled at him.

"Of course," the lady said, then looked up at her husband, whose face made the most remarkable transformation Conroy had ever witnessed. Clearly, Viscount Granton was a man very much in love with his new wife.

Chapter 16

Lilian arrived at Mount Carlyle with a small army of servants and a stomach roiling with nerves. Marcus was attending a meeting in Birmingham, and she'd assured him it would be a simple matter to go to her sister's home and collect all her belongings. Mabel was getting to know her cousins, one of whom was just her age—a girl—and the two had taken to one another almost immediately.

Still, this was not an errand she looked forward to. The familiar sight of the grand estate made her slightly ill, though given her meeting with the constable, she felt a bit more confident than she would have otherwise. In hindsight, fleeing that night might have been foolish, but if she hadn't, she wouldn't have met Marcus nor have Mabel in her life. Lilian's mother had always told her that things happened for a reason—even the bad.

Mount Carlyle was a lovely home, completely renovated in this century so that the white stone front gleamed richly in the morning sun. It stood three stories high with massive square towers at either end, built in the baroque style of Blenheim Palace, a home greatly coveted by Weston. He'd wanted something grander, lovelier than the Duke of Marlborough's famous palace, and had nearly succeeded. As beautiful as it was on the outside, the inside was even more lavish, and she'd felt like a visitor in some museum the entire time she'd lived there. For nearly three years, Lilian had lived in the east wing, far from her sister and the duke, and had felt almost as if she were living alone. It might have been lovely had the duke not wandered over to her side far too frequently. Only two things had prevented her from leaving: her sister and the sad fact that she had nowhere else to go. Each time she'd mentioned leaving, her sister would dissolve into tears and beg her to stay, and so she'd stayed, feeling more and more trapped as time went on.

Now, stepping down from her carriage, Viscountess Granton felt an overwhelming sense of sadness that everything had gone so wrong for her sister. Theresa had always been spoiled. As the youngest, she had been doted on, and so when Weston had turned his favor toward Theresa, her mother, knowing she was dying, had given her blessing. It hadn't really mattered which daughter married the duke, for if either one was well settled, the other would also be taken care of. Desperation and fear had driven her mother to accept Weston's suit for Theresa.

Lilian stepped down from her carriage, noting a second carriage with six servants, including two footmen, followed closely behind. Within moments, the large double doors opened, revealing the dear face of Weston's butler, Mr. Dawson. If he was surprised to see her at the front door, he did not show it.

"Lady Granton, a pleasure indeed." Lilian smiled at the proper use of her title. "I do apologize, but Her Grace is not at home."

"No matter, Mr. Dawson, I've only come to collect my belongings, not visit. I left in such haste the last time I was here, I hardly had time to collect them."

Lilian walked up the shallow steps, and Mr. Dawson stepped out of the way, saying blandly and not meaning a single syllable, "Oh dear, Lady Granton, I must insist you do not enter the house. Please do stop."

Lilian grinned up at his somber face, and she could tell he was using his best butler mien to not smile. "I assure you we'll only be a few minutes." Turning to the servants who had gathered behind her, Lilian said, "Please follow me."

She got as far as the edge of the grand foyer, where the curving stairs to the second floor began, when the first screech was heard. Everyone except Lilian immediately froze.

Her Grace, the Duchess of Weston, then appeared at the top of the staircase, her hair a mess and her belly—Lilian opened her eyes wide—her belly large and showing an obvious pregnancy. "Heavens," Lilian whispered to Mr. Dawson, "Her Grace is—"

"Not," he finished with authority.

How very curious, for Lilian couldn't help but concur. When she'd left her sister not two weeks ago, Theresa had not been with child—and if she had been, she certainly wasn't as far along as the woman glaring down at her from the stairs.

Collecting herself, she said, "I've come to get my belongings."

"I had them burned," Theresa said.

"No, she did not," Mr. Dawson said softly, but not softly enough that the duchess did not hear. She glared at the butler but said nothing.

"Theresa, please. Let me collect my things and then I'll leave."

Theresa lifted her chin imperiously. "Very well."

There was something a bit odd about the way her sister was acting, and it wasn't just that her usually meticulously groomed sister looked more like an overworked chambermaid than a duchess. She had dark circles beneath her eyes and her face was unusually pale. Perhaps the strain of all that had happened was affecting her more than Lilian would have thought. After all, she'd truly believed her older sister had murdered her husband. Of course it would have affected her, and Lilian felt a sharp twinge of guilt that she hadn't given a thought to how Theresa must have suffered through all this.

Lilian led the servants to her suite and directed them where to go to collect all her belongings. She went immediately to the little shelf that held her rock, and she picked it up, feeling unaccountably relieved that it was untouched, before placing it in her pocket. Theresa hovered just outside her door, looking young and lost. Despite all that had happened, she loved her sister, and seeing her looking so forlorn touched her heart.

"Would you like to visit for a bit?" she asked, and her sister started, as if she'd forgotten Lilian was in the room.

"Yes, that would be nice."

"Perhaps in the sitting room. That way if the servants have any questions, they'll be able to easily find me."

When they were seated, Lilian eyed her sister warily, then looked pointedly at her belly.

"Oh, that. It's a pillow." Theresa said the words almost listlessly, as if she hadn't any idea how odd it was that she'd stuffed a pillow under her dress.

"Why?"

"Weston hardly provided for me. A silly small house in the village without even gaslight and only enough income for a handful of servants. If Lord Standish believes I may be carrying the duke's heir, he'll stay away at least for a time."

"Lord Standish, oh yes."

"His Grace's brother. He's next in line, as you know, and he wants to move into Mount Carlyle. But this is *my* home."

Lilian studied her sister a long moment. She was only eighteen years old, still a child, really, and here she was, alone and widowed. "Regardless of how long you stay here, we shall be neighbors. Cannock is a charming little village, and even if your home isn't what you would have wanted, it will still be yours. As a widow, you'll have far more freedom than a single girl would. You'll see, everything will work out." Lilian eyed the large bulge beneath her sister's skirts. "How long do you think you can hold Lord Standish off? I think you should have perhaps used a smaller pillow." Lilian smiled and hoped Theresa would too.

But Theresa looked down and patted the pillow, frowning. "Lord Standish already saw me. He was quite surprised." Theresa giggled.

"Is there any chance you could be with child?" Lilian ducked her head so she could see her sister's expression.

"No." And Theresa's eyes filled with tears. "I had so hoped. Oh, Lilian, you had no idea how I hoped. What was I to do? Lord Standish wanted to move in immediately, the cad."

Lilian smiled sadly at her sister, so young and now so lost.

"It is the way of things, Theresa, you know that. Think of what happened to poor mama when Father died. Many women would be happy to have a home of their own and servants. And you can always remarry; you are so young."

And then Theresa burst into tears. "I don't want to marry just anyone."

"Of course not."

Theresa sniffed. "You don't understand. I'm already in love."

"You are?" Lilian asked cautiously.

She nodded, dabbing her eyes with a handkerchief. "With John Munroe," she said with a sniff.

"Mr. Munroe? Weston's secretary?" Lilian asked, dumbfounded. She'd lived in the same home as her sister and never suspected a thing. Then again, she'd spent most of her days wandering the grounds or in her own wing of the massive house, so it wasn't entirely impossible the pair could have kept such a secret.

"We love each other. Oh, Lilian, it's wonderful. He had to leave to make arrangements, but he'll be back and then we can marry. I haven't heard a word from him in two weeks, and I suppose I'm a bit weepy from missing him. I do hope I can find a new maid before he returns. I'm such a sight."

"Marry? But Theresa, you've only just become widowed. You can't possibly be discussing marriage at this time. It's, well, it's unseemly."

Theresa laughed. "Unseemly? I don't care. We've been planning to run away together for months."

Lilian furrowed her brow. "Months?" Weston had been dead for less than a month.

"Well, not really *planning*," her sister said quickly. "Just dreaming, really. Oh, he's so wonderful, Lilian. I know you'll adore him as much as I do. He's so gallant and he loves me, truly, truly loves me as much as I love him. I know what you're thinking, that it was awful of me to have an affair right beneath my husband's nose, but was he not doing the very same to me? And not just with one woman, I might add."

"How fortunate for you that Weston died," Lilian said, only half joking.

"Nothing could be more fortunate," Theresa said with enthusiasm. "As soon as John returns, we're off to America. Can you imagine? This," she said, indicating the pillow, "is just to keep Standish away until John returns. I think it's brilliant. It was John's idea, you see. He is brilliant. And so handsome."

Lilian forced a smile. "I'm so happy for you, Terri, but why America? Why not stay here?"

"John thinks it's best to get a brand-new start. I miss him so much, Lilian. He should be returning this week, if all has gone well. Just in time for the birth!"

"Birth?"

Theresa patted her stomach and giggled. "I daresay as soon as John returns, my baby will be born. I loathe this house. I'm here alone and no one cares about me. The servants hate me, I know they do. My maid quit." She motioned to her hair and dress as proof. "They're all hateful and awful." She looked suddenly distressed.

"What is it, Theresa?"

"What if John doesn't return?"

"If what you say is true, he will."

Theresa frowned. "Why would I lie?"

"You misunderstand, Terri. Of course he loves you, and I'm certain he will return." This seemed to brighten Theresa's mood, which only made Lilian wonder at her sister's mercurial moods. Lilian didn't care for the situation at all. What sort of person talked of marriage not three weeks after burying her husband? It didn't matter a bit if Weston was an awful husband. Society had rules, and one of those rules was one had to wait at least a year before remarrying, particularly if one had been married to a peer. It also was rather unseemly that her sister, a duchess, was considering marriage to a commoner. She wondered at this man that he could have influenced her sister so. It didn't speak well of him at all. Still, her sister may have been a spoiled girl, but she had not deserved what she had got when she married Weston.

Despite her misgivings, Lilian put on a bright smile. "You haven't congratulated me on my own marriage, you know."

"Congratulations."

Theresa didn't sound at all sincere, so Lilian let the subject drop.

Marcus descended from his coach in Birmingham, where he'd agreed to meet with Kathryn Cates, his dead wife's former maid. He would do nothing with the information she had for him, but perhaps knowing who sired his daughter would one day be valuable. How, he couldn't say, but he had just enough curiosity to agree to meet with the woman.

She sat on a bench overlooking the large pond in Cannon Hill Park, her back ramrod straight, her hands clenched tightly in her lap. Just seeing her brought back ugly memories of his wife, and he tried to push down his dark thoughts. When she saw him approaching, Miss Cates stood immediately and waited in silence until he'd reached her. Then, she sat, her lips pressed thin, her pale blue eyes on a small group of ducks that were making their way across the pond. Marcus sat beside her, giving her a curious look before turning his attention to the ducks as well.

"Thank you for meeting with me, my lord. It has been a difficult time, these past years. A trial. I'm not one for secrets, and working for your wife . . ." She let her voice trail off. Yes, Marcus was well aware that his wife had held many secrets, but he'd never actually given a thought to what this would have meant to the woman who was keeping them for Eleanor. "It has weighed heavily on me, knowing that poor little mite was left behind with that awful woman in Northumberland. How is she?"

"She is healthy and seems to have been well cared for. You needn't worry on that account, though I don't believe her childhood was as it might have been had Eleanor not resorted to such subterfuge."

Miss Cates nodded, but her demeanor did not change; she still looked as if she were about to bolt from the bench and run away.

"You have knowledge of who the father of the child is?" he prompted, wanting this interview over as quickly as possible so he could return to Lilian. The sun was shining brightly, after all.

"Yes," she whispered, and something about the way she said it, or perhaps the way her hands tightened in her lap, making her knuckles white, put Marcus on edge.

"Miss Cates, please be assured that whatever my wife did, I hold you in nothing but the highest esteem. You were put in a difficult situation, and for that, I apologize." It was clear the poor woman was distraught. "The name of the child's father, if you please."

She took a deep and shaking breath. "The youngest Mr. Dunford, sir."

The blood fled his head so suddenly that Marcus's vision momentarily darkened and blurred. "What did you say?" he asked, his voice low.

The poor woman twisted her hands together and looked up at him, and he knew by the look in her eyes that she pitied him nearly as much as she feared him. "Stephen Dunford, sir. Your brother."

It could not be true. It could not. The pain slicing through Marcus at that moment might have felled another man, and even as he sat there, deathly still, Marcus wondered that he was able to breathe, to look out and see those ducks swimming, to hear the sound of a child's laughter. Everything, *everything*, changed at that moment. "Are you certain? It is vital that you are certain." He sounded normal, like a man discussing some mundane topic and not the fact that his brother had stabbed him in the back.

Miss Cates's eyes filled with tears. "She told me so herself. And I was . . . aware of the goings-on. She wasn't very discreet, at least with me. He visited her room more than once and I—"

"You what?" he asked, more harshly than he intended, but he could hardly feel sorry for the woman even when she flinched.

"I saw them. Together. One morning. She screeched at me, and I ran from the room, but not before I saw him. It was Mr. Dunford, sir. And then, when she realized she was going to have a baby, she wailed and cried and told me all, about how angry you would be, about how you'd kill her and Mr. Dunford, too. I'd never seen another soul so afraid. She asked me what to do, where to go, and I, God forgive me, I helped her."

A strange calm enveloped Marcus at that moment, almost as if he'd stepped outside himself, leaving behind the man whose heart and soul had just been ripped to shreds. "Does Stephen know about the child?"

Miss Cates shook her head briskly. "No. He never knew. No one knew except myself and Lady Granton. She was very clear that no one should know."

"Particularly not me."

"No, sir. I mean yes, sir."

Marcus stood, though he wasn't at all certain his legs would be able to support his weight. "Thank you, Miss Cates. I realize this was not an easy discussion, but I do appreciate your honesty."

"I'm so sorry, sir. Truly I am. I wish there was something else I could have done. You never deserved any of this."

For some odd reason, Marcus felt a smile tug at his lips. Perhaps this was exactly what he deserved.

Marcus entered Hallstead Manor with exaggerated calm, though inside he was a seething mass of emotions. Funny, the house looked the same, smelled the same. In the distance, he could hear the soft murmuring of the maids as they cleaned somewhere. A large grandfather clock ticked, its heavy pendulum swinging back and forth, as if time hadn't stopped when Marcus had learned the awful truth about his brother.

Handing off his coat and hat, he inquired as to the location of his youngest brother.

"I believe he is having luncheon with the rest of the family." The footman eyed Marcus warily, and Marcus realized he wasn't as good at hiding his emotions as he'd thought.

"And the children?"

"Are in the nursery, my lord."

Marcus thanked the footman, then headed directly to the breakfast room, where the family often had luncheon as it was a smaller, more intimate room for family gatherings than the large, ostentatious dining hall. He wasn't certain what he would do or say; he only knew that he had to see his brother, the same brother who had been so very worried about Marcus disappearing to Merdunoir after Eleanor had died that he had followed him there, written heartfelt letters full of concern. The same brother who had greeted him with a warm embrace when Marcus had finally returned home.

Marcus stopped at the entrance to the breakfast room, taking in the homey scene. Most of his family, including his father, his brothers, Georgette, and Lilian, had gathered around the table and were chatting about something mundane and unimportant. Lilian looked up and smiled a smile that froze in place when she saw him. Her eyes widened. Stephen looked happy, sitting there, laughing at some joke Adam had made. As if nothing in the world were wrong.

Without thinking, without even knowing what he was doing, he strode up to Stephen, grabbed him by the collar, and smashed his startled face with his fist so hard, his brother was ripped from his grasp and fell to the floor, his chair upending and landing atop him

"Bloody hell, Marcus, what was that for?" Stephen asked from the floor, as the others around the table stood in shocked horror.

"How could you?" He knew his words were laced with anguish, but it couldn't be helped. Not now.

Stephen's look of confusion soon turned to one of dawning, terrified realization. "Oh God, Marcus. How did—"

It was not the correct thing to say, as Stephen quickly realized, for he snapped his mouth shut. Marcus wasn't certain what he'd expected, but for Stephen to ask—or start to ask—"How did you find out?" was not quite what he was looking for.

"How could you *do* it? *I want to know!*" Marcus said this last with so much raw intensity, his throat hurt, as if the words had been ripped from his throat by brute force.

"What is the meaning of this, Granton?" his father asked, coming round the table to stand next to his oldest son.

"The meaning?" Marcus asked politely, calmly. "Let's see, the meaning. Oh, yes, I know. I wanted to know why my *brother fucked my wife.*"

The women in the room gave a collective gasp, and Marcus's father jerked his head back as if the words somehow hurt him. Stephen, still lying on the floor, started weeping silently, tears falling unbidden.

"Is this true, Stephen?" his father asked, his face gone white. Stephen could only nod his head, and Marcus had the terrible urge to punch him again. "My God, Stephen."

"I was nineteen, Father. And she . . . she told me she loved me. Marcus, I'm so sorry. More sorry than I can say. Please, Marcus." His pleas fell on deaf ears.

Marcus swallowed heavily, suddenly feeling ill. "You have betrayed me in the worst possible way. You have taken *everything* from me, do you understand that? *Do you?*"

And then, his little brother had the audacity to say, "But you didn't even love her."

It was almost as if everyone in the room froze, waiting for Marcus to explode, which surely he would. He could feel it building, building. Instead, the same strange calm that had come over him in the carriage ride from Birmingham settled around him. "I wasn't referring to my whore of a wife. I was referring to my daughter."

"Marcus." Lilian had come up beside him and laid her hand on his arm, which no doubt felt like a steel rod beneath her palm. He ignored her, unwilling to release the growing rage in his heart.

His brother looked momentarily confused, as if he couldn't fathom why Marcus was bringing Mabel into the conversation. Then, again, the dawning realization came, and Stephen braced himself, no doubt expecting another blow. "I didn't know, Marcus. I didn't. I swear to you."

"Do you think that matters? She was my daughter and now she's yours." Marcus could feel his eyes burning, feel his throat tighten on that last word, but he'd be damned if he cried in front of his family like some weak little boy. "I'm going to be sick," he said distractedly, and staggered from the room, feeling everyone's pitying gaze on him. At that moment, he felt everything good he had managed to salvage from his ruined life had suddenly been snatched away. He flung open the door and stumbled down the steps, his stomach heaving. He barely made it to the small shrubs lining the drive before he lost the contents of his stomach, retching painfully.

He was still bent over, swallowing convulsively, when Lilian came up to him and laid a hand on his back. "I'm so sorry, Marcus."

"We're leaving. Now. Have your things packed immediately."
He stood, bracing himself, suspecting she would argue.

"Of course. I'll go fetch Mabel." She turned and headed toward
the steps.

Just hearing his daughter's name made his stomach clench painfully.
"She stays."

Lilian spun around so quickly, her skirts twirled, wrapping her
legs momentarily before settling back down. "No, Marcus. She belongs with us."

"She belongs with her father."

His wife marched up to him, and he recognized the stubborn set
of her jaw. "*You* are her father," she said, pointing a finger into his
chest, not ungently.

Just hearing those words caused the rage he'd felt all day to surge.
"I am not, Lilian. Saying it does not make it so. My God, she's only
been with me for three weeks. She'll forget about her time at Merdunoir, she'll forget that I was supposed to be her father. She's a child.
She'll forget."

Tears flooded Lilian's eyes, and Marcus somehow found the
strength to meet her gaze unflinchingly. "Will you forget, Marcus?
Do you think for one moment that *I* will?"

"It doesn't matter. The fact is that Mabel is not mine. And she's not
yours." He knew he was being cruel, but he had to make her understand. When Mabel was the daughter of some nameless, faceless man,
it *hadn't* mattered. Hell, even if he'd known who it was, it wouldn't
have mattered. But Mabel's father was his own brother. *That* mattered, more than he could ever possibly explain. From the corner of
his eye, he saw a servant and called to him.

"Robert, please tell them to ready the carriage."

"Yes, sir."

"Marcus, no. Please." Lilian sounded on the verge of losing whatever composure she had left. He turned and in that moment, he almost gave in to her, almost told her to have her things packed and to
fetch Mabel so they could return home and pretend all of this was
some horrible nightmare. But he knew that whenever he looked at
Mabel, he would picture his brother with his wife. It was too much to
bear.

"I can't," he said, unaware of how very disconsolate he sounded.
"Please try to understand."

"Marcus, no. Don't make me choose."

He stepped back, her words a physical blow, the silence behind them seemingly endless. He hadn't seen that coming, hadn't thought in a million years she would say such a thing. Marcus knew she'd be sad and angry and perhaps would hate him for a little while, but he never thought she would even think of choosing to stay and allowing him to leave. "Don't worry, my love, I won't make you choose. I'll choose for you." He gave her a mocking bow. "Good-bye."

He turned, ready to mount the first horse in his father's stables, ready to ride to the ends of the earth so he might forget the look in Lilian's eyes when he'd said that last word. He thought she might run after him, might clutch at his arm and make him stop. He thought she might beg him to stay. But she was silent and he knew he'd made the right choice.

For both of them.

Chapter 17

"He's gone."

Lilian stood at the entry to the breakfast room and looked from one shocked face to the next. They had the look people got when something truly horrid had happened, like an unexpected death. Indeed, that was how Lilian felt. How could she have been so happy not one day before, and now everything had gone wrong. She was here, alone, with a family who tolerated her at best, abandoned by the husband she loved with all her heart.

At that moment, Lady Chesterfield stepped into the room from behind her, smiling a greeting that quickly turned into a look of worried puzzlement. "Oh God, who's died?" she asked, holding her hands over her heart.

"Nothing like that," Lord Chesterfield said, walking to his wife and placing her hand in the crook of his arm. "I'll explain everything, my dear, in private."

She looked back at the group even as Lord Chesterfield drew her away. "What happened to Stephen's face?"

"In due time, my dear."

Lilian was left alone with the younger Dunfords. Georgette stood next to Adam, and Stephen stood alone, his red-rimmed eyes tortured.

"Did he say where he was going?" Adam asked.

"No. He wanted to leave Mabel and I could not do it. And so he left." Lilian's eyes burned from unshed tears and her throat felt on fire.

"He just needs to cool off. And if he doesn't return by tomorrow, I'll go find him. He'll either be in London in his townhouse or Merdunoir."

Lilian hugged her arms around herself. "I couldn't just leave her. She called me Mama last night, you see." Then, the tears that had been threatening fell from her eyes, and she spun around and attempted to pull herself together. When Georgette came up to her and laid an arm across her back, Lilian began crying in earnest. It was such a sisterly gesture, and she couldn't help but think about what had happened earlier that day with Theresa. Everything seemed to be crumbling around her and she had no one to run to. That arm around her back was more comforting than Georgette could ever know.

Georgette handed her a handkerchief, and Lilian dabbed at her eyes and cheeks. "I'm so sorry," Lilian whispered, mortified that she'd cried in front of the Dunfords.

"Don't be. Granton is being foolish, but he'll be back."

Lilian shook her head. "You didn't see his face. He was so hurt."

"Bloody hell." This from Stephen, who looked close to crying again.

"What in God's name were you thinking, Stephen?" Adam asked angrily. "If Marcus hadn't already ruined your pretty face, I think I would do it for him."

"I've no excuse other than the fact I was young. She came to my room one night. Of course I told her to leave, but she kept on. I . . ." He looked at the women as if trying to gauge whether he should continue or not. "I was inexperienced and she made me feel as if I was something special. A man, I suppose. I kept telling her to leave. Of course, she didn't and after, she threatened to tell Marcus if I didn't do as she said. It was horrible and wonderful and wrong, and it went on for far too long. I was so ashamed. I couldn't even look at Marcus, and she would give me these looks behind his back. Looking back, I think I was a little bit mad."

"And now you have a daughter," Adam said, shaking his head in disgust.

"No. Mabel is not my daughter." He looked to Lilian. "I'd never seen Marcus so happy as he was when he arrived. He adores that little girl, and I know he loves you. I can't take that away from him too. Please, you have to convince him to keep Mabel."

Lilian swallowed past a growing knot in her throat. "I shall try, but I fear this has hurt him more than anything could."

"I wish I could make it all go away, but I can't. I need to talk to Marcus, to convince him," Stephen said.

"Bad idea," Adam said. "I think if he sees you anytime soon, he'll likely do more than punch your face. Let me speak with him once I find him. I'll try to reason with him."

Lilian had only known her husband for three weeks, but even she knew reasoning with him about this would be difficult at best.

Chapter 18

Constable Conroy was finishing up a tedious report about a burglary. The station was quiet, and the only sound was the scratching of his pen and the ticking of a clock above him. His desk was clean and neat, but on one corner sat a thick pile of papers, bound together with a strap, with the red ink CLOSED stamped on top of the cover sheet. He had no idea why the report was still on his desk, and he certainly had no idea why, when Smithers had come to file it away, Conroy had stopped him.

"Not yet," he'd said. *Not yet. Why?*

Conroy put his pen in the stand and closed his ink pot, then sat back in his chair and closed his eyes. *Why, why, why?*

He suddenly sat forward and stood, his heart pounding in his chest. Walking over to the registry, he looked at the names of those who had signed in the day prior, stopping when he got to the Maines. He stared at those names a long moment, breathing harshly. M-A-Y-N-E.

Conroy ran back to his desk, back to that large stack of papers still lying on the surface with the word CLOSED stamped upon it, and began riffling through the stack until he reached Silas's suicide note.

"You son of a bitch," he said beneath his breath. "You brilliant son of a bitch."

Then Conroy took the cover sheet, crumpled it up, and threw it in the trash.

Marcus got as far as Cannock before he stopped, which wasn't saying very much, for Cannock center was but a ten-minute ride from his home. He would have gotten farther if he hadn't seen them, the little girl with her mother, walking across the street. There was nothing at all remarkable about them and nothing at all to remind him of Lilian and Mabel. The woman was stout with bright red hair and the little girl quite a bit older than Mabel with blonde braids swinging down her back. So he couldn't have said why the sight of them stopped him cold, made him realize that he couldn't leave—or at least not go as far as he'd intended.

Marcus turned his horse toward the Cow and Plow, a small inn he'd frequented as a young man, an inn that drew locals, gentry, workingmen, and peers alike. He was suddenly so weary and the sun was about to set, so he dismounted and handed his horse off to a stable boy, flipping him a coin for his trouble.

When the barkeep saw him walk in, he came around the front and greeted him. "Lord Granton. Good day, sir." The barkeep's smile, at first quite sincere, turned into something less so after a time, and Marcus realized his remarkable talent for hiding his emotions had somehow been misplaced.

"I'll need a room if you have one available," Marcus said, knowing how ridiculous it was for him to ask for a room when he lived only walking distance away.

The barkeep's thick brows rose a bit, but he said nothing and grabbed up a key with a wooden square attached to it and the number 2 carved inexpertly into its surface. The inn had but two rooms to let, so a number was hardly needed, but Marcus took the key and headed up the stairs where the inn's two rooms were, his feet feeling nearly as heavy as his heart.

"Can I send a supper up for you, my lord?" the barkeep called as he trudged up the stairs.

Marcus waved him off. "I'll come down." For now, he wanted nothing more than to sleep, perhaps forever, or at least until he lost memory of what he'd discovered that day. But sleep would not come. No matter how hard he tried, he could not stop the images that crowded his mind: Stephen weeping, his father's shock, and Lilian, the way she'd looked when he'd said good-bye. And yet, she hadn't called to him, hadn't tried to stop him from leaving. Hell, he hadn't left, not really. When Eleanor had died, he'd run from the snide remarks, the smirks, the humiliation. His pride, he supposed, couldn't take such a pummeling.

This, though, this was different. This time it was his heart that had been pummeled and he knew the only way to heal it was to go back, face what had happened, try to fix what he'd done. Had he truly thought he could leave Lilian? Or Mabel? God, just the thought of her little face when Lilian told her he was gone forever caused the ache in his chest to flare.

He turned onto his back and stared at the ceiling, illuminated only by a gaslight outside. It was raining, and the rivulets on the window created a shimmering pattern on the ceiling. A flash of lightning brightened the dark sky outside, followed a few seconds later by a rolling rumble of thunder. It was just as well, he thought. He wasn't certain he could face his family this night. Tomorrow, after a good night's rest, God willing, he would go back home, collect his family, and try to repair the terrible damage done this day.

His stomach rumbled, protesting the fact that he hadn't eaten since his breakfast. Despite everything that had happened that day, or perhaps because of all that had happened, he was starving.

Though he dreaded the thought of seeing someone he was acquainted with, Marcus made his way down to the taproom, where he knew he could get some good, hearty country fare. He'd no intention of drinking, as he'd rarely been a man to embrace the bottle even in the worst of times.

Thankfully, the room was nearly empty when Marcus entered; the only other seat was taken by a well-dressed gentleman Marcus did not recognize, thank goodness.

"Good evening, Lord Granton," the barkeep called out. Upon hearing his title, the other gentleman lifted his head, but Marcus ignored him.

"What has Sally made for dinner this evening?" Marcus asked, trying to sound jovial. Sally and Peter Riordan had owned the Cow and Plow for as long as Marcus could remember. They kept the place clean and served the finest ale in Cannock, and Sally was a splendid cook, but he'd never spent the night there. He knew Peter must find it odd that he'd taken a room, especially given the fact that it was well known that he'd just married. No doubt rumors would abound that he and his new bride had suffered some sort of tiff.

"Roasted chicken with Brussel sprouts and boiled potatoes, my lord."

At that, the other gentleman turned fully toward Marcus. "Lord Granton?"

Marcus gave Peter a smile that was more like a grimace at having been recognized, then turned. "I am. I don't believe I've had the pleasure," he said with the utmost politeness. A true gentleman would have taken the correct meaning from his cold response and wished him a good evening and gotten back to his meal. But Marcus could tell that, for all the fine clothing the man wore, he was not a gentleman.

"You're the bloke with the sister what ran away from Weston."

Marcus gave the man a steely look but said nothing.

Apparently, the man had no ear for subtleties, for he continued. "I worked for Weston. May the man rot in hell." He lifted up his glass, filled with an amber liquid, and Marcus gave a mental shrug. He wouldn't be averse to talking with the man, particularly as they shared the same opinion of His Grace. When Marcus sat, the man extended his hand. "John Munroe, at your service. I worked as Weston's secretary for ten years, the bastard. Ten years and only a half day off a week. He wouldn't let me go visit my poor mother when she was on her death bed."

"You don't say."

"Whoever killed the man deserves a medal."

At that, Marcus smiled. "A similar thought had occurred to me. Unfortunately, the man in question is dead and unable to accept any accolades."

Mr. Munroe frowned at that, then smiled. "What are you drinking?"

"Tea, I'm afraid," Marcus said, casting a quick glance at the bottle next to Munroe's glass. It appeared to be half empty, and the man's cheeks were unnaturally flushed. He was clearly in his cups, for no sober man would say such things about a member of the peerage in such a public place, even if it were deserved.

"Don't tell me you're a teetotaler. I'll have to find me another dinner companion," Munroe said before letting out a laugh. "Ah, don't mind me. I'm celebrating. I'm gettin' married soon. Going to America with my sweetheart." He'd leaned forward and lowered his voice as if he were imparting a secret.

"My felicitations."

Munroe grinned, and winked. "You'll never guess who it is."

"I couldn't begin to."

"It's the duchess herself."

To say that Marcus was taken aback would have been a massive understatement. This man thought he was marrying the Duchess of Weston? He was either delusional or drunker than Marcus had thought.

"You don't believe me," Munroe said, then let out a cackle. "It's true, though. She's a lively thing, she is. And to think she was married to that whoreson Weston. Makes my stomach crawl, it does. You don't know half. No one does, what that man did. He deserved what he got and more. Too bad about Silas, though. Just too bad."

Munroe, who had been laughing not five seconds prior, looked about to cry, and Marcus very much regretted his decision to sit with the man. Perhaps he'd make his excuses and have his meal brought up to his room after all. He turned to indicate as much to Peter, but the barkeep was nowhere in sight.

Munroe was a fidgety sort of fellow, and Marcus couldn't imagine that he could have attracted the duchess. He was wiry, with close-set eyes and a mop of curling hair that gave his head a bit of a pointed look. His clothes were expensive and well-tailored, and had a look of newness to them, as if he'd walked out of the haberdashery just that day with his new wardrobe. Even the man's bowler, lying on the worn wooden table by the bottle, looked as though it had never been worn. Yet his fingers were ink-stained, marking him as a man who worked as a secretary.

Theresa, if he recalled, was a pretty little thing, a smaller version of his own wife.

Munroe's bleary eyes took on a contemplative look as he took another sip. Marcus cast another look about, hoping to see Peter.

"I remember your sister," Munroe said abruptly. While they talked, Munroe had taken an object out of his pocket, brought his hand to the table, and begun picking up and dropping the object over and over, making a staccato beat and driving Marcus a bit mad with the motion. But when Munroe dared mention his sister, Marcus slammed his hand on top of Munroe's, stopping the irritating noise immediately. "Hey! You'll break it."

"You are not to discuss my sister in a public place, Mr. Munroe. Do I make myself clear?"

Munroe rubbed his hand, leaving behind on the table the annoying something he'd been playing with. Marcus had a good mind to take it up and throw it from the—

There are times in life when it seems as if every clock stops ticking and every heart stops beating. As Marcus looked down upon the object on the table, it indeed seemed as if time had stopped.

"A worry stone." Marcus picked the object up, fingering its

smooth surface. "I saw one just like it recently." On Constable Conroy's desk. Next to the file on Weston's murder marked CLOSED. It
could be a coincidence; it could mean nothing at all that this man
who worked for Weston had the same type of stone found near another man's body. Marcus schooled his features as quickly as he
could when he realized he could very well be sitting across the
table from a murderer. Or perhaps not. But he realized he should do
nothing to alarm Munroe, and so he placed the stone back on the
table as if he'd lost interest in it.

"Nah, you couldn't have seen one like this. My grandpappy got
that in Turkey for me. You can't find them around here. Used to have
two but . . ." Munroe let his voice trail off and gave Marcus a hard
look. Marcus smiled blandly as if politely interested in his story. "I
lost that one years ago. Years." He looked at his drink and fiddled
with the glass for a time. Finally, he cleared his voice. "I'd like to
find another one like it. Did you see it in a shop? I would like to purchase another if I could."

"I don't recall where I saw it," Marcus said. "And now I recollect,
it was a different type of stone altogether." He heard a noise behind
him and turned, grateful to see Peter coming from the kitchen with a
steaming plate in his hands.

"On second thought, I think I'll take my meal in my room, Mr.
Riordan." He turned to Munroe. "I do hope you don't mind. I'm terribly tired and very poor company."

Munroe smiled and lifted his glass. "It was lovely chatting with
you," he said grandly, then took another drink. Marcus figured he'd
be sleeping at his seat within the hour. In the morning, he might send
word to Constable Conroy about the stone, though he doubted anything would come of it. They had a man's confession, after all.

Chapter 19

Lilian awoke the next morning, her eyes gritty from crying, but it took a few seconds before she remembered why she'd been crying, and when she did, she pulled the covers up over her head.

"Mama. My lady."

So that was why she'd woken. Pulling down the covers, she peeked out to see Mabel standing next to her bed, her hair all bed-messy. "Where is Papa? He promised to take me to see the swans today."

Lilian pulled the covers back up, unable to face Mabel and her questions so early. Mabel giggled, thinking she was playing a game. "He had to leave on business yesterday. It was an emergency and he didn't have time to say good-bye. So your visit to the swans will have to wait. Unless you want me to take you?"

"I'll wait for his lordship," she said. It was something she did now, interchanging my ladies and my lords with Mama and Papa, and Lilian thought it was the sweetest thing. She had Sadie to blame for this. When talking to Mabel, she always referred to Marcus as Papa and herself as Mama. And now, mostly, Mabel also referred to them as Mama and Papa, which almost broke Lilian's heart. No doubt it would tear Marcus to pieces.

Though Lilian had prayed for Marcus's return, he had not come back to Hallstead Manor, and Adam had promised late the prior evening that he would go out and find him. And drag him home.

"I should have gone with him," Lilian had said. "He was so upset. I don't know what I was thinking, letting him go."

Georgette had held her hand throughout the evening, telling her that all would be well and that of course she couldn't have left Mabel, that she'd done the right thing.

"He's like a wounded bear trying to run from his pain," Adam said, which only made Lilian want to cry even more. For Marcus was hurt, terribly so, not only by Stephen, but now by her. But what should she have done? Abandoned Mabel?

Worse, her sister was never far from her thoughts. It seemed a lifetime ago that she'd sat with her sister, her stomach large with pillow. Theresa had seemed so fragile, on the verge of some terrible breakdown, and Lilian felt helpless knowing she could do nothing to help her. Lilian felt torn in too many directions.

"Marcus cannot continue to run away every time something goes awry with his life," Georgette had said.

And Adam, who rarely disagreed with his wife, shook his head. "This is not something going awry, this is finding out your brother betrayed you. Georgette, you cannot know how much that must have hurt Marcus. If you had done the same with Stephen, I think I'd be as far away from him as I could possibly go."

"That doesn't change anything," Georgette said stubbornly.

"Of course not. But what would you have him do? Shake Stephen's hand and offer forgiveness?"

"Yes," Georgette said with a nod, seeming completely sure of herself. Then, a sigh, and "No, I suppose not."

"Be damned if I would. As it is, I cannot stand to look at him and he did nothing wrong to me."

And so it had gone on for several long minutes, Lilian not listening, thinking only of how Theresa had acted the last time she'd seen her.

"You've broken her heart, you know."

Marcus groaned, immediately recognizing Adam's voice, and pulled the pillow over his head. He needn't ask how Adam had found him so quickly, for in a town as small as Cannock, word that Lord Granton was staying at the Cow and Plow when he lived not two miles away had no doubt caused a stir in the village.

"Drink too much, brother?" Adam asked, chuckling.

"Not a drop," came the muffled reply. He hadn't needed to drink; he'd just needed sleep, still did. "Sod off and leave me alone."

"She's outside the door, Marc."

Marcus sat up like a shot, his bleary eyes finding Adam, who was grinning like an idiot at him, which immediately told him his brother was lying. "Can you not leave me alone?"

"No. Not this time." Adam was sitting comfortably on a chair, one leg propped on the other. "And if you truly wanted to be left alone, you wouldn't have stopped in Cannock. You'd be halfway to Merdunoir now. Or in London."

Marcus rubbed at his day-old beard and scowled at his brother. So frightened was Adam by that look that he laughed out loud. Damn brothers. And then the day's previous revelations hit him like some rogue wave, and he felt like crying. It had been there, of course, that deep sadness that made him feel as if a large weight was in his chest instead of a beating heart, but just thinking the word "brothers" made him think of Stephen and what had transpired.

"Mabel wanted to know where her papa was," Adam said with brutal cruelty.

"Don't." Marcus pressed the heels of his hands against his eyes. He would not weep again. He. Would. Not. But when he took his hands away from his eyes, they were wet.

"Hell, Marcus, I know it's difficult. Actually, I don't know. I don't know what it's like to have a wife who doesn't love you, who cuckolds you. I don't know what it's like to find out you have a daughter who isn't truly your daughter but whom you love enough to die for. But I do know what it's like to have a wife who loves you. And now you do, too. Don't ruin this, Marcus. Don't throw it away."

"Christ, Adam, are you trying to make me weep?" he asked, and indeed two tears slipped from his eyes. "Why in hell did she start calling me Papa?" He shouted this at the ceiling, as if God would have some answer for him.

It was a rhetorical question, but Adam answered it anyway in a way he must have known would either break his brother's heart even more or put it back together. "Because she loves you."

Marcus looked away and squeezed his eyes shut, swallowing convulsively. "Stephen." He barely managed to get that one word out.

"Feels like hell. As you might expect. Looks like hell too, thanks to you. And he doesn't want her, Marcus. She's *your* daughter."

"She's—" He was about to say Mabel was not his daughter, but he could not because, in his heart, she was. Marcus might have lied and said he didn't want Mabel either. But he wasn't a man who was given to lies, so he remained silent. "Let me get my clothes on," he said wearily, and scowled when Adam gave him a brilliant smile.

Lilian paced back and forth under the watchful and bemused eyes of her new sister-in-law. Every once in a while, she would stop and bite her thumb, look at Georgette as if she was going to say something, then continue her pacing. Thank goodness Mabel had been kept occupied in the nursery with her cousins.

Following breakfast that day, a footman had appeared and discreetly called Adam over. Within minutes, Adam was out the door and headed to Cannock center, promising not to return without Marcus. Lilian couldn't help but think that was a promise Adam might not be able to keep, and told him so.

"If Marcus truly wanted to disappear, he would have," he said. "He's in Cannock. He didn't get any farther than *Cannock*." Adam had grinned, and even though she'd thought the two brothers didn't look alike, at that moment Lilian's heart had wrenched, for that grin was so much like Marcus's.

And Lilian had been pacing ever since.

It seemed like a lifetime ago when Marcus had sat beside Miss Cates and learned the terrible truth about his brother. As he rode in the carriage on the way back to Hallstead Manor, Marcus flexed his right hand, realizing for the first time that it was slightly swollen from striking Stephen's hard head.

"Stephen's eye is swollen shut," Adam said, obviously noting Marcus's perusal.

"He's lucky that is all I did. If the ladies weren't in the room, I daresay I wouldn't have stopped with a single punch."

"He's devastated, you know. And gone to London, at Father's behest."

Marcus sighed. "If this is an attempt by you to mend fences, you are wasting your breath," he said darkly. "At least for now." This last was said begrudgingly, though in his heart he knew he could not remain at odds with Stephen indefinitely. In truth, he regretted his punch and his words; Stephen had been little more than a boy and Marcus had no doubt who the aggressor had been. Still, the betrayal smarted and it would take longer than a single day for him to come to grips with all that had happened. For now, he wanted to go home and hold his wife. And bring Mabel to see the swans as he had promised before he'd left to talk to Miss Cates.

Adam gave him an innocent look. "I'm thinking of Mother. She was hysterical all yesterday, fearing she would never see her eldest son again. I knew better, though."

"Did you."

His brother grinned. "You're my brother, and I've never seen you so idiotic over a woman in my life. Reminds me of me."

Marcus widened his eyes in mock horror. "Never say that."

Adam chuckled, and the two brothers shared a moment of companionable silence, exchanging curious looks when the carriage stopped midway between Cannock and Hallstead Manor.

"I'll see what's happened," Adam said, then opened the door to stick his head out.

It happened so quickly, Marcus wasn't certain what had occurred even when he saw Adam slump over, then tumble from the carriage.

"Adam!" he shouted, lunging to try to stop Adam from hitting the ground. And then, a searing pain in his chest and the sickening sound of his flesh being pierced to the hilt by a knife. Stunned, Marcus fell back, glancing off his seat and ending up in the narrow space between the carriage seats. He stared blankly, first at the knife, and then at the man standing outside the carriage and smiling.

"Curiosity killed the cat," John Munroe said cheerfully.

Marcus tried to get up, but he lacked the strength to pry himself from between the seats and the pain the action produced was excruciating. Munroe frowned, as if he was sorry to see him in such agony. Marcus looked down, his vision swimming, to see a heavy stream of blood coming from his wound, his hand thickly covered with it.

"Funny, it gets easier with every one. I vomited after His Grace, but Silas was easier, and this, well, this has been very nearly a pleasure."

"You'll hang," Marcus said, struggling to remain conscious. He looked down at the gruesome wound, saw the blood pouring from him, and knew he was going to die. Adam lay unmoving on the ground in a heap, perhaps still alive, and he could do nothing to save him, nothing to save himself. Ah, God, Georgette and the children. It could not end this way, he thought, and yet with each breath he felt weaker until it was a struggle to keep his eyes open. He would never hold his wife again, never tell her how sorry he was, never make love to her with the sun shining sweetly on her pale skin. Mabel would grow up without him, perhaps might even forget the man she'd thought of as papa for such a short time. *Oh, God, it was too much to bear.*

Munroe watched him for several long minutes, his head tilted a bit to one side as if fascinated by the process of death. After a time, he let out a sigh. "I suppose I should go now. I am curious, though, whether Lady Granton was with you when you saw that worry stone. Not that she can tie it to me, of course, not with you dead, but one can never be too careful. There's a thought to take to your grave." And then he chuckled softly, and Marcus's eyes widened in horror.

"Do not touch my wife," he growled. The effort of saying those five words cost him dearly, and his vision turned momentarily black. It seemed impossible to draw a breath.

"Touch her? I don't have to touch her at all," Munroe said, as if explaining a simple lesson to a child.

Marcus found the strength to attempt to sit up, but Munroe laughed and shoved him back down with ease. "You cannot save her, you know. Just think. You'll soon be reunited! Good day, sir. I do apologize for leaving so hastily."

After Munroe left, Marcus tried to move, but he felt so weak, so tired, and his last thought before he slipped into unconsciousness was that Lilian was in terrible danger, and he could do nothing about it.

"What could be taking so long?" Lilian asked, biting her thumb again.

"Adam hasn't been gone all that long. Marcus probably needed to get dressed, perhaps break his fast in the inn."

"What if Marcus has already left? What if he refuses to return? I should have gone with your husband."

"Please do not worry, Lilian. I'm sure everything will work out."

Lilian wasn't quite so certain. She would never forget the look on Marcus's face when she'd begged him not to make her choose between him and Mabel. But what was she to do? Abandon Mabel, forget that for one brief time she'd had a daughter? It had been an impossible choice to make so quickly.

Finally, the two women heard a carriage, and Lilian froze in place. "He's here," she breathed, then smoothed down her skirts. Lilian gave Georgette a wide-eyed look. "Where is Stephen? He—"

"He left right after breakfast for London."

"Good, good." Lilian worried her bottom lip. Would Marcus be terribly hurt that she had stayed behind? Would he be angry? "I can't wait a second more." Lifting her skirts, she ran out of the room and flew down the stairs, her feet beating a quick staccato on the marble steps. If Marcus was angry, she'd make it so he was not; she'd let him know how much she loved him and how very sorry she was for letting him leave without her. And then she'd tell him that he was never allowed to leave again and certainly not without their daughter. Oh, Lord, she didn't know what she was going to say to him. Not that she loved him, because she was uncertain how he would react to such a proclamation, given he had told her not to expect love from him.

She stood in the foyer, hands clasped in front of her so tightly it hurt, and stared at the door. When it opened, she screamed.

Adam stood there swaying, his face covered with blood, so much blood that as he stood there, a small puddle formed at his feet. "Call the doctor," he said, right before his ability to stand deserted him. Thankfully, a footman caught him before he fell and laid him carefully on the hard marble floor. Behind Lilian, she heard Georgette's shout of anguish, her hurried footsteps on the stairs.

"What happened? Oh, my God, my darling," she said, kneeling down beside her husband. "He's dead. He's dead."

"He's not, Georgette," Lilian said, rushing to her side. "Look he's breathing. Breathing. See?"

Georgette frantically looked for signs that her husband was still alive, and began sobbing when she saw proof of life. "What happened, Lilian? Was there an accident?"

"I don't know. He came in, told me to call a doctor, then collapsed. I have no idea—oh, no. Marcus." Cold fingers of dread moved up her spine as Lilian stared out the door at the carriage outside. One carriage door was open, revealing a pale hand, marred by blood, hanging out, unmoving.

"I cannot look," she whispered, staring as a drop of blood dripped off a man's index finger and landed in the gravel below. "Georgette."

Her sister-in-law, face ravaged by tears, looked up at Lilian and then followed her horrified gaze, giving a sharp gasp when she saw what was in the carriage. "Oh, no. Oh, no."

The foyer had quickly filled with servants, who stood there momentarily in shock before Mrs. McColl, the housekeeper, clapped her hands loudly. "Has someone gone for a physician? Good. You and you there, lift up Mr. Dunford and bring him to the main parlor. You, go get some clean cloths and get some water boiling. The rest of you go about your business. Mary, go fetch Lord and Lady Chesterfield immediately."

The servants were quickly dispatched. "Please, can someone check on the carriage? There's a man." Lilian couldn't bring herself to say, *Lord Granton*. She didn't want to believe that unmoving hand could belong to her husband. It was a stranger. A stranger who had stopped to help Adam. Or the driver. It was someone, anyone, other than Marcus. It had to be.

A burly footman immediately ran out the door, and Lilian forced herself to follow. It had only been a matter of seconds since she'd seen that bloodied arm hanging out of the door. Only seconds. *Please be alive. Please be alive. Please don't be Marcus.*

"It's his lordship." His voice broke as he said the words, and Lilian thought she might faint. Another young man appeared by his side, climbing inside as Lilian stood there watching, praying, until she couldn't watch and stand anymore. She ran to the carriage, just as the man inside called out, "He's alive." She could see the servant's brown eyes, and though he'd just said Marcus was alive, the servant's eyes said something different entirely, and Lilian found it was quite impossible to breathe, even as she took Marcus's bloodied hand in hers and lifted it to her cheek, willing him to live. "My lady, please, do not look."

It was too late, of course. Lilian did look and what she saw would be etched into her mind for the rest of her days. A knife, an impossibly large knife, was still sticking out of her husband's chest, thick blood seeping from the wound. "Get him inside," Lilian said, and the two men maneuvered the unconscious Marcus out of the carriage. When Lilian saw the huge amount of blood left behind on the floor of the carriage, she very nearly retched.

Just then, a young maid, her eyes wide and fearful, looked about the carriage, at the driver's seat, even beneath. "Where is Mr. Ashton?"

Mrs. McColl put her arm around the young maid. "We don't know. I'll send one of the boys out to look for him, shall I?"

"But where is he? What's happened?" The young maid started crying, burying her head in her hands. "Did they just leave him there? Leave him there to die?"

"I'm certain they did not," Mrs. McColl said sternly, and led the maid back into the house.

"Then he was already dead. Because they wouldn't have done that. Not Lord Granton. He never would have left Will to die. Oh, God."

Chapter 20

The two brothers were laid on facing settees that were both too small for their tall frames. The other seats in the room were filled with family members, stoic or crying, depending upon their sex or fortitude. Lilian was not crying. She stared, dry-eyed, at Marcus, feeling more helpless than she could ever remember feeling.

Lady Chesterfield, faced with two gravely injured sons, had to be led out of the room, her growing hysteria deemed far too distracting for the physician who had been called in.

Dr. Landsdowne had returned to England from America just three years prior, urged to do so by Marcus, who had met the gentleman in New York when he had gone there to fetch Rose home. So impressed had he been by the physician's skills, Marcus had promised to help his practice grow if he returned to England. Now, Lilian wondered if it had been some dark premonition that had led him to bring Dr. Landsdowne home. He was a quiet, solemn man who went about his examinations with measured assurance. The grotesque sight of Lord Granton, the knife still protruding from his chest, did not faze the man in the least.

He first attended Adam, determined there was little he needed, and then directed his attention to Marcus.

"What of Mr. Dunford?" Georgette asked in a panicked voice.

"Mr. Dunford has suffered a concussion, Mrs. Dunford. His pulse is steady and he responded to the light when I opened his eyes. I suspect he will regain consciousness shortly and may suffer from nausea and headaches for a few days. It is my belief he will live, and the damage to his skull appears to not be overly grave, but with such head wounds it can be difficult to provide a certain prognosis. Lord

Granton, on the other hand, is in far greater danger of succumbing to his injury."

Lilian stifled a sob at the doctor's plain speech, but was oddly grateful to be told the truth. Marcus might die.

Dr. Landsdowne carefully cut open Marcus's shirt and Lilian did all she could not to cry out. He bled still, though the bleeding had lessened, and Lilian prayed it was because he wasn't so badly injured rather than he was running out of blood.

The doctor held a stethoscope over Marcus's heart, his entire body tense as he listened. "It is good you did not attempt to pull the knife out," he said into the silence. He straightened and his eyes sought out Lilian.

"Lady Granton, your husband has lost a great deal of blood, and I've no doubt the knife has punctured his lung but I'm uncertain as to the extent of the damage. As it's impossible to know how large this knife is, I cannot say for certain how serious the wound is. Unless you are immune to the sight of blood, I would suggest you and your family remove yourselves from this room as you are about to see a great deal more of it."

"What are you going to do?"

"Remove the knife, of course. Clean the wound. Dress it." The doctor seemed genuinely confused by the question. "Unless you believe his lordship would rather keep the knife?"

Lilian narrowed her eyes. "I do not, Dr. Landsdowne."

"Very well. I would suggest you all leave."

"I'd like to stay, if you don't mind," Georgette said, her voice wavering slightly. "I'll keep my head averted. I cannot leave my husband."

Dr. Landsdowne considered that for a moment. "To be honest, madam, I'd rather not have a third patient, so I suggest you leave. The spray, you see. I'm not certain how far it will travel, and—"

"You have made your point, sir," Georgette said, leaping to her feet. She bent and gave her husband a kiss before taking Lilian's hand and leading her out of the room. "Please call us back in as soon as you are finished."

The two women stood outside the door, their eyes mirroring one another's anguish. "What a horrid man," Georgette said finally.

"I pray he is a good doctor. He seemed capable. Perhaps when faced with such dreadful things, one must not show emotion."

"I recall Marcus telling me that he cared for Rose when she was ill in New York. Marcus must have been impressed with the man if he urged him to relocate here."

Lilian hugged her arms around herself. "What do you suppose happened to them?"

"They were accosted, obviously." Georgette shook her head. "Cannock is such a peaceful place, and there's been such violence of late. It's frightening, it is."

Somewhere in the house, they heard quiet weeping, and Lilian wondered if they'd found the driver who had been with Adam.

"Lord Chesterfield sent for the constable." Lilian swallowed heavily. It seemed so unlikely that anyone could have done such violence on two men as fine as Mr. Dunford and Marcus. Poor Lady Chesterfield must be beside herself with worry, to see two of her sons so injured, and so soon after the terrible drama that had played out the day before. Thank goodness Mabel had been on an outing with her cousins' nanny and had no inkling of what was now happening. It was all so awful, and Lilian had a fierce longing for Merdunoir, which now seemed a haven from all that was wrong and bad.

They heard a small exclamation from inside the room, and both women turned, ready to rush in, when they heard the doctor call out. "All is well, ladies. I was just a bit startled."

Lilian's breath caught in her throat and she stayed frozen, waiting to hear more, praying with all her being that Marcus would live. He'd looked so pale, so helpless. But he could not die. She needed him. Mabel needed him. The one thought she held close was that he'd been on his way home to her when he'd been attacked. She held on to that thought, the hope that when Marcus did recover, they could be a family and go home.

After what felt like an eternity, Dr. Landsdowne came to the door and opened it, a grim look on his face; his once white shirt was covered with bright red blood.

"No," Lilian gasped.

Immediately, the doctor schooled his features into a more appropriate expression. "My pardon, Lady Granton. He is well as can be. Take no heed of this," he said, indicating the blood on his shirt.

"Sir, you need to practice your expressions," Lilian said, her hand on her heart.

"It is a deficiency on my part, you are correct. Ah, Mrs. Dunford, your husband appears to be regaining consciousness." He turned, and Lilian gave Georgette an exasperated look before Georgette hurried over to Adam, who was, indeed showing signs of awakening. He was moving his hands about restlessly, and his eyes were fluttering, as if he was trying to open them.

Marcus, on the other hand, was terribly pale and so still, for a moment Lilian thought the doctor had simply been trying to spare her feelings. But there, his chest moved ever so slightly.

"Adam. Adam," Georgette said, sounding overcome with happiness. "Oh, darling. Hello."

"Marcus."

"He's here. Right over there and recovering. Oh, Adam, I was so frightened," Georgette said, half lying atop her husband and letting out a sob when he managed to weakly bring an arm up and pat her back.

Lilian stood and walked over to the pair, both happy and filled with despair. "Do you know who did this thing?"

Adam put a weary hand on his head. "No. The carriage stopped and I stuck out my head to see why. The next thing I knew, something had struck me. When I woke up, poor Mr. Ashton was dead and Marcus . . ." He swallowed heavily and squeezed his eyes shut. "Marcus was stabbed." He turned his head, seeking to confirm that his brother still lived. "Are you sure he's . . . ?"

"He lost a great deal of blood," Dr. Landsdowne said, then muttered something about the inadequacy of the study of blood transfusions. "I believe he will recover."

"You believe?" Lilian asked.

"It would not be prudent of me to be overly optimistic. While I do not believe death is imminent, I cannot say with certainty his lordship will live. His heartbeat has slowed, which is a positive sign. But dealing with wounds to the lungs is always difficult. Yes, I should think it is more likely he will live than die. Unless infection sets in. Then his recovery will be a bit more challenging."

The physician looked wholly satisfied with his response and didn't seem to notice that those around him were completely unsatisfied.

"What should we do?"

"Leave him be for now. Keep his feet elevated. Don't change the bandage; I will return later this evening to see to that. If blood comes through the bandage, you may place another atop the one I have in place. If Lord Granton awakens, you may give him water but absolutely no spirits of any kind and do not allow him to move. This is imperative."

Lilian looked over to where Marcus lay, his feet propped up on the settee. He looked quite uncomfortable. "When can we move him to a bed, sir?"

"When I direct you to," he said. "Now, if you don't mind, I'm delivering a child into this world this afternoon. I'll return when I can. Oh, and if he does expire, please do not call me. At that point, there is nothing I can do." With that, he placed his bowler hat on his head, collected his bag, gave a smart bow, and left.

By the end of the day, Adam, with the help of Lord Chesterfield and a footman, was brought up to his bedroom, where he could better rest away from the activity in the house. Though his head pained him, he was able to sit up and walk carefully around the room, while Georgette hovered by his side continuously. He'd argued that he didn't want to be far from Marcus, but Lord Chesterfield had put his foot down, brooking no argument.

Marcus was unchanged, which Lilian chose to believe was a good sign.

Lady Chesterfield had sent a cable to London asking that Stephen return immediately; she'd decided that Marcus should have the chance to see his youngest brother if he so chose. The unspoken reason for this was not lost on Lilian. Lady Chesterfield did not want her oldest son to die without giving him the opportunity to forgive Stephen. The older woman had informed Lilian of this, her eyes filled with such anguish, Lilian nearly lost the last of her control.

She'd pulled a chair over and stayed by his side all day, her throat burning from unshed tears. If only his eyelids would flutter. Or his hand clutch hers when she held it to her cheek. Lilian spoke to him as if he could hear, trying to sound lively and happy, even though her heart was breaking. If he were to die without giving her a chance to tell him how much she loved him, she wasn't certain she would have the strength to go on. She told him now, of course, over and over whilst looking at his dear face. His jaw was darkened by a two-day beard, and she noticed for the first time it was sprinkled with lighter, reddish hair. If he ever chose to grow a beard, it would be far lighter than the hair on his head. Suddenly, she desperately hoped that she would one day see how he looked with a beard. She wanted to see what he looked like when he held their baby, when he was old and gray and wrinkled and perhaps even a bit fat. They would grow old and fat and wrinkled together. Please, God, that this could be true.

Constable Conroy alighted from his buggy and looked up at the grand house, hoping that Lady Granton was at home. His first stop had been at Mount Carlyle to see the duchess, but he'd been told in no uncertain terms that Her Grace was far too distraught to speak with him.

Now, standing in front of Hallstead Manor, he didn't have much hope that Lady Granton would shed any light as to who had killed the duke, but did know one thing: old Silas had had nothing to do with it. Silas had left a clue in plain sight by incorrectly spelling his own name on the so-called suicide note. That note, with its shaky penmanship and cryptic words, had haunted Conroy for weeks, both when he'd thought Silas had written it of his own accord and more now when he realized the man had been forced to pen those words. Whoever had killed the duke knew about Silas's daughter, knew she'd been raped by Weston, and had taken advantage of that terrible knowledge. *I killed the duke because of what he done to my daughter.* And he'd signed his name: *Silas Maine.*

Only problem was, Silas's last name was spelled Mayne. What a brave and brilliant thing he'd done at a time when he must have been under terrible duress. Conroy might have missed it if he hadn't happened to look at the register where Silas's daughter and wife had signed in. To be doubly certain, he'd visited the Maynes to confirm the spelling of their last name. Of course, they'd given him the correct spelling and assured him that Silas knew how to spell his own name. And that left him where he now was: at the beginning of a murder investigation that seemed to have been solved twice.

He'd had one hell of a month, and it didn't look as if it was going to get any better. How many times could one murder investigation be solved incorrectly? Never in his career had an investigation taken so many wrong turns. It was downright maddening. And frustrating. The last thing he wanted to do was tell his chief that he'd been mistaken about this case from the beginning. He thought back with more than a bit of chagrin to the CLOSED stamp he'd placed on the file. Next time, and pray God there would not be another case like this for as long as he worked, he would listen to that tiny voice in his head. That voice had whispered: *This is not over, Toby. Not even close, my lad.*

The house was preternaturally quiet, and a sense of foreboding struck him. He looked at the boy who had tied up his horse and saw that the lad looked unusually solemn. Frankly, Conroy was done ignoring his gut feelings. "Has some tragedy occurred here?" he asked the boy.

"You haven't heard? His lordship and his brother were attacked, they were. It were awful."

"Has anyone died?"

The boy looked frightened to be questioned so, but he shook his head. "Mr. Ashton, the driver. But no one else, sir, at least not as I know."

When Conroy twisted the bell, it seemed to take an unusual amount of time before the butler opened it. One look in the man's eyes, and Conroy's stomach dropped.

"Constable Conroy. I'm here to see Lord Chesterfield."

The butler's eyes widened and he took a step back.

"Is there a problem, sir?" Conroy asked, and he could smell the distinctive and rather ominous odor of bleach in the foyer.

The butler composed his features immediately. "No, sir, but I must say I am amazed at how quickly you were able to come. From Birmingham, is it?"

"I was on my way here on other business, and I had no knowledge of the events that apparently occurred today until just a moment ago. I understand there has been some trouble?"

"I'm not at liberty to say, sir, but if you will wait here"—the butler cleared his throat, clearly distressed, and indicated a small parlor to the right—"I will return shortly with Lord Chesterfield."

This house seemed as though it lacked only black creping and a wreath on the door for it to be completely in mourning. Conroy entered the narrow room, which held a small fireplace and had space but for two chairs and a long, gleaming mahogany table placed beneath a hunting scene. It was a room, Conroy figured, that was rarely used, though it was meticulously clean. His wait for Lord Chesterfield was brief, and the man went right to the point.

"Constable, my sons were accosted this morning coming on the road from Cannock. My younger son was struck on the head and is recovering. Unfortunately, he did not see his assailant. Lord Granton . . ."

The older man paused briefly. "...is still unconscious. He was stabbed in the chest and our physician is hopeful he will recover. Their driver was murdered. His body is in the stable; the mortician is coming to fetch him tomorrow. I apologize, but that is all the information I have. Until Lord Granton awakens, I'm afraid we will not know more."

Conroy took out his pencil and pad. "Do you know where they were before they were attacked, my lord?"

"The Cow and Plow. Lord Granton spent the night, and Mr. Dunford went there this morning to bring him home. A family matter of no consequence, I assure you. My middle son is resting, but you may interview him tomorrow if you need to, though I don't believe he will be able to enlighten you much further."

This was startling news, indeed. "Lord Chesterfield, do you know of anyone who has a grievance with either of your sons. Has anything unusual transpired? A visitor? A fight?"

Lord Chesterfield hesitated a moment before saying, "No, nothing like that."

"Is there anyone here close to the driver who was killed? It could be that he was the target of the assailant and your sons were simply in the wrong place at the wrong time."

Lord Chesterfield shook his head. "I find that difficult to believe, sir, as Mr. Ashton is not my regular driver and no one would have been in wait for him. It was quite unusual for him to drive, you see. Given what occurred, I have to believe Lord Granton was the target, though I could not say who or why. He hasn't even been in residence here for more than a year, and only a few knew he was home." The earl swiped a hand through his thick, graying hair with frustration. "It makes no sense."

It made no sense to Conroy, either. "I would still like to talk to the other driver if I might. Perhaps it was a case of mistaken identity. Then I will go to the Cow and Plow. Before I go, I must tell you that the reason I came here originally was to interview Lady Granton. It seems there has been a change in the case of the Duke of Weston's murder." Lord Chesterfield's brows rose in question. "We thought the case closed, but it seems it is not. Lady Granton is not a suspect, but she may know something that can help solve the case."

"She is in no condition to talk about anything at the moment, sir. She is by her husband's side and is quite distraught." Lord Chesterfield lowered his voice. "I very much fear we may never know who attacked my son." The lord's words hung there, full of meaning and terrible sadness.

"I am so sorry." His gut told him that Lady Granton had nothing to do with the murders or the attack, but she'd had motive and opportunity for both the duke's and Mayne's murder. Conroy didn't press for now, given the day's events. He put back his pad, disappointed at how little he'd learned. It would be a long evening, for he would have to go immediately to the inn and interview whoever had been there last evening. "If you have news, I will be at the Cow and Plow for the evening. Please send for me immediately should Lord Granton awaken."

"I will. Thank you, Constable. You cannot know how imperative it is that you find who is responsible for murdering my driver and harming my sons."

Lord Chesterfield held out his hand, and Conroy grasped it in a firm handshake that seemed to give the older man strength.

"This will end well," the earl said firmly, and Conroy wished he felt as sure.

"My lady, perhaps you should rest."

Lilian looked up from Marcus's still body to Lord Chesterfield. "Oh, no, I'm perfectly well." She was not well, not at all. Guilt and grief tore at her. If she had done something more, begged Marcus to stay, gone with him, none of this would have happened. If he died, she would forever blame herself. The servants had done their best to clean him, but his beard was still speckled with dried blood and his shirt, now in tatters, had been tucked around him beneath a warm blanket.

"My lady, I fear if Marcus were to awaken at this moment, you would cause him no small amount of fear." At her puzzled expression, his lordship explained. "You have blood all over you," he said finally, unable to look at her.

"Oh." Lilian looked down at her dress, her hands, and, indeed, she was quite a mess. Of course, she'd been aware that she had blood on her, but she hadn't realized quite how much. All of a sudden her dress felt stiff and heavy with it.

"Your face, madam."

Yes, she had held his hand to her cheek, she remembered now.

Undoubtedly she looked as if she were the one accosted. "Very well, sir, I will change and wash. Will you be able to stay with him? I don't want him to awaken alone." *Or die alone.* She pushed that terrible thought away.

"Of course. Mabel is staying with the other children in one of the tenants' homes this evening. They are good people who are used to having children about. The nanny is with them as well. I thought you should know."

Lilian nodded. It was for the best, she knew, but she wished she could hold Mabel, smell her soapy scent, and braid her hair.

She stood, her eyes once again moving to Marcus, willing him to wake up or at least stir. He was so very still; not even his eyelids flickered from a dream. Tearing her gaze away, she forced herself to walk from the room, telling herself he would be fine while she was gone. He would not die. Yet every step she took was like a step toward a forever that would be without him. *Do not think such things,* she admonished herself.

Lilian headed to her room and called for a maid to assist her. She wanted the dress off desperately. When she stepped in front of her mirror, she let out a sharp gasp, and then looked quickly away, for her stomach heaved at the sight. Her face and her gown, a lemon yellow day dress that had been one of her favorites, were covered in blood. She needed the dress off—immediately. She couldn't wait for a maid, couldn't stand the stiff feel of it on her person, the coppery smell. Twisting and contorting her arms, she frantically tugged at the buttons that ran up along her back, trying to undo them as quickly as possible, tears streaming down her face, her breath coming out in short, audible gasps. The dress felt heavy and sticky, and the buttons endless. Wrenching her arms behind her, she tried to reach those in the middle, but she could not, and finally she hung her head, leaning her hands on the vanity as great wrenching sobs wracked her body.

"Please allow me, my lady," came the soft voice of the young maid who had been assigned to her. She laid gentle hands on her shoulders and helped her to straighten, then made quick work of the remaining buttons. "All done," the maid said, pulling the dress forward and allowing Lilian to step out of the garment.

"Please have it burned, Sandra."

"Of course, milady." The maid bundled it into a ball of stained yellow fabric and white lace.

Fearfully, Lilian looked down, praying that her undergarments had not also been soiled, and sighed in relief when she saw nothing but white fabric. Still, she wished she could soak her entire body in scalding water, but she had to settle for the tepid water in the wash basin. Dipping her hands into the water, she swallowed thickly when the clear liquid immediately turned pink, then red.

"Here, milady," Sandra said, bringing her a fresh pitcher of water. The maid poured clean water onto a cloth so that Lilian might clean her face. Afterwards, Sandra chose a brown plaid day dress and helped Lilian don it.

"How is Mr. Dunford?" she asked the maid. "Have you heard?"

"Well enough to complain about the broth brought up to him," Sandra said with a smile.

Lilian returned her smile weakly, her heart too heavy to do more than that. She was glad Adam was recovering, but she couldn't help feeling a bit envious of that fact. Dr. Landsdowne had said Marcus would likely recover and she prayed he was correct, that Marcus's wound would not become infected. He was so weak, she wondered whether he would be able to survive such a thing.

A flurry of footsteps sounded down the hall, followed by a quick rapping on her door, and Sandra hurried over to see who it was. A young maid, her cap askew, stood outside the door with a large grin on her freckled face. "His lordship is awake," she said breathlessly.

"Thank God," Lilian said. "Sandra, quickly, do you see any remnants of blood?"

Her maid gave her a quick but thorough look, then reached up with the wet cloth and scrubbed at her hairline near her ear. "All gone now, milady."

Lilian picked up her skirts and ran down the hall, uncaring that someone might see her acting so unladylike. Marcus was awake. He wouldn't die. He wouldn't. Her heart sang, and she suddenly felt as if she could fly up to the clouds. Coming to a skidding halt just outside the library, Lilian caught her breath as she smoothed her skirts, then walked into the room, her eyes, blurry from tears she hadn't even realized she was shedding, immediately on Marcus.

It felt as though he had an elephant sitting on his chest. An elephant with thorns. Marcus slowly came back to the world, aware first of his father's voice and then of Lilian. He drifted, in and out, the elephant growing lighter or heavier depending on his level of consciousness. It was the heavy scrape of a chair that finally awakened him fully. The first thing he thought was, *I'm damned uncomfortable.*

"Marcus." His father stared down at him as if the act of opening his eyes were miraculous. It was, actually, quite a feat considering how hellish he felt at the moment.

"Wha—"

"Don't try to speak," his father said quickly. "You are injured. Stabbed in the chest by an unknown assailant. You are home, in the main parlor."

"Adam." It came out as no more than a whisper.

"He was struck on the head but is recovering."

Marcus did nothing more than flex his stomach muscles to sit up when a searing pain had him crying out.

"Do not move, Marcus. It is imperative that you do not. Dr. Landsdowne was summoned and he has dressed your wound, but if you are to recover, you must listen and follow my orders, son."

Marcus smiled, thinking he must be bad off, indeed, if his father was calling him anything other than Granton.

"Lilian. Where . . . ?"

"I'll have her fetched. Don't move." His father disappeared for a short time and returned, looking grim, and in that time Marcus felt himself slipping away, unable to keep his eyes open, unable to speak. He was aware of his father returning to his side and, oddly, placing a hand on his shoulder. He couldn't remember the last time his father had touched him other than to shake his hand. "Do you know who did this to you?"

Marcus couldn't answer, though he willed his eyes to open and his tongue to say the words. *John Munroe.* But he could not. Instead, he fought to remain cognizant as he tried to recall that morning's events, which passed through his mind like a stereoscope: the carriage stopping, Adam looking out, the horror of seeing his brother's head bashed in. Searing pain. Ungodly pain.

Curiosity killed the cat. Those words danced in his head, low and mean. Who said them? Oh, yes, Weston's secretary. John Munroe.

"Marcus." He tried to open his eyes upon hearing his father's voice. "Do you recall what happened?"

John Munroe tried to kill me. And Lilian, my God, Father, Lilian is in danger.

These thoughts swirled around his head as he tried to focus on waking up. *Open your eyes.* He could hear Lilian, her soft tones soothing, and his father's low murmur of reply. What were they saying? He wanted to tell them to call the constable, to hide Lilian and Mabel. *Open your eyes, you damn weakling.*

But he could not. His mind was working, he was breathing, though for some reason even that was damnably difficult, but Marcus simply could not open his mouth or move his tongue to speak.

He had to warn them about Munroe, tell them the duchess's life might be in danger. No, that wasn't right; Munroe thought himself in love with her. His mind swirled endlessly, in and out of conscious thought.

"He was awake briefly, doctor, but hasn't moved since. Or said a word." Lilian, sounded worried.

"Yes. A bit, then he fell unconscious again."

Open your eyes, Marcus. Open. Your. Goddamn. Eyes.

Marcus became aware of a terrible pain in his chest. Someone was poking at him with a hot iron or some equivalent. "He has developed a slight fever."

"Is that bad?" Poor Lilian, she sounded so worried. He had to wake up to tell her not to worry, to tell her . . .

"I don't understand it. I cleaned the wound quite thoroughly. The wound does not yet look infected so perhaps it will pass. It is a low fever and not entirely unexpected." *Oh, Dr. Landsdowne. The knife wound. Of course.*

"Lady Granton, I do beg your pardon, but there's a Mr. John Munroe to see you. He claims to know something of the attack."

"John Munroe?" Lilian asked. "That's Weston's secretary. Of course I'll see him."

No! Why couldn't he get his mouth to move, why could he not wake up? He felt as if his world was about to end and he could do nothing but let it happen. His panic grew. The terrible inability to speak, to move, was driving him mad. *No. Lilian, no. Don't talk to him.* Why wasn't his tongue forming the words?

"I'll bring him to the parlor just off the foyer, my lady."

"Thank you, Mr. Fletcher, I'll be there shortly."

Wake up, you damned fool. Open your eyes. Speak, for God's sake. Please, God, Lilian, don't go. I beg you, please. Oh, God, help me.

"This is good news," Lilian said, her voice tinged with excitement.

Marcus felt a hand on his forehead, no doubt Dr. Landsdowne, and then the low rumble of his voice as he said, "Hmmmm."

"I'll return momentarily, sir."

"Would you like me to accompany you, my lady?" his father asked.

"I know Mr. Munroe quite well; he practically lived at Mount Carlyle and sometimes dined with us during informal occasions."

No, no, no, no, no "No!"

"Ah, as I thought," Dr. Landsdowne said. "He's regained consciousness."

Lilian turned abruptly and hurried back to where her husband lay, his eyes open, his face a mask of fear. "What is it, Marcus?"

He simply stared at her, moving his mouth as if trying to form the words he needed to say, his eyes filled with a terror that was devastating. "It's all right," she said, trying to soothe him. Perhaps, she thought, he'd had a nightmare about the attack. His eyes were glazed and not quite focused and he seemed agitated. Lilian looked up at the doctor to see if he could enlighten her on her husband's condition.

"Munroe attacked me." He spoke hesitantly, as if each word required all his strength to form.

"Wh-what?"

"Munroe."

Lilian clutched his hand. "You're certain."

"Yes." A whisper, barely heard, as if he'd expended too much energy speaking those few words and was now slipping away again. His eyes slowly closed, his features relaxed.

Dr. Landsdowne leaned over and slapped him, hard, and Lilian let out a sound of dismay and shot him a look of disbelief. But when she saw Marcus open his eyes and give the doctor a look of anger, Lilian forgave the physician. An angry Marcus was much better than an unconscious one.

"John Munroe attacked you?" the doctor demanded.

"Yes. And murdered Weston."

Lilian drew her breath in sharply. "Oh my God. Terri."

"Who is Terri?" Lord Chesterfield demanded.

"My sister, Theresa, Duchess of Weston. She's in love with Mr. Munroe." The full scope of what she'd just learned hit Lilian, but was so terrible, she could hardly believe where her thoughts were taking her. Was it possible that Theresa had helped plan the murder of Weston and Silas? It was too awful to contemplate. Her sister was spoiled and self-centered, but could she have been party to such a nefarious plot?

"We need to get the constable," Lord Chesterfield said. "And we need to deal with Mr. Munroe first. I will see him and tell him you are far too distressed to speak to him."

"If I may," Dr. Landsdowne interjected. "I believe it would be best if you allowed Mr. Munroe to believe Lord Granton is dead." He ignored Lilian's sound of distress. "If he believes his lordship is dead, he will have less reason to fear discovery. You might even add that he never regained consciousness."

"Indeed. Thank you, doctor," Lord Chesterfield said. He went over to Marcus and laid a firm hand on his shoulder before leaving to speak with Munroe.

When he was gone, Lilian knelt on the floor, her head by Marcus, needing to be as close as possible to him. "You can rest now," she whispered. "Are you in terrible pain?"

He turned his head, wincing as he did so. "I am more sorry than I can say."

Lilian leaned over and gently kissed his cheek, closing her eyes. She was overcome with the relief of hearing his voice, seeing his beautiful golden eyes. "I'm sorry too, Marcus. If you don't mind, I'm not going to let you out of my sight for some time."

"I can hardly escape," he said, so softly Lilian hardly made out his jest.

She kissed him again and he closed his eyes. Within minutes, his breathing was steady and he was asleep.

"He shall be quite weak for some time," Dr. Landsdowne said. "But his heartbeat is near normal, an indication he is recovering. The knife's blade was short and I believe the damage to his lordship's lungs was minimal. If his fever remains low, I believe his chances of full recovery are excellent. I've brought a stretcher with me. If you could fetch two of your strongest footmen, we can have him moved to a more comfortable location."

"Thank you, doctor."

The doctor gave detailed instructions, and was admonishing Lilian not to allow him to move, not even to sit up, for at least a week when Lord Chesterfield returned. His eyes went directly to his son.

"He's asleep."

"Ah. Just as well. Mr. Munroe has been dealt with. He seemed remarkably calm for a man who has just committed murder. Said he saw a redheaded man talking to Lord Granton at the Cow and Plow and that they seemed to be arguing. The lie tripped off his tongue as if he believed what he was saying. I've sent for the constable." He drew out his watch. "He should be here within the hour, I'd say. And I pray this business will be over soon."

"And Mr. Munroe? Did he say where he was going? I fear for my sister, you see."

"Munroe? Why he's tied up and gagged in the wine cellar being guarded by Mr. Fletcher."

Lilian let out a laugh. "How on earth did you manage that, my lord?"

"I could hardly let the man who tried to murder my son walk away, could I?" He pulled out a small pistol. "This did have a way of convincing him he should listen to me. This and the fact I had three footmen standing outside the door waiting for me to give them the word to enter." Chesterfield chuckled. "Rather exciting, yes?"

"Yes," Lilian said, laughing again. "You are quite the hero, sir."

Chesterfield blushed and harrumphed a bit. "Man's lucky I didn't kill him after what he did to my sons. Now, if you will excuse me, doctor, my lady, I do believe I'll visit with Adam to see how he is faring. God willing, we'll have no more excitement today."

Throughout the long night, Lilian stayed by Marcus's side, lying beside him, sleeping fitfully. Each time she woke up, she laid her hand lightly on his chest to make certain he was still breathing before touching his cheek to ascertain his temperature. He'd awoken only briefly when the footmen moved him from the settee and onto the stretcher, in what was obviously an excruciatingly painful process. But with the calm direction of Dr. Landsdowne, the men successfully transferred him to the stretcher, then carried him to his own room, where they gently moved him onto the bed, all while Lilian hovered to make certain he wasn't dropped.

At some point, Stephen, looking exhausted, came into the room. "I'm sorry to disturb you, Lilian, but I wanted to see how Marcus is faring." Lilian got up and lit a lamp, then turned the light low so as not to disturb her husband before sitting on the bed beside him.

"The doctor is pleased with his progress and he hasn't developed a high fever, so we think he will recover."

Stephen laid a hand against his own forehead, as if trying to contain the emotions he was feeling. His eyes filled with tears as he looked down at the prone form of his oldest brother and shook his head. "It's my fault. If he dies, it will be my fault."

"I daresay the man at fault is Mr. Munroe, Stephen."

"But he wouldn't have been home if none of this had happened. He very nearly died, and I would have been to blame. I can never forgive myself."

Lilian stood and went over to Stephen, laying her hand on his arm. "You must forgive yourself, Stephen. And remember, if the events of five years ago had not transpired, we would not have Mabel. And that would have been terrible, indeed."

Stephen nodded, but his face was still a study of anguish as he looked at Marcus. "He didn't deserve any of this."

"No one deserves this," Lilian said forcefully. "But Munroe is in jail and will no doubt pay for his crimes." Lilian couldn't help but wonder if Theresa would somehow be tied to her husband's murder. She prayed not. "You look exhausted, Stephen. Go to bed and visit in the morning."

"Good night." He stood there a long moment, looking down at Marcus, his eyes tormented, before turning and leaving the room.

The next morning, Lilian awoke to the sound of a goldcrest outside the window, its high-pitched trill making her smile. Beside her was the warm, masculine body of her husband, and her mouth turned up even more. *Thank God he's alive*, she thought, and was surprised to see his golden eyes looking at her.

"Good morning," he said, and she hurt to hear how weak he sounded.

"Good morning." She was close enough that she could see the golden hairs of his beard, the light lines near his eyes that showed he had been in the sun. "How are you feeling?"

"As if a murderous maniac stabbed me with a very large knife."

"That's about right," she said. "We've got him, you know. Munroe. Your father held him at gunpoint and tied him up."

"Truly?"

"Truly. They put him in the wine cellar until Constable Conroy could come fetch him. He's in jail and safely put away."

"Wonderful news," Marcus said. "Adam?"

"Recovering nicely but suffering from a terrible headache. Dr. Landsdowne said he had a concussion. And Mr. Ashton, I'm afraid, was killed."

Marcus let out a curse. "Three men, he killed. Three. My God."

Lilian snuggled a bit closer, not wanting to think it might have been four men killed if Marcus hadn't been very lucky. Lilian felt tears burn in her eyes and she swiped them away and laid a hand on his cheek, rough with stubble. "I'm so sorry, Marcus. I should never have let you go. I feel I'm to blame over what has happened."

"No." She could hardly recognize his voice, so thin and raspy did it sound.

"I shouldn't have let you leave," she said in a rush. "What if you had died, Marcus, and I never got the chance to tell you I was sorry?"

"No, you shouldn't have. And I should not have left. Not as I did, at any rate."

He took a deep breath and turned his head so she could no longer see his eyes. "I need to say something to you, Lilian."

A feeling of calm stole over Lilian. Nothing had truly been resolved between them, and Lilian was afraid of what he might say. For a moment, she wondered if she should tell him how very much she loved him, simply to stop him from tearing them apart. "Go on," she said, sounding calm even though her heart was pounding, pounding in her breast.

"I know that this marriage was not by choice." He stopped, his eyes still on the ceiling above them, while Lilian's eyes were on him. He was being so serious, it was scaring her. She didn't want to think of their troubles, of Mabel, of the fact he had left her. She had a terrible feeling he was going to say good-bye. "Which is why I don't understand what has happened."

Lilian furrowed her brow; he'd confused her completely. What didn't he understand?

He let out a humorless laugh, and turned his head toward her, the effort to do so obvious in his strained expression. "Do you realize we've only known one another for less than one month?"

Lilian nodded uncertainly.

"Then perhaps you can explain this, because I certainly cannot. When I left you here, I thought I was leaving forever. I was hurt and angry, and I didn't think I could bear to see Mabel again. And then, in a remarkably short time, I realized what I truly could not bear was being apart from you. Or Mabel."

Lilian placed one shaking hand over her mouth, her eyes immediately filling with tears. For a woman who took pride in not crying in front of others, she seemed to be doing quite a bit of it lately. It wasn't a proclamation of love, but it was as close as one could get, and Lilian couldn't stop the surge of hope that nearly staggered her.

He found the ceiling fascinating once again. "I apologize if this proclamation makes you uncomfortable."

"Uncomfortable?" Lilian asked on a small laugh. "Uncomfortable? No, Marcus, it does not make me uncomfortable in the least."

He closed his eyes briefly and took a bracing breath. "I'll never leave you again, Lilian. I swear it."

"Good. And I shall never let you leave."

"Tie me up, will you?"

She let out a watery laugh. "With heavy chains."

It was on the third day of his bedrest that Dr. Landsdowne finally pronounced that Lord Marcus Granton would live. There was much cheering throughout the house, and it seemed as if the dark cloud that hovered over Hallstead Manor and all its inhabitants was whisked away. The doctor left, admonishing Marcus to stay abed for several more days and to be patient with his recovery.

"You are not to travel for another two weeks at least or get out of bed for another week," he said before snapping his bag closed.

Marcus settled back into his pillow and frowned. Seven more days of lounging about was not particularly enticing.

The only benefit of bedrest was that Lilian was in the habit of curling up beside him and reading him *The Times* or a periodical or a book, or simply entertaining him with stories from her childhood or the goings-on of the house. Waking up with her beside him was quite nice. He decided after the third day that his wife could use her own room as an overlarge wardrobe; she was sleeping with him from now on.

On the seventh morning, he woke to a tickle on his lips and smiled. How many mornings had he woken up with a smile on his face? Lilian was painting his lips with the tip of her braid, and when he turned to whisper good morning, she kissed him softly.

"Today we go for a stroll about your room," she said, as if they were planning a grand adventure for the day.

"How invigorating. Do you think I can make it all the way to the window?"

Lilian looked at the window, which, to be honest, looked to Marcus to be miles away. He still felt uncommonly weak, something the doctor had told him to expect. It would take some time for his body to recover from the loss of blood, but he hadn't counted on feeling so weak for so long.

Mr. Courtland knocked and walked in, and Lilian took the entry of his valet as her cue to leave Marcus to take care of his private matters. Marcus made a mental note to have a talk with his valet. Walking into his room in the early morning was fine for as long as Marcus was incapacitated, but it would not be seemly when Marcus had recovered his strength, not when he was waking up to his beautiful wife and her enticing body. But for this day, he allowed her to leave so that Courtland could help him to use the chamber pot. It was humiliating, but necessary.

"You'll be well and strong soon, sir," Courtland said when Marcus was finished. Just pissing in a pot had completely drained him, leaving him light-headed. How would he ever manage to walk?

"I hope so, Mr. Courtland. I still feel as weak as a babe."

Lilian returned, followed by a footman carrying a tray laden with breakfast foods. One thing that had definitely recovered was his appetite, and his stomach rumbled appreciatively at the smell of sausages.

Once they were settled, Lilian said, "I saw Stephen in the breakfast room."

"I thought once he realized I wasn't going to die he would have departed for London. What is he still doing here?"

Marcus could tell Lilian did not like his reply, for she pressed her lips together in displeasure. "I think you should speak with him. You cannot refuse to see him forever."

"We have nothing to say to one another, Lilian. Let it be."

She sighed and dropped the subject, for which Marcus was vastly relieved. It seemed everyone in the household felt sorry for poor

Stephen, who was suffering mightily from some well-placed guilt and regret. *Let him suffer*, Marcus thought, *just a bit more*. He still was not at a place where he could even contemplate forgiving his brother; the betrayal was too raw.

A light knock on the door distracted him from thoughts of his brother. "Enter."

Mabel, followed by the children's nanny, peeked through the door. "Her ladyship thought you might be up for a visit this morning," the nanny said shyly.

Mabel stood there, looking so small and sad, staring at him with her big, hazel eyes, as if she knew how difficult this moment might be for Marcus. But it wasn't difficult at all, not even a smidgeon, damn his soft heart. God, he felt like weeping, so happy was he to see her. Lilian had thought it best that Mabel not see him when he was so very ill, and Marcus had agreed.

"Of course. Mabel, come here. Thank you, Nanny."

Mabel hurried to the bed and scrambled up, her eyes on the bandage on his chest. "Are you better?"

"Much. Still a tiny bit sick, but I'm getting better."

"Did it hurt terribly?"

"Awfully. Very nearly as much as pricking one's finger on a thorn. A very big thorn."

For some reason, that made Mabel smile, as if she knew just how much he was downplaying his injury. Then her brows furrowed. "They said you might go to heaven."

Marcus put on a look of shock. "Who said? Someone was telling tall tales, Mabel. The only place I'm going is over to that window there to look out and watch you play with your cousins."

That seemed to satisfy her, and when Marcus looked over the girl's head, he found Lilian looking at him as if he'd just given Mabel the moon and stars. Really, she ought to stop looking at him so every time he did even the smallest kindness. Made a man think he *could* give away the moon and stars.

"By God, did someone come in overnight and double the size of my room?" Marcus glared at the window, his legs shaking, his forehead bathed with sweat, his breath labored as if he'd just run to Cannock and back. Lilian hovered next to him, and he wondered if she thought she'd be able to catch him when he collapsed to the floor.

The window was open, and he could hear the sound of the children playing. For some reason, it was imperative that he get to that window and call down to Mabel.

"Are you . . . are you unable to . . . ?"

Marcus shot his wife a look and she stopped speaking, but she was clearly frustrated with his refusal to abort their mission. He would get to that window if he had to crawl. "I can make it." Strong words from a man who felt weak as a kitten. One shuffling step after another, he made slow progress, stunned by how he felt. Perhaps this trip had been a bit ambitious after all, he thought as the room began to swirl a bit, his vision darkening slightly.

Suddenly, a strong arm was wrapped around his waist and a shoulder was thrust under his arm, steadying him.

"Get the hell out, Stephen," Marcus snapped, just as he felt his knees buckling beneath him.

"Whoa, there you go," his baby brother said, standing him up and strengthening his grip on him. "I'm not leaving, Marcus, and you're too damned weak to do anything about it."

"I'll leave you two alone, shall I?" asked Lilian, sounding overly bright.

"Do not dare leave," Marcus said, and Lilian promptly ignored him and left, giving him a cheerful wave as she closed the door. Had he lost all control of everything? "Hell, since you're here, help me to the window."

With Stephen's help, the way was much smoother and in a few moments, Marcus was at the window, looking down at the children in the garden playing some game with Nanny. "Hello, Mabel," he called, and was gratified to see Mabel stop immediately what she was doing to run beneath the window and wave wildly, as if he couldn't see her at all. "What are you playing?"

"Duck, Duck, Goose. You have to run really fast and if you get caught, you're the duck."

"The goose," her cousin called.

"The goose," Mabel corrected.

"Go on and play now. I'll watch from here."

Marcus stood at the window for several minutes, resting heavily on his hands, his legs hardly holding his weight. He wasn't sure how he'd be able to get back to bed, even with Stephen's help. To his credit, Stephen hadn't said a word, just stood silently behind him as he watched Mabel play. Every once in a while, she'd look up and wave and he'd wave back.

"She's a good girl," Marcus said.

"Yes."

Marcus clenched his jaw because it hurt so much to know Mabel was his brother's daughter in blood. But she was his daughter in heart.

"She's your daughter, Marcus," Stephen said as if reading his thoughts.

Marcus nodded. "Help me back to bed before I collapse, will you?"

Without another word, Stephen positioned himself to help Marcus walk back to his bed and stood silently while he settled against the pillow and drew up a blanket.

"Thank you," Marcus said, keeping his tone neutral.

Stephen's head jerked slightly, as if Marcus had struck him or wounded him with a harsh word instead of expressing his gratitude. His brother's eyes filled with tears and Marcus had to look away. "If you had died, I never would have forgiven myself. I'm asking you now for your forgiveness. I don't deserve it. I know that, but I'm asking anyway."

"What you did, Stephen—"

"I know. God, I *know*, Marcus."

"I will try."

Stephen let out a long breath. "That is all I ask." He hesitated a moment. "Can I get you anything?"

"My wife."

Lilian gave Stephen a curious look when he found her in the library just as she pulled *Frankenstein* off the shelves to read to Marcus. He did enjoy the macabre, nearly as much as she did. Stephen looked slightly more at ease, and though he didn't say anything in particular, Lilian sensed that the brothers had made up a bit.

"Marcus would like to see you."

"Is everything well?"

"As well as could be," Stephen said, giving her a weak smile.

Lilian tucked the book in her skirt and hurried up the stairs. Constable Conroy had stopped by briefly and given her news of Theresa, and Lilian was excited to tell Marcus. When she entered the room, he was abed, looking tired but pleased to see her.

"I've news of Theresa," she said, coming to the bed and climbing up to lie beside her husband. He lifted his arm so that she might snuggle close by his side.

"Oh?"

"It is the constable's opinion that Theresa had no knowledge of what Munroe planned. He mentioned that my sister would have been the finest actress in the kingdom if she was lying, and apparently Munroe said the same. She had nothing to do with Weston's murder. I'll have to visit her soon. She must feel awful about what happened. She loved Munroe and he murdered three men for her, two completely innocent. Theresa must feel horribly guilty."

Marcus drew her toward him and kissed the top of her head. They lay there with their own thoughts for a time before Lilian drew out the copy of *Frankenstein*. "I found this in the library."

Marcus smiled. "One of my favorites. I haven't read that since I was at the university."

"Shall I start?"

"I have a better idea," he said, moving one hand to cup her breast and making Lilian smile.

"Oh? Shall we play cards?"

His hand slipped beneath her dress and Lilian's breath grew shallow as he kissed her jaw, her neck. "No, not cards."

"Chess?" she asked, then dissolved into helpless giggles.

"The sun is shining my dear, and it's been far too many days since I made love to you."

Lilian turned and gently placed her hand on his chest near his wound. "You have been a bit under the weather." She bit her lower lip and Marcus's eyes dropped to her mouth. "Are you certain you are up for such . . . activity?"

"Very much so," he said, chuckling and looking down pointedly at the small tent in the covers. Lilian followed his gaze and giggled.

"Yes, indeed, but that's not what I meant and you know it."

Marcus sighed. "You are probably right. I am not able to make love to you." Lilian felt a stab of disappointment until he said, "But you can make love to me."

Lilian pulled back, brow furrowed, for she had no idea what he meant.

"Here." He pulled back the covers and lifted up his nightshirt, revealing his member, bold and strong and clearly in need of attention.

His golden eyes were hooded with desire. "I need you, love. I need to feel you."

Lilian hesitantly brought her hand down to his member and trailed a finger from the base to the tip, and Marcus hissed in a breath.

"Here," he said, and took her hand so that she was holding him, her fingers wrapped around. Velvet surrounding steel, she thought. He guided her, moving her hand up and down, showing her how to please him, and he closed his eyes, his face taut, his body rigid. "God, my God. I don't think . . ." He stopped her hand and let out a chuckle. "I want to be inside you, but I fear I don't have the strength. I must leave it up to you."

"I'm not certain what to do," Lilian said.

"Ride me, love." Heat suffused her body as she realized what he was asking. She hadn't realized such a thing was possible. "Undo your buttons so I can see you. I need to see you."

Lilian slowly undid the buttons of her dress, thankful that she'd opted for one of her simpler gowns. As she loosened her clothing, Marcus's eyes darkened and he swallowed heavily. "I like watching you undress," he said, his voice low and gruff and sending a sharp stab of desire through her. Impatient, he brushed her hands aside and made quick work of the rest of the buttons, then pulled the ribbon on her chemise and pushed her undergarments down until her full breasts popped free. "Much better," he said, before drawing her down to him so that he could suckle one taut nipple. He let out a sound, low and rumbling, and Lilian arched her back at the pure pleasure coursing through her. It had been too long since she'd felt Marcus's clever tongue on her breasts, and her body sang beneath his caresses. For several long minutes he made love to her breasts, until Lilian could feel the moisture between her legs, until she was moving her hips to somehow find some relief from the building pressure.

"Ride me," Marcus said, urging her up and helping to position her over him. "Take me in your hand like—" Lilian had it well in hand and he let out a harsh breath as he slid inside her, filling her, helping to ease the growing ache. She felt so wanton, so exposed, sitting atop him, his manhood inside her, thick and hard, her breasts displayed for his heated look. She moved slightly and he groaned. "Yes. Move, love."

Lilian lifted her body up, reveling in the power, the sensations she was creating. It felt so good, so wonderful and right, and so she smiled. "Lovely."

"Yes, lovely." Marcus sounded out of breath, but he held on to her hips and guided her, up and down, setting a rhythm that she easily followed. She watched him, his eyes, his mouth, and knew she was pleasing him as much as she was pleasing herself. What a marvelous thing this was. "Oh, God, Lilian."

One of his hands moved to a breast, the other between her legs, and what a clever hand it was, teasing her, back and forth as she lost herself in the rhythm she was creating. Somehow, Lilian forgot to think and only felt. Her body took over, wanting, needing release, and so she let go, followed what her body was telling her, moved with abandon nearer and nearer to that place where she would explode into a million beautiful pieces. There. Now.

Lilian let out a long, keening cry just as Marcus thrust deep inside her, arching his back and emitting a harsh, masculine sound, his manhood throbbing as they both found release.

Lilian collapsed on top of him, completely sated.

"Ouch!"

"Oh! Sorry. I forgot." Lilian made to scramble off him, but he held her in place, still inside her.

"Lie still," he murmured, wrapping his arms around her. "Like this. Forever."

Lilian giggled. "I fear we would eventually starve."

"I could live off this for quite a long time," he said, sounding drowsy.

After a time, Lilian slid off him, but stayed pressed against his side, uncaring that her breasts were still exposed and that her skirts were a wrinkled mess and still rucked up about her hips.

"I'm quite angry with you, Lilian." He didn't sound angry, so Lilian smiled. "Don't you want to know what you've done?"

"Not particularly."

"I'm going to tell you anyway," he said, and kissed her forehead. "You've made me love you, confound it, and I'm not at all happy about it."

"You love me?" Lilian asked.

"Yes." This said nearly begrudgingly. "I can hardly warrant it. I didn't plan to, you know."

Another woman might have wished for something more flowery and romantic, but Lilian knew the fact that Marcus had made such an admission was like another man frolicking about a room and declaring his undying love. It was perfect. "Did you know, I saw you years ago at a house party? You were having a push-up contest with Adam. You won."

He furrowed his brow as if not following what she was saying.

"I was hiding from Weston and there you were, shirtless. I fell in love right then and there."

"The Barrington party. Yes, I remember. But I don't remember seeing you."

"No, you didn't see me. And even if you had, you were married. Something that I found rather vexing at the time."

Marcus lifted one brow. "And you fell in love?" He sounded quite skeptical.

Lilian felt herself blushing. "Perhaps not. But I did fall in love at some point. And that was quite vexing too."

"Oh?"

She pulled up and looked down at him, giving him a frown. "Do you not recall telling me that you were quite incapable of loving me?"

"I don't recall saying any such thing."

She scowled and said in her deepest voice, *"I wouldn't want you to expect me to love you."*

"Ah. That does sound familiar." He made an effort to take her into his arms, but lay back down and sighed. "Kiss me, will you? I'm too weak to do it myself." Lilian complied, kissing him softly, tasting him, and he groaned. "I cannot make love to you again today, but as soon as I can without feeling as though I've run a hundred miles, I will do so, madam."

Lilian kissed his nose and giggled. "I shall look forward to it, my lord." He was quiet for a long time, gazing up at the ceiling, so long, in fact, that Lilian began to worry that something was wrong. "Marcus?"

"Would you mind very much, even when I am well, sharing my bed? I've grown used to having you by my side, you see. I know it's not the done thing, but I would very much like it to continue."

Lilian's heart, already nearly a puddle, melted even more. "Do you snore?"

"I have never been accused of such."

"Then, yes. I will sleep by your side all the days of my life." Lilian kissed him again, softly, and lay back down.

After a time, Marcus let out a long sigh. "I have another request."

"You are very demanding."

"Indeed." He turned his head and kissed the top of her head. "I'd like to go home as soon as possible. I need to be at Merdunoir. Would that be all right? I daresay I should be fully recovered in a few days."

"Dr. Landsdowne says weeks, Marcus. The knife pierced your lung."

He frowned. "As soon as I can travel, then. I need to be home." He swallowed thickly. "With my family."

The room was suddenly unnaturally quiet. Perhaps it was because Lilian found herself unable to breathe, and if there was a tiny bit of her heart that hadn't been filled with love, it was now overflowing. "Yes, Marcus. Let's go home."

Epilogue

"**P**apa, when can I see the baby?"

Marcus, who'd been pacing a path in the carpet of his study at Merdunoir, looked up at his ten-year-old daughter and smiled. "As soon as he or she makes an appearance."

Stephen, Adam and Georgette, their five children, and Lord and Lady Chesterfield, all sat pensively in his study, awaiting news from upstairs, where his wife was giving birth. She'd been up there for hours, though once in a while Dr. Landsdowne would come down and give them news of her progress. Servants came and went, and his butler, Mr. Dawson, formerly of Mount Carlyle, seemed to make every possible excuse to come into the room and hover about. Everywhere Marcus looked, there was a person.

Mabel grinned and raised her eyebrows. "Unless one of the maids secretly has a baby, I believe my little brother has arrived."

"Or sister," Marcus said. "Wait, you're not jesting? You heard a baby?"

Mabel gave a happy little jump. "Yes. Can we go? Can we?"

Marcus grabbed Mabel's hand and the pair ran up the stairs, leaving the others behind, only to nearly bowl over the doctor as he was coming out of the room, his face unreadable.

"A son, milord. Both mother and son are well."

"Thank you." Marcus pushed a hand through his hair in relief, then brushed past the doctor to where his wife and son lay. Servants bustled about, but when they saw Marcus, they hastily finished what they were doing and left the room.

"Come see your son, Marcus. And your little brother, Mabel."

Marcus walked almost hesitantly to his wife, unable to believe she was lying in their bed, holding their child. Her hair was neatly braided and she looked lovely, her cheeks flushed, her eyes bright. They had both given up long ago on ever having a child, but there he was, a red, ugly thing with a smooshed-up face and downy dark hair. "Isn't he beautiful? The most beautiful boy in the world," Lilian said, gazing down at her son as if he truly were beautiful. Marcus and Mabel exchanged looks of doubt, and Lilian laughed. "He is beautiful," she insisted.

Just then, he opened his eyes, revealing the stunning shade of blue Marcus had seen only twice in his life: on the wings of a morpho butterfly and in his wife's lovely eyes.

"He's got blue eyes," Mabel announced. "I wish my eyes were blue."

"If everyone had blue eyes, the world would be quite boring," Lilian said.

"He is cute," Mabel said, gazing down at her little brother. She held out a finger and the baby grabbed onto it, making Mabel giggle. "He's strong. What's his name?"

"Thomas, after my grandfather," Marcus said. "This was his home. And now it is my son's."

Mabel furrowed her brow. "That's not fair."

Marcus chuckled. "What I mean to say, Mabel, is that this is his home, in the same way it is your home."

"Our home," Lilian said, kissing the top of her son's head.

Marcus had come to understand that the ache he felt in his heart at times like this wasn't necessarily a bad thing; it was simply his heart making a bit more room for those he loved.

And so the man who'd wanted nothing more than to live by himself, found himself with a houseful of people bustling about, making noise, and generally being annoying. And he wouldn't have had it any other way.

JANE GOODGER

Behind a
Lady's Smile

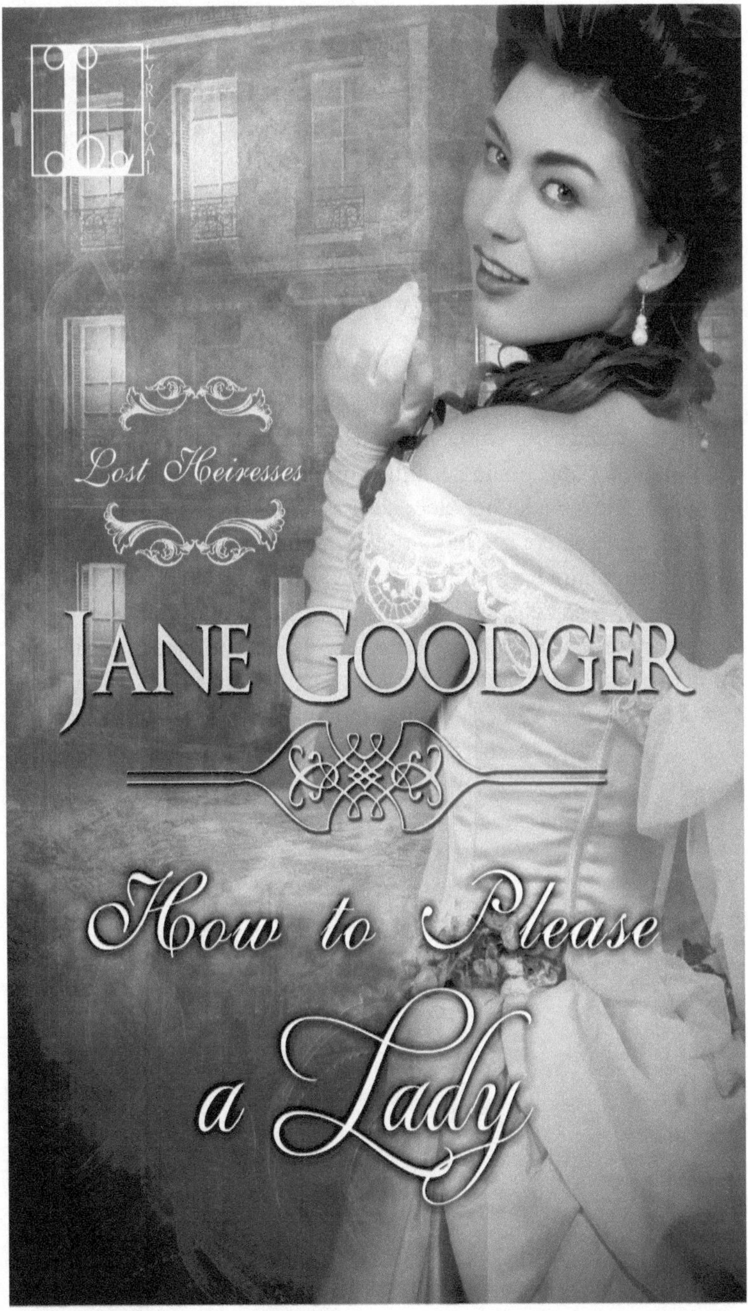
LYRICAL
Lost Heiresses
JANE GOODGER
How to Please a Lady

Have you found the other Lost Heiresses?

BEHIND A LADY'S SMILE
Available now from Lyrical Press

It's one thing for a girl to lose her way, quite another to lose her heart...

Genny Hayes could charm a bear away from a pot of honey. But raised in the forests of Yosemite, she's met precious few men to practice her smiles upon. Until a marvelously handsome photographer appears in her little corner of the wilderness and she convinces him to take her clear across the country and over the seas to England, where she has a titled grandmother and grandfather waiting to claim her. On their whirlwind journey, she'll have the chance to bedazzle and befuddle store clerks and train robbers, society matrons and big city reporters, maids and madams, but the one man she most wants to beguile seems determined to play the gentleman and leave her untouched. Until love steps in and knocks them both head over heels ...

HOW TO PLEASE A LADY

The Lost Heiresses
Run though they might, love will find them . . .

Lady Rose Dunford is shocked—and titillated—by the number of female visitors coming and going from her mysterious new neighbor's Manhattan brownstone. Recently widowed by the death of her very sweet, but not very exciting husband, Rose finds it difficult to imagine just what the attraction could be.

And then she meets the bachelor in question. Not only is Charlie Avery dashing and outrageously good looking—she knows him! He is none other than the man who once helped her escape the dreary matchmaking plans of her father, the man she once dreamed she could love. Can Charlie's presence next door be an accident? Or has he come to show her everything he has learned about . . .

HOW TO PLEASE A LADY

Praise for the novels of Jane Goodger

**"Fun, delightfully romantic—and sexy."
—Sally MacKenzie on *The Spinster Bride***

**"A touching, compassionate, passion-filled romance."
—*RT Book Reviews* on *A Christmas Waltz***

ABOUT THE AUTHOR

Jane Goodger lives in Rhode Island with her husband and three children. Jane, a former journalist, has written and published numerous historical romances. When she isn't writing, she's reading, walking, playing with her kids, or anything else completely unrelated to cleaning a house. You can visit her website at www.janegoodger.com.